THE VIEW
BEYOND
EARTH

by Cary Neeper

Penscript ®
PUBLISHING HOUSE

Characters and alien species depicted herein are trademarks of
Carolyn A. Neeper. The Penscript® logo and calligraphy are trademarks and
Penscript is a registered trademark of Shawne A. Workman, DBA Penscript
Publishing House.

Publisher's Cataloging-in-Publication
  Neeper, Cary.
    The view beyond earth / by Cary Neeper.
    p. cm. — (The archives of Varok ; 1)
    Includes bibliographical references.
    SUMMARY: Microbiologist Tandra Grey finds new hope for an ailing
    Earth and her own future when she makes first contact with alien
    neighbors too intelligent, too nosy, and too near to ignore.
    LCCN 2014911362
    ISBN 978-1-62222-016-8 (hardcover)
    ISBN 978-1-62222-017-5 (trade pbk.)
    ISBN 978-1-62222-018-2 (pbk.)

    1. Human-alien encounters—Fiction.
    2. Extraterrestrial beings—Fiction. 3. Sustainability—
    Fiction. 4. Science fiction. I. Title. II. Series:
    Neeper, Cary. Archives of Varok ; 1.

Originally published as *A Place Beyond Man* (Charles Scribner's Sons, 1975).
Revised as *The View Beyond Earth* (Penscript Publishing House, 2014).
Published by Penscript Publishing House, San Jose, California.
http://www.penscript-publishing.com

For Don, who knew Conn first—
with thanks to those who have contributed
invaluable guidance and encouragement:
Bonnie, Betsy, George, and Sarah in 1975,
my editor Shawne Workman, and the Center for the
Advancement of the Steady State Economy
(http://steadystate.org).

CONTENTS

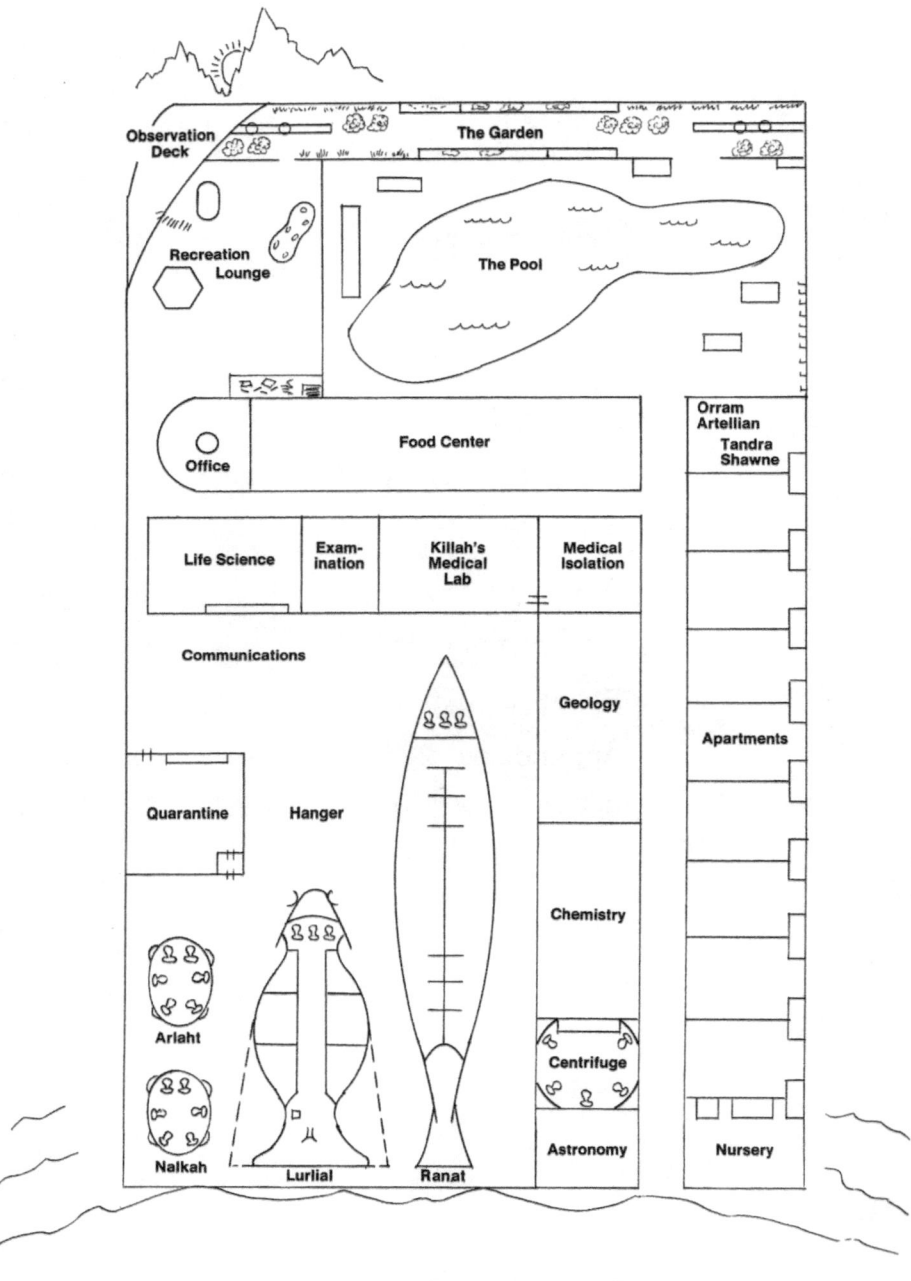

E111-Varok Observation Base

I. Flight of Fancy

Beyond the moist, vibrant Earth and pocked Mars; past wild Jupiter and its veiled living stepchild, Varok; far from the cold regions of skirted Saturn and tiny Pluto flies a hot, watery planet. Rudely kicked out of the Oort Cloud into a 12,000-year orbit around Sol, it hides buried in the midst of the hollow black void between the Kuiper belt and the Oort cloud. The planet grew large enough to glow dimly in the deeps with its own internal warmth. Luckily, it stayed small enough so that powerful creatures could evolve out of its mild ooze to lounge and play in its weighty waters. Ellls they called themselves, handsome creatures who toyed with time as nature toyed with them, enlarging their wit to ridiculous extremes and adding unnecessary but charming decorative touches. They became creatures with an enormous capacity for joy, and sometimes for much more.

Occasionally an elll like Conn came along. . . .

To Trust a Stranger

High above the North American Spaceport, a sleek parachute deployed. A humanoid shape with large flat feet hung from the rig, landed with a thump, then disappeared into the desert, mumbling to himself.

"If this isn't the goofiest stunt we've pulled! If I didn't trust Jesse Mendleton so much, I'd never have agreed to do this interview."

The elll Conn stopped for a moment and allowed himself to enjoy the darkening turquoise sky. The half moon shone with a warm tone, and he thought of his colleagues up there beneath the d'Alembert Mountains at the Elll-Varok Observation Base, swimming and fooling around in the base pool.

"Who do I think I am? Super-elll? Is the water in this nasty isolation suit going to last the evening? I'm in the middle of the flattest, driest, emptiest piece of real estate in the solar system, and I've got to walk another kilometer to the Spaceport. I'll tear every toe-web to shreds before I get there. And what if Jesse's human scientist lady doesn't show?"

– Δ –

The previous day microbiologist Tandra Grey received a voice call.

"Tandra Grey here."

"Tandra, it's Jesse Mendleton. Clear your calendar for this weekend. You're needed at the spaceport."

Tandra tucked the communicator into her shirt pocket and sat down next to her adopted two-year-old girl sitting on the floor. Three-D puzzle pieces lay in heaps around them.

"Here, Shawne," she said to the child, "look for blue on the edge, like this one."

The child took the piece and started hunting for another.

"Okay, Jesse," Tandra said. "What's this really about?"

"Someone wants to interview you for a . . . project."

"At the spaceport? They must have money. I wouldn't get along with their clients."

"I know, but this is not about spaceport clients. Money is not . . . part of the deal. It's a project that requires your skill as a microbiologist."

"I'm busy teaching, Jesse."

"I know that, but this is a chance you don't want to miss. It's right on target for what you care most about."

"Shawne."

"And her future. They need your expertise, Tandra."

"In germs? Have your friends at the CDC told you something I should know? Have the die-offs spread, Jesse?"

"No, it's not that. I mean, yes, there's another outbreak, but this is something different. You've got to trust me. Just come to the spaceport cocktail party Saturday night."

Tandra sighed. She had no wish to spend her Saturday night at some stuffy marketing party, away from Shawne.

"It's the opening of their Spacewalk Expo. Their sales team is show-ing off all the newest safety gadgets and trying to attract a few more clients. The vendors will have new gadgets on display—the usual spacesuits, cameras, all that. You'll be interested in the isolation suits. The spaceport is serious about avoiding outplanet contamination."

"C'mon, Jesse, find someone else. I've got midterms to grade, and I just got back from collecting the latest designer germs in Darfur. I re-ally don't want to be away again so soon."

"It's just this one Saturday. My friend has a proposal you won't want to refuse. Anything that comes after the party will be up to you. And Shawne can be a part of it. It could change her life, Tandra, and yours."

Tandra hesitated.

"I wouldn't ask you to do this if I didn't know you so well."

"So when are you going to pick me up? I'd rather not drive all the way down there alone."

"How about two p.m.? Get a baby-sitter that will stay all night. You may not want to leave."

"You're serious." Tandra reached into her pocket to stare at the face on her com. "You'd drive me? That's a six-hour trip."

"Or more." Jesse's image looked back at her with steady eyes. There was no hint of jest on his rugged face. "I'd drive to the moon and back to be sure you showed up."

"Okay. Deal. How fancy is this? What do I wear?"

"Something comfortable. It's warm desert, you know, but bring a sweater for the evening. Slacks are fine. There will be all kinds of people there."

"I can't leave before three—naptime for Shawne."

"See you then."

"This better be good, Jesse. I don't like to lose my Saturdays with Shawne." *Or a night of sleep.*

Tandra sank back to the floor and set Shawne on her lap. "Try this one," she said, placing a puzzle piece in the toddler's tiny hand.

"Dat's too broad, Mommy. This one here." She reached for another and fit it into place.

"Right." Tandra gave her a squeeze. *How lucky to have found you,* she thought, remembering the agonizing wait for the adoption authorities to accept her application. *Nothing Jesse can imagine will steal more time away from you. Promise.*

– Δ –

The drive down the length of New Mexico on US 25 with Jesse Mendleton gave Tandra a chance to finish grading midterms. The miles disappeared as she sat with a vintage keyed-screen in her lap, thankful that Jesse was not one to require conversation.

They stopped for dinner in Truth or Consequences and arrived at the spaceport's cocktail party an hour later. A crowd of paid passengers and prospects already filled the hangar and adjoining rooms. Some of the guests trying on space suits had escaped to the weightless training pool to cool off.

"Look for someone in a full isolation suit," Jesse said. "I've got to go—the exobiology session is scheduled for seven-thirty. I'll find you here or on the patio no later than nine."

"So how will he-she-it know me?"

"It will." Jesse actually laughed.

Tandra socked his shoulder.

"I described you as a beautiful young woman of nondescript ethnicity wearing long cool hair and slacks."

"Thanks a lot, Jesse."

He took her by the shoulders and put on the fatherly look that always got her attention. "This will demand everything you've got, Tandra. Don't blow it. I didn't mean to make light of it."

She watched him disappear from the main hangar into a smaller conference hall. Then she walked outside a short ways to get a feel for the spaceport campus. The launch pad was visible in the distance as a smooth spot in an endless landscape dotted with waist-high creosote bushes. The sky surrounded her with a magnificent dome of deepening turquoise, and the moon, like a golden jewel, filled her with its beauty.

– Δ –

Just after sunset, the elll Conn reached the spaceport, checked his parachute backpack at the booth near the hangar entrance, and busied himself ambling through the crowd, studying the postures and mannerisms of those wearing isolation or space suits. Trying to imitate them, he almost missed the warm (brown, humans would say) delicate beauty with the cold, probably black, long hair and slacks.

This had to be Tandra Grey, the microbiologist. She was dressed more simply than most, and was busy studying the suited guests and vendors. Her sweater was a medium bright, the color of the early evening sky. He followed her at a distance as she looked over the crowd, obviously concentrating on those demonstrating isolation suits. Finally she made her way to the periphery of the crowd on the patio.

Like a cat on padded flippers, the elll moved toward the shadows at the far corner of the patio. There, he waited his chance, enjoying the colorful variety of passers-by.

When no one was facing his direction, he moved toward the woman. He bumped her arm gently in passing, and assumed a casual slouch by the punch bowl.

"Excuse you," Tandra said and smiled at him.

No one else had noticed him amidst the jumble of bright and dim clothes. Most of the space suits on display were probably safe in a vacuum but inconveniently bulky.

He poured a glass of punch and offered it to Tandra, as if disinterested.

She took it, said thanks and moved a few steps away.

He looked longingly into the liquid in the punch bowl. Where was Ellalon right now? Probably in the pool with Killah. *Ae-o-o*, wouldn't that feel good? On the other hand, Killah rarely had a chance to get away from Moonbase, poor *eloid*. He'd like it down here. Good to be

surrounded by living things again. Beats that *kaehl-din* hot dust and
dry rock up there.

A tall man and a woman in brightly patterned cloth approached
Tandra as if they knew her. *Yes. They used her name. Good.* Now he could
be sure she was the right person.

Someone pushed passed him, mumbling, "'Scuse me, skin diver,"
and the elll saw Tandra glance up at him. Was that an invitation? He
wandered closer and listened. Apparently the older couple had en-
gaged her in an argument.

"There is nothing in evolution's rulebook that says accumulated
knowledge will lead the human species into a more sane social order,"
Tandra was saying. "Distortions in human thinking can be unbelievable. Our misguided priorities are leading us straight over the cliff. We
need to respect our natural gifts."

"You mean you intend to raise that adopted baby of yours like a
wild animal?" said the large man.

"I trust her God-given instincts. She'll need them."

"You'll produce a spoiled brat and a social misfit, if you ask me,"
said the woman in bright cloth.

"I don't think so. I teach her that she must never impose herself on
anyone—that she never hurt any living thing, physically or emotionally. She's got to decide for herself the best way to live. I want her to
grow up trusting her own integrity."

"That's crazy. There are proper ways, time-tested ways, of raising
children—for very good reasons."

Conn could no longer remain silent. "And what are they?" he said,
stepping into the group.

"Restraint, for one," the woman said, giving Conn a look, "not just
following every impulse to act, or speak. Don't you think so, Tandra?"

Tandra looked more closely at Conn as she answered.

"Children need lots of unconditional love and consistent limits,"
Tandra said. "I'm sure we could all agree—spaceman. Is your suit one
of the new spaceport designs? I'm not familiar with spacesuits, but that
looks more . . . flexible than most others here."

"It's designed to secure microbial isolation," he said, "while we . . .
do whatever we need to do."

Conn's isolation suit, designed by varoks, was sleek and trim, as if
tailored to fit his lean body. Only on its small, slightly squared helmet

were there hints of electronic gadgetry and hardware. The suit's material, a fine, natural cloth, was randomly marked with muted colors that served as excellent camouflage for Conn's long torso and limbs.

As Tandra's appraisal lingered over the nonchalant newcomer, she thought she saw him smile. Too bad she couldn't see the man's face through his faceplate. She concluded he was her intended contact. *Where could he be from?* She had never heard such a melodious, strangely accented voice. She imagined men of Slavic tongue imitating Japanese language students speaking English. Though his syllables were slightly angular, they slid over each other in a charming progression.

"I don't think we know all the proper ways of doing things," Conn said. "At least, I don't—other than not hurting others, as Dr. Grey has suggested. Theories of how best to raise children seem to keep changing every ten years."

Tandra laughed. "I've been reading some of those old books since I adopted my baby. Once in a while they actually agree."

"Oh, you know what I meant," said the lady.

Conn moved close to Tandra. "Seriously, I'm interested in Dr. Grey's thesis. I've often wondered if the wisdom of genetic instinct is more ancient, perhaps more to be trusted, that the current trends in human society."

"So we should revert to our animal nature?" the man challenged.

Conn let out a hoot of laughter. "But we *are* our animal nature," he said. "You couldn't possibly escape that fact."

His comment delighted Tandra, but sent the lady off in a huff. Her companion shrugged and walked away, leaving Tandra alone with Conn.

Tandra felt bright with expectation. Here was someone she could talk to. *The conversation could have gone nowhere with those people,* she thought. *Why couldn't they argue sensibly without getting so emotional? Why did it matter so much?*

"The term 'human society' is a semantic myth," Conn continued with mock stiffness in his voice, "certainly not an absolute reference for good conduct. The phrase merely refers to the habits, good and bad, of the current swarm of *Homo sapiens*. Don't you agree, Dr. Grey?"

Tandra laughed, entering Conn's light mood. "I don't believe I know you," she said, offering her hand. "You talk as if your mouth were connected to your brain."

"I'm afraid it's connected to more than you'd like to imagine," Conn muttered.

"I doubt that's possible."

Conn looked at her closely, remembering Jesse Mendleton's warning that she could be idealistic. "How possible?" he asked.

"Im-possible, after what you've just done for me. That argument could have left me stewing all week. Besides an understanding heart, your mouth could be hooked up to sixteen crossed eyes and great hairy teeth, and I wouldn't mind a bit."

An easy laugh tumbled out of Conn's helmet. "I'm not that weird."

"How weird are you? Jesse Mendleton insisted I meet you here, but I can't guess who you are. Do I know you?"

The elll hesitated. "You will, I think," he said.

"I'm correct? You wanted me to meet you here, for an interview?"

"I am interviewing you."

"O-o-okay. I see."

An insistent beat began to tease from the patio loudspeaker.

"Can you dance in that suit?" Tandra asked.

"It's designed not to slow me down."

He took her hand.

"We spacemen pull . . . eh . . . a mean beat, lady," Conn said as casually as he could. "Think you can keep up?"

"Try me."

They began to move rhythmically to the music, and Conn gradually coaxed the quiet, soft woman into his arms, imitating other couples dancing on the patio. To his delight, he found he could easily cue her responsive body with gentle nudges and tugs as he followed the beat. Soon they were sensing it as one. They floated together on the thread of sound in a harmony so complete they lost awareness of everything but the matched and answering movement of their bodies submerged in the rhythm.

"Where did a lady scientist learn to dance like that? You speak the language of ellls."

"Are you an elll?" Tandra tried unsuccessfully to match the sound Conn made for the word. "You couldn't be a man; your dancing is . . . almost meaningful."

"Almost? Don't belittle such meaning, my lovely *kaehloid*. You may have need to understand it some day." Conn paused, suddenly tempted

to take her from the party and reveal who he was. She seemed ready
to accept the fact of his alienness. She seemed even to want it. Then he
noticed her broad grin. "Are you laughing at me?" he asked.

"I've never been called that name—kiloid?—before. Where does that
expression come from?"

"It's Varokian, but I enjoy using the colloquialisms and slang of human languages, too," he said. "They are a hobby of mine."

"Will you tell me where you're from? I can't place the accent."

"I am from Ellason," Conn said. "I am an elll." The rolled *ll* was a
tuneful, lapping sound and the rolling triple *lll* made Tandra laugh. "I
am an elll," he repeated, "and my name is Conn."

CONN

At the sound of a heavy Latin beat, the elll pressed Tandra to his
lean body and guided her into the music again, effectively silencing
her next question. They danced with an absorbing, syncopated rhythm,
while her mind followed its fancies. *What fun if this lanky figure with
the attractive slouch were actually alien—if Ellason were somewhere far from
Earth. His 'l' had a strangely beautiful sound.* She quietly tried to imitate it.

Conn's voice jolted Tandra to awareness. "Don't try to say *elll* that
way. You'll get a cramp in that fat tongue of yours."

She laughed. "You said you specialize in human languages. What
other kinds of languages do you speak? Dolphin?"

"Yes. Some. Enough to get along." He sounded serious. "And all of
the Ellasonian and Varokian languages we've figured out."

"Ellason. Ellason. That's somewhere beyond Orion's Belt, right?"

"Wrong. We couldn't have come that far. Speed-of-light travel is a
myth—too much energy and way too much time. However, Ellason is
far beyond Jupiter, even near perihelion."

Conn lead Tandra into a quick spin and back into his arms. "I've
risked my bones and pooled my green blood just coming here from

Varok, then to the moon and then here, to shop for help from sympathetic human microbiologists. Still interested?"

"Who wouldn't be?" Tandra laughed.

"Your name came to our attention from two different sources. You have published well-regarded work in comparative immunology and bacteriology, yes? And you enjoy music, play flute and piano. But best of all, you have beautiful brain waves."

"Really? You can see them?" With a teasing smile, Tandra weaved to the side, trying to see into his faceplate. "What do my waves tell you?"

"They indicate a good measure of adaptability, spiced with some stubborn willfulness, a fantastic imagination, and a sense of humor. Moreover, your low voltage patterns have a strong romantic twist that might be compatible with the notion of extraterrestrial life."

"Daydreams put out strong voltages?" Tandra asked.

"Not exactly. We've been spying on you with an EEG amplifier. I hope you don't mind."

"So! You're very careful in picking your contacts." Tandra quit dancing and stepped back.

"Extremely."

"But you don't much care who you dance with."

"What is that supposed to mean?"

"I asked *you* to dance."

"Clever of me, wasn't it?" Conn touched a finger of his glove to her chin. "Understand me well, I honestly intend—"

Tandra took his hand, examining it as part of his isolation suit. Then she dropped it. His gloves had six digits. Conn admired the way she covered her surprise.

"I wondered when you would notice," he said. He offered her his hand again, and she gingerly explored the six digits. Then she stared out into the sage brush.

"Here, take this." Conn poured another glass of punch from the nearby bowl and handed it to her.

"I do have to drink alone, don't I?"

"'Fraid so, though the *lohn* bird knows I'd break this smothering disguise if I could. The filters in the helmet make breathing more like work, and I don't like to rely on lungs alone for very long."

Tandra smiled. "Then we should go soon." She held out a hand to him. "Let's dance one more."

Conn looked down at her. "You're not living up to your reputation for cool."

"I'm not reserved with people I like," Tandra said. "Tell me more about your suit. It protects you from our bacteria and viruses, too, I assume."

"Of course." He pulled her to him, and they moved to the music. "The isolation suits are worn as a routine precaution, though all of us at Moonbase have been immunized to your infectious diseases and carefully exposed to your normal flora."

"You're very thorough, Mr. Ellrunian."

"The adjective is elllonian, but call me Conn for short. Come, let's relax on yonder bench, and I'll tell you a story about us alien space-types." He led Tandra inside the hangar, motioned for her to be seated, then sprawled beside her.

"Once upon a time," he began, cocking his head at Tandra's grin, "on a large, floating haven of life not too far from here, lived a people called varoks. Their home was a dry place, hidden within gigantic swirls of colored mist and dusty crystals of auroral light, a place called Varok by its grim, hard-working inhabitants. On this planet, an aging poet, an astronomer by trade, tackled mathematical deviations in the orbital paths of various heavenly bodies. At his urging, and with a great deal of compromise from more conservative minds, great silver vessels sailed into the black, mindless space and found that it was, indeed, not mindless.

"A self-heated dark body, sporting thirty moons, was found to exist in physical, not just mathematical, reality. It was home to aquatic beings with a fascinating take-it-or-leave-it attitude toward most of life's bothersome details.

"The varoks worked for thousands of Earth-years at the puzzle of how best to talk to these creatures, my ancestors, the ellls. Like most of their descendants, the ellls preferred pressure signals in water to their more extensive ultrasonic vocabulary. Finally a compromise was reached.

"The ellls agreed to utter a pattern of throat sounds in order to communicate with the varoks, within the latter's audible range and air-constrained capabilities. Thereafter—through the millennia, an intimate partnership developed between the two species.

"Meanwhile, hominids grew a bit straighter and less hairy on the blue paradise some called Earth. Then, as the *Homo* genus began to move about, leaving intelligible scars, the two species from further out decided to keep a closer watch on that third planet. In time, not so long ago, a laboratory home was buried beneath the wall of a small crater on the surface of Earth's moon. The ellls and varoks settled down in appropriate comfort to watch what happened on Earth. Needless to say, lots happened, but they didn't care much for it."

Conn stopped, glanced at Tandra, and shifted uncomfortably on the bench.

"Here." Tandra took his helmeted head into her lap.

"EEG patterns don't lie after all." He nestled down. "Gentle, sweet human."

"I'm not as cold as some people think. It's just that I make no pretenses. I've always been quick and definite about what I liked."

"Or what you thought you liked."

"I'll try to remember that." Tandra chuckled to herself. "Now please go on. You've touched my most romantic soft spot. How I would love to know of life beyond Earth! Let's go into the weightless room where it's less noisy, and you can tell me more."

"I'll tell you all I can." Conn followed her into the weightless training room, so encouraged he nearly took her into the nearby pool to begin their adjustment. It was all he could do to talk calmly. "After some ten decades—we operate on Greenwich Mean Time at base, so it's easy to keep track of things down here—an aggressive young fool named Conn arrived at the observation base on Earth's moon and began his own review of your planet's affairs via UHF radio. I've exchanged information—digitized and encoded as entangled bursts—with a kindly old coot on Earth named Jesse Mendleton. He has become our official contact down here, a great help in obtaining good, current data without causing a ruckus. We're very careful, as you might guess. We come down here only when we must."

Tandra's magnificent brown eyes widened with amusement. "Ha! No doubt you ellls are responsible for some UFO sightings." She glanced around the open space, and chose a spot in the observation stands to sit down.

"Yes, some of them, I suppose, in the San Luis Valley," Conn said, sitting down next to Tandra. "Our ships have a low radar cross-section, but occasionally we use ionic or electrical display decoys when we visit our favorite lake in the San Juans to pick up water or steal fresh fruit."

"So here you are now, snooping around up close and personal. But what exactly do you want with me, Conn?"

"I want to get you good and drunk, then capture you as my prize specimen."

Tandra laughed, and her hands reached out hesitantly to explore his helmet.

"Actually, we are considering making official contact with Earth," he said, capturing her hands. "Your stress from overcrowding has shaken us up lately–nasty wars, disease, water problems, climate. You know them all too well. If we can stimulate the human capacity for self-control, we might have an outside chance of helping you put a lid on a few of the more explosive issues."

"I wish you luck," Tandra said darkly, abruptly dropping her play-ful mood. "Just don't forget that the human conscience is made of money. No matter what political or economic or religious philosophy is touted, in practice, maximizing the bottom line in one form or another is the basis of all our morality."

Conn looked at Tandra carefully. Was she serious? He couldn't tell. She seemed as stolid as a varok now.

"I didn't mean to spoil your evening with my cynicism."

"Your cynicism may help us identify how we can help. Now, where was I?" Conn settled into Tandra's lap and left his long legs dangling. "As you know, before we decide whether to contact Earth formally, we want to be sure there is no danger of exchanging pathogens. If you come with me, you'll have a small lab to help us complete tests in comparative microbiology."

"In quarantine, I hope," Tandra said.

"Yes, unfortunately. After you have done an analysis of our normal flora and received our immunizations, you can begin Killah's–he's our medical expert—exposure procedures and, hopefully, leave quarantine to join us for a few months on Moonbase. Our life requirements are roughly similar to yours. Our natural cycle is about thirty hours, and the varoks evolved in a twenty-hour system, so we get along on Earth's twenty-four-hour rhythm. We use oxygen, eat anything organic. There shouldn't be any major problems. Of course, it's unavoidable; you'll be something of a . . . "

"Guinea pig," Tandra said.

"Yes. We would say *kaehl*. We think there is little danger of transmitting lethal organisms between our species. Our biochemistry is different, but we can't be sure it's *that* different. Carbon, water-based biochemistry has its boundaries. Eventually we should test the pathogenicity of our parasites on Earth's other species. We have vaccines prepared for humans from all of our potential pathogens. Killah will keep you updated, and he'll run any tests that you feel are necessary."

"Sounds like a good plan, so far."

"Big question," Conn said. "I'm supposed to ask if you would be willing to submit to personality studies, behavior patterns and such—a psychological analysis of yourself as a representative of the human species."

"In captivity?"

"Absolutely not. If the situation blows up your stress balloon, or if we piss you off for any reason, we can have you back home in less than thirty-six hours. We won't even cut out your tongue. No one would believe you anyway. Of course, you could always start a cult and make some money."

"Now there's a brilliant idea. You have been watching Earth, haven't you?"

"Second big question—will you bring little Shawne with you? We'll help you educate her as best we can, but the experience will make an unusual person out of her, a change—"

"For the better. I have to trust that, Conn. Can you guarantee it?"

"Of course not, but I'll do everything I can to be sure she has a good experience."

"You should understand that she will be my first priority, in any situation."

"You sound like an elll, Tandra." He saw that his easy laugh delighted her, but he wasn't sure if she had sensed in his words a strong desire to be believed. Not yet. "You have ten minutes to decide if you want to come to the moon with me. I'll get you another drink to help you make up your mind."

He ambled out to the reception room bar, paused to exchange banter with some other guests, and returned to the weightless training room with a beer.

Tandra looked relaxed and happy sitting on the observation stands surrounding the pool, and she watched him with unabashed admiration. "I'm telling myself not to be silly," she confessed. "Here's a real one. Do yourself a favor. Don't let your daydreams get in your way. I wish you would unmask and join me, now that your story is finished. I want to know you."

"You like me? I thought so."

"I don't often find someone I can talk to, someone who loves the things I do. I shouldn't tell you how long it's been—I would like to know who you are."

"I have told you who I am: Conn of Ellason, an elll with two Varokian degrees. You should be honored."

"Come on now—"

"Just sit here beside me and look through the skylight. There's the moon, right? What constellations do you know? Tell me where they are, and I'll tell you if I can see them, too. My visible spectrum does overlap yours but goes farther into the infrared."

It soon became obvious to Conn that they were seldom referring to the same stars. They finally gave up, arose together from the stands, and danced with unrestrained warmth around the pool.

"How long has it been since I've met a man I could like so well?" Tandra was standing on no ceremony. "Life is too short and love is too scarce. I won't let you go, you know—not easily."

"Good, and back at you, as humans used to say. I'll give you a better view." The elll took her about the waist and, with a low hoot, toppled backwards into the pool, taking her with him. Tandra screeched and struggled briefly to free herself, but he carried her to the bottom.

There in the dimly lit water, before he released her, she looked into his face plate. She saw his pleasant smile flashing gray-green and warm in a wide face framed with intricate plumes, the huge black eyes happily expectant—but totally alien. Her mind cleared. She scrambled to the surface, pulled herself out of the water, and stood beside the pool, stunned.

Conn coasted toward her and gave her foot a playful tug, before he sprang effortlessly onto the deck beside her.

"Other people mustn't know," she said quietly. "They might harm you, entrap you." She was serious. "We must go now, immediately, before anyone else suspects."

"Hold on," he said, taking her hand.

"That was no story you told," Tandra said in a tight whisper.

"No story."

Their fall into the pool had precipitated a noisy melee of disrobing, splashing, and dunking games, and it took several minutes to work their way through the crowd and break free to look for Jesse Mendleton.

Doubling Back

"What time is it?" Tandra fumbled in the small pack she wore slung on her left shoulder.

"Let's see. Inside, there on the wall, it said five minutes to nine," Conn said. "Sit down, Tandra, before you fall down. I'm coming home with you or Jesse. Your choice. I need a ride back up north to catch the next ship back to Moonbase. You'll have plenty of time to think about my offer."

She couldn't stop shaking. "What kind of coward am I?" she muttered.

Conn slumped awkwardly onto the bench and placed a broad glove on Tandra's shoulder. *Is it a hand, fin or paw*, she wondered.

"Are you warm enough?" he asked.

She didn't answer, incapable of focusing on the reality that sat next to her, but she could hear the real concern in his voice. She nodded. Reality was now in that concern, as it had been in the touch of his sensitive body while they danced, in the understanding he had shown her, in the pleasure they had shared with stars, in the warm smile behind the face-plate.

"Tell me what you're thinking," Conn said. "How are you? I can't sense enough through this *kaehl-din* suit."

As he spoke, she began to relax. His voice rolled slowly and gently at first, then faster and more easily as he sensed that this woman, who had somehow come to mean more than just success to him, was staring at him intently.

"You're in danger at this party," she said. "Don't you realize the people here—anywhere on Earth—wouldn't hesitate to capture an alien being?"

"Tandra, put yourself in my place. I have decided to risk contact with you only because my evidence supports the conclusion of our informant, Jesse Mendleton. I believe you are the person to give us the help we need. I know I am in considerable danger here. Though I mean no one and no thing on Earth any harm, you should know that I am armed."

He stretched out both arms toward Tandra and turned them outward. There was a long, narrow pocket in each sleeve of his isolation suit. "Under no circumstances will I allow myself to be captured. I can hold off a sizable attack with the paralyzing gas in this ejector. Or, if cornered, I can activate this hypodermic and disintegrate into pea soup so fast and so completely that no one would be able to ascertain what I was, or that I had been anything at all."

"I . . . I don't know what to say," Tandra stammered. "I had decided that you were a man I could . . . could care for. She stopped. "But now, how can I know that you won't suddenly turn—"

"Turn into what?" Conn chuckled. "I'm already a monster from outer space." He touched her hair. "Take me home with you. I won't do anything to compel you to go to Elll-Varok Moonbase with me. You can take as long as you like to decide."

"I am a fool to go and a fool not to. Your offer is too attractive if it is real, and I truly believe that no one—no thing—could fake being you so well."

"You can be very sure of that," Conn said. "I'm no fake. A bit weird perhaps, for an elll. They call me a loner, one of the new breed, but not a fake. We'll take good care of you, Tandra."

She took his glove in her trembling grasp, and felt something like prehensile fins tighten in response.

"At this party you saw what provincial minds we have," she said. "Few people see themselves in the larger context, but I think you do—whatever your context is."

"That's an indirect way to ask more than I can tell you, Tandra. My context is very different from yours in some ways and yet very much the same in others. It's all one: Earth and Ellason and Anywhere Else. We live, and some of us breathe, and all of us need love." He paused. "You see yourself in proper perspective."

"Do I? I doubt it; I'm far too cynical now. I'll find a way for my daughter, Shawne, to survive. That's all. That's my only real purpose in life."

Conn shifted uneasily. "Let me understand you, Tandra. Mendleton warned us that you had rejected political solutions, but I'll bet you're worried about how politics will affect your child, probably the way she has to live, right?"

Tandra nodded.

"I understand very well. Ellls are notorious for doting on their children. Have I caught your wave length? You sit there like a warm afternoon with not even a long, misty hair out of place. Your voice shook more during that argument at the party than your body shook when you realized what I am. You're cool as the proverbial cucumber, but you run deep—deep and hot where Shawne is concerned. I'd like to expose that heat. I love the elllonian-like passion in you."

"My acquaintances would laugh at your description 'deep and hot,' though my few friends might agree with your analysis. I may be indifferent too often, but 'cool' never, at least not now. Can't you see how nervous I am?" She laughed. "Here, let me hold on." She reached out to touch his hand again. "You're the source of my fear, but you're also its best cure."

Together they sat in silence. When Jesse Mendleton approached a few minutes later, he treated them to a knowing smile.

They stopped at the check booth to retrieve Conn's backpack and made it to Jesse's car without incident. Tandra had little trouble talking Jesse into letting her drive.

"You're not in shock, are you, Tandra?" he asked.

Tandra held out her hand for the keys. It was no longer shaking. "I have some serious thinking to do, Jesse," she said, and she opened the back door for Conn.

The elll emptied his pack and spread out his electronic gear on the back seat.

"You think it's wise to radio in from here?" Jesse asked.

"The signal is scrambled," Conn said, "but I'll wait until we're on the highway. You going up Interstate 25, Dr. Grey?"

"Yes." She almost laughed. "I can't believe who's . . . what's sitting in the back seat. Just ignore me for a while, you two."

They drove on in silence for several miles, then Tandra cut loose. "I can't take Shawne to the moon. I can't put her at risk. God, what am I supposed to do?"

"Tell me what He says, Sweetheart," Conn said. "I've got to make my report to EV Science, and learn my options. Maybe that will help you, too. Tell me when we're on the highway so I can call Moonbase."

"I'm on the entry ramp."

"Do what you need to do, Conn," Jesse said. He sat in the front passenger seat, his eyes fixed on Tandra. "We're okay up here."

Conn radioed to the EV Science Directorate at Moonbase. The conversation took place in Varokian. "We've been worrying too much about contaminating Earth and finding a foolproof way of influencing its fate," he argued. "We should jump in blind and see where it will lead. Jesse Mendleton has found a human expert on the parasites and infectious organisms of Earth's biota . . . No, she's not in government. Jesse says she teaches at Southwest University . . . I haven't asked, but she is an independent soul . . . someone creative enough to work well with Killah at Moonbase . . . Yes, make it official."

He switched to English. "I, Conn, recommend the human microbiologist Tandra Grey for the job Killah has described. We'll need time to clarify all the details. If she accepts our offer, I'm convinced she would be committed and reliable. She has the expertise to help us decide whether direct contact might seriously endanger any Ellasonian, Varokian, or Earthly forms of life."

"Jesse Mendleton seems to have made a good choice," came the reply in English from Moonbase. The annoying delay between exchanges set Conn to tapping his thumbs rhythmically on his knees, which reached up to his shoulders as he sat in the back seat.

The voice continued. "We have confirmed that she has experience in medical immunology, understands the effectiveness of immunization and the possibility of allergic reactions."

"Yes!" Conn gently kneaded Tandra's right shoulder with his gloved fingers. "Did you hear that, Tandra? They've already followed your leads, Jesse, and done a thorough background check."

"However." Another EV Moonbase official spoke in Varokian. "The Directorate has decided that before we bring this person to Moonbase, you should make an independent evaluation, Conn. Are you prepared to stay alone, as long as ten days on Earth? We repeat. Alone? Suited for biological isolation while you make the evaluation?"

"What language is that?" Tandra asked.

"It's Varokian," Jesse answered, "the native language of the varoks, the ellls' partners on Moonbase. They use it when talking official jargon, though it's considered somewhat rude in front of us."

"Really," Tandra said. "It has a nice sound. I'd like to learn it . . . maybe, someday. Did you understand what they said, Jesse?"

"Some of it. It's just business as usual."

The woman's right hand left the driver's wheel and grasped the ellll's glove still resting on her shoulder.

"Conn?" The elll recognized medical officer Killah's voice, tied into the transmission from somewhere on Earth. "Tallyn and I have agreed to stay up here at the lake until snowfall. We'll stay in touch, but you're on your own at the University, or wherever you decide to reconnoiter. State your health—and your mental health in that blasted isolation suit, *aloon*. How are you? Any problems landing or walking to the Spaceport?"

"I think I'll be just fine," Conn said in English, as Tandra's grasp tightened.

"Likely location?"

"With Jesse. I rather like being chauffeured around. Jesse has four-wheel drive on this thing, and snow tires. He's committed."

"Location."

"Southern San Juan Eco-region."

"Confirm support from Jesse Mendleton."

"Confirmed. I'm right here," Jesse said.

"Then you agree with the original plan—that I should observe Tandra unaware?" Conn asked Jesse in Varokian. "I don't like it."

Tandra interrupted. "I heard my name. You're talking about me."

Conn nodded in confirmation, and gestured toward the transmitter.

"It's okay," Jesse said to Tandra in English. "They're just being careful." Then he continued in Varokian as best he could. "There's too much at stake for her, Conn. I know you'll be kind, but go slowly. Look her over carefully. There's no doubt she is expert at her work, but she's a dreamer, this one. That's why I think she'll take the job. Actually, her idealism might be helpful. At least she won't scare easily."

Jesse paused and continued in English. "Tandra Grey might cause you aliens trouble, though. She put too much of herself into politics when the World Environmental Charter was drawn up. She got turned off pretty badly when she finally woke up to the double-think going on."

"Double-think?" Conn's eyes lit up at the promise of new English slang.

"Read George Orwell if you want to understand twenty-first century humans," Jesse said.

Tandra glanced over at Jesse. "That was impressive. Should I know what else you said?"

"No, it would compromise the results," he said honestly. "I have your back, Tandra. Your job is to worry about what this means for Shawne."

"You got that right," she said.

Killah signed off. Conn sat back in his seat but kept one hand kneading Tandra's neck until he felt her muscles begin to relax. So the Directorate had decided that he should further evaluate the woman without her knowledge? His years of study had left him the uncontested master of human custom on Varok. He had perfected his English and could effectively control the long rolling *lll*'s in his accent, if he had to. He felt ready to stay and do whatever was necessary to recruit Tandra.

When they arrived at Tandra's house, Jesse took over the driver's seat. Conn sensed that Tandra needed time alone with Shawne. "I'll come by soon," he said. "I would love to meet your daughter."

Tandra look relieved. "I do need some time for . . . for all this to sink in."

"For just what to sink in?" the elll asked.

"I wish I knew," she said.

FAILED RECONNOITER

Late the next day, Jesse drove Conn to a clearing surrounded by ponderosa pines near Tandra Grey's home. The elll set off at dusk on feet padded thickly with the softest boot stuffing they could find.

"She asked for you this morning, Conn," Jesse had said. "Hoped you were okay. Wanted to know if the job offer was still good. You can't do any better than that for now. Just be sure she's ready before you approach."

The elll, a thin, dark, deceptively humanoid figure in his isolation suit, climbed silently past old wooden houses scattered in the pine trees. He was glad that the suit did not mute the sound of cricket legs. During his pauses to listen he became conscious of the delicious feel of soft pine needles beneath his broad boots. Through the visor of his helmet, he also managed to enjoy the cold silhouettes of distant pines against the darkening sky.

What was that brilliant cool color? Teal, Jesse called it. It reminded Conn of the skies of Varok just before the dark periods. The trees were a different shape there, more like the fruit trees of Earth. It was Earth's oak bushes that resembled the untidy web fields of Varok.

How different both planets were from the Ellason he remembered, with its internal watery glow, its broad sky dominating the low profile of the land and the complex dance of thirty bright moons behind restless cold mists. He couldn't remember much more, but his isolation here on Earth had triggered an odd longing for home, his biological home. He had been gone too long from his native planet Ellason, educated and adapted to Varok since his youth.

He had never missed Ellason while on Varok. His life had been good there. That's where he would choose to take Tandra, if such an option worked out with her. She would like Varok with its lightning-drenched skies, its rolling hills and hidden villages in long valleys. The varoks had changed very little during the long Jovian years—living proof that intelligent beings could find a way to maintain a comfortable steady-state. From what he knew of her concerns about Earth, she would feel safe there.

Empathic being that he was, Conn felt no small pain in watching a progressive deterioration in Earth's life quality. In 2050 CE he saw little remaining he could call beautiful, outside of the pine forests he had visited. Few moments had been peaceful in what humans called the twenty-first century. Most human beings still let their differences and old hatreds downgrade other considerations. Stress and extreme weather were also taking a large toll. Conn and his colleagues saw lowered minimal standards for air and water purity slowly squeeze thin any possible chance of escaping the worsening health statistics.

In the 2040s, the international accords on human population control and food distribution had broken down. Many feared a precipitous decline in numbers, like that experienced earlier on the African continent. Though temporary aide sometimes surfaced, the ravages of malnutrition on nearly a billion humans were largely ignored. The brightest spots, globally, were the trends toward increasing economic cooperation and focus on regions that shared ecological features.

Conn checked his bearings as he climbed the hill behind Tandra Grey's house. For a moment he paused beside the textured bark of a large pine to enjoy his infrared view of the crescent moon. His dimming lenses had done their job, making the brightness of Earth's full daylight tolerable. Now he was glad to be rid of them.

He startled when a grasshopper bounced out of the grass and landed on the sleeve of his isolation suit.

"Hi, pal," he said. "Want to go to the moon with me?" He bent down and lifted the insect to his helmet, but it hopped off into the grass and disappeared. "Guess I'll have to improve my approach," he told himself.

He moved swiftly through scattered ponderosas toward a single-story wooden house on the brow of the gentle hill. Jesse had described its fireproof green metal roof.

The elll crouched behind a Mountain Mahogany bush for a few moments, listening. Then he checked his coordinates. Good. Tandra Grey lived here. She would be alone with her adopted daughter, Shawne.

He was less cautious now. His stride lengthened as he neared the back of the house. Then he tripped on something in the grass. His primary blood chamber sped up, and everything went quiet except for its annoying slush.

He was about to move on when a gentle rustling noise sounded immediately to his left. His infrared vision picked up the silhouette of a warm mammalian female as she lay sleeping on a lawn chair.

Conn started to move away, when something let out a cry. This time Conn did not hesitate. He jumped clear and rolled away.

"What's that, Mommy?"

"Probably a raccoon, Shawne. Go to sleep now. He won't bother us again."

As Tandra and her two-year-old daughter settled back into their sleeping bags, Conn heard the nearby rasping song of another cricket join the whispering of night breezes in the pine trees. The woman drew out a flashlight, and its beam of light chased after the insect into the dark.

Aeyull. The Elllonian invective raced silently through Conn's mind. He was tempted to end this game and simply make himself known. Tense and frustrated, he lay in the grass as Tandra's light circled near him.

The beam swung away as she homed in on the cricket and rolled over to stare into its large complex eyes. "Hi, pal," she said.

Conn nearly lost all caution. It was confirmed—this woman was a kindred soul. Tandra Grey might not share gills and sonar melons and befinned digits, but she was no alien to an elll's love of life's remarkable experiments.

Tandra turned away when the muffled ring of her communicator interrupted her communion with the insect.

Not one to lose a moment's enjoyment, Conn eased over onto his back and watched the quarter moon shining radiant behind the dark lace of pine boughs. There was the constellation Alleoon, stretching like a great eel above the pine trees. He longed to show it to Tandra, but realized they would never share anything again, if he kept botching his independent study of her.

He listened carefully as Tandra talked into the com unit. Standard English, as before. Easy to understand.

She laughed. "It's beautiful out here. I don't intend to sleep in the house this fall if it continues so warm. . . . I don't want Shawne to miss a chance to see the stars, that's why. A little snow on the ground won't hurt her. . . . Yes, I'll be there after I take Shawne out for a few trick-or-treat visits. . . . Of course—Halloween was fun when we were kids. I'll be there, in something like a costume." She laughed nervously. "You'd better remind me how to get to their home . . . After the bridge and a cattle crossing, turn left. Is it the second or third gravel road off the pavement? . . . Tanner's Road. The third gate on the left? I'll find it." She shut down the phone with a resigned sigh and settled into her sleeping bag.

A plan quickly formed in Conn's mind. When Tandra's breathing indicated sleep, he made his way quietly down the hill and stopped beneath a ponderosa. He spoke into his communicator, using Elllonian, the elll's throat language. "Killah, I'll be moving a short distance tonight. Give me the position for Tanner's Road, and find it on the sectional. Okay, I've got twenty-four hours, half of them will be in daylight, and I can't see a *kaehl-din* thing when the sun's out. Twenty-five kilometers? That's more than a thousand *pallons*. I'd better call Jesse for a ride."

"I heard you say 'Tanner's Road.' Why don't you just drive there with me, Conn?"

Every nerve in the hexlines between Conn's tiles fired at the sound of Tandra's voice.

"That is, if you really want to crash the Halloween party." She came out from behind a large tree. "Come on back up to the house. I thought you'd never get here. I've been promising Shawne—"

"I'm not supposed to make contact yet."

"Jesse keeps me well informed. I know everything you had for lunch yesterday, every thing you've had to—you know. He wouldn't let me walk into this contact blind." Tandra held out a steadying hand. "Hurry please. I shouldn't leave Shawne alone any longer."

THE VISIT

Conn took her hand and was grateful for its support as they climbed back up the hill. The rocky ground was tough on his toe fins.

"I can't imagine why your alien friends would send an amphibioid on a trek through these mountains," Tandra said.

"You'll get it, as soon as you know us better."

Tandra smiled. "An amphibioid with attitude. All right. Should we rest?"

"No. Let's get this walking over with."

"Too bad you can't soak your feet at the house. You're flippers are more designed for swimming than walking. Right?"

"This irritating isolation suit is no fun, either. Too bad I can't get out of it."

"Of course that would defeat the purpose of our mission. When my European ancestors first invaded this country, they killed off a lot of Native Americans with their germs."

Conn didn't miss her use of the phrase *our mission*. "We know your history all too well," he muttered. "And apparently you have done some homework. Did Jesse provide information about us ellls and the Elll-Varok Moonbase?"

"All of it. You don't need to tiptoe around me, Conn."

Near the house they found Shawne still fast asleep in the lawn chair. Tandra scooped her up in her sleeping bag. "Did you stay in Jesse's home?" she whispered, as Conn held open the back door. "Any problems? Questions?"

He gave a negative shrug.

"Don't hesitate to ask. Anything goes. We've got to be sure, both of us, right? First, satisfy your curiosity. Look around while I put Shawne to bed. Pick out some things you'd like to know more about."

"Are you going with me?"

"I don't want to refuse, but we both need some more time together."

"I'm supposed to observe you, unnoticed. We have an uncertainty principle to deal with here."

"I understand. I'll keep our lives on track for now, but we'll have trouble ignoring you. Also, if I decide to go, I will have to arrange for a leave of absence from my teaching job. It could take some time."

When Tandra disappeared up the stairs to tuck Shawne into her bed, Conn made a detailed survey of the house, noting her stacks of professional books and some interesting electronic devices. He then surveyed the kitchen cabinets and selected what looked like jars of preserved foods, perhaps fruit. They would be convenient to eat, if he could manage it aseptically.

As Tandra came downstairs, she called, "Conn? Where are you?"

The elll was turning under the full-spectrum lamp in the bathroom. "Feels good to see again. This lamp is too bright, but it's much better than your LEDs. Come here, Tandra. Let me look at you." He took her hand and turned her slowly around. "Your skin is a lovely shade of cool-warm." He made a purring sound as he clasped her shoulders. "I wonder how different our vision is. We'll be able to tell better when we dim Moonbase light to Ellasonian levels."

Tandra smiled and touched his helmet. "I wish I could see through your faceplate again," she said. "I feel as if I'm talking to a ghost."

Conn wrapped his long arms around her and pulled her into a comfortable hug.

"Yes, you are really in there, aren't you?" She rested against him. "Nice muscle tone."

"Not normal. We lose a lot in low gravity. When you're safely wrapped up in one of these isolation suits on our ship, I'll exchange this miserable suit for nature's own, and you'll see up with just what you've got to put."

Tandra laughed. "You have been studying English, haven't you?"

"One of the most hopeful signs we've seen in this century is the widespread use of a common language, global communication networks, all that."

Tandra's curiosity peaked, and they talked for another hour, checking out each other's view of the current trends in human culture. They agreed that the potential for individual integrity provided hope, but the tendency to attach absolutes to ancient paradigms was still dangerous. Good evidence was too often ignored.

"It makes my teaching difficult," Tandra said, with a huge, infectious yawn that coiled Conn's tongue in reflex. "Let's sleep now. We'll forget the Halloween party tomorrow night and spend as much time as we can together. The guest bedroom is downstairs here just off the living room. I'll—"

"Would you mind if I slept in the bathtub?"

"You're serious."

"Eighty-degree water will do. Floating relieves this suit's rubbing on my pressure plates. I'm an aquatic biped, Tan, Dr. Grey. I'm an elll."

"Of course. I can't seem to remember—"

"Maybe that's why we need to learn all we can about each other, before you make a decision."

"Don't you need something to eat?"

"Not for the next ten days. Then my resources run low, and I'll have to run for the hills. Jesse knows—"

"I get it. I've got nine days to make up my mind. Let's go run your bath. I'm exhausted."

In the following days, Tandra worked to imagine the advantages of taking Conn's job offer. Weighing all the risks she could imagine proved easier.

Conn, a being immersed in the present, bombarded with a cacophony of senses, was not much help—except with Shawne. The toddler and the elll delighted in exploring every new idea and sensation that came along.

Tandra began to make arrangements for her leave of absence from the university, so Conn set a date with Jesse Mendleton, who would help them get to the waiting spaceship. That's when new fears surfaced.

For a long moment, Tandra stood looking into Conn's blank helmet. "It's true isn't it? We've talked about it? We've talked for so many hours, Conn, and I still can't find enough faith. I feel Shawne knows you better than I do. The hugs help . . . a lot . . . but something is missing. Maybe I need you to convince me that trusting our lives to ellls—and varoks?—will change Shawne's life for the better."

"I believe it will."

"Where is the guarantee, Conn?"

"Mommy." The serious tone of the conversation upset Shawne. She began to cry and reach for Conn.

The elll picked her up in his arms. "You know I can't guarantee anything, Tan. Maybe you'll have to trust Shawne's instincts."

"I wish I could. When you are with me, I know I can trust you. Even Killah. I've had some good talks with him, discussing the horrendous job we need to do. He's seems very professional."

"There's no way you can do a fool-proof job. We realize that, but we feel that the risks are manageable."

When they had put Shawne down for her nap, Conn took Tandra's hand and led her to the living room, where he selected one of his favorite composers, Debussy, on Tandra's sound system. "You'd be nuts to come away with us without some fear," he said. His warm, firm touch found her hands. "But if we're going to follow protocol and take reasonable precautions against contamination, I'll have to leave you and Shawne alone when you first enter the ship. You'll be in quarantine for weeks."

"Can you and Killah put up with my concerns, Conn? I can't put away all my fears, but I do want to go. I feel we must."

Conn looked down at the human hand in his. The physical contact reassured them both.

"I've committed everything I am, Tandra, to make this work. You have all the promise I can deliver."

The days together passed quickly. Conn knew he had endeared himself to both Shawne and Tandra. The toddler consistently sought him out for music and games and stories, and he responded tirelessly. Conversations with Tandra ranged from her difficult family history to her frustration with human failures.

Tandra continued arrangements for departure, but still the elll could not be sure that she would accept the job at Moonbase. Finally, the morning of day eight, he decided to ask.

"I've got to call for a ride back to the ship, Tandra. Have you made a decision?"

"I can't say no, can I?" She smiled. "You said ten days, and that's the day after tomorrow, when the renters will arrive. We need to be gone very soon. I've arranged for my leave of absence. It started today."

Conn had a hard time containing his joy. The hug she gave him helped, but too soon she pulled away. She was all business.

"Now, Conn, you'd better do your morning story with Shawne, and then you'll have to tell me how much stuff we can take with us. What do I need to survive on the moon for six months? I don't have a clue."

"Jesse can tell you better than I can. He offered to give us a ride north and arrange for a pack horse."

"A pack horse! Where are we going?"

"Just a ways into the San Juan Mountains, to our favorite lake."

After they had read stories and tucked Shawne in for the night, Tandra led Conn into the living room. Soon her Navajo rugs were heaped with things the elll collected from her shelves.

"Do you really intend to take all those old discs—my grandfather's CDs? How would you play them?"

"We could build something. I've worn out the music library at base in my five years there. I'd like to try experimenting with some of these if I may—convert the bass line to ultrasonics—" Suddenly the elll stopped, his gaze riveted on the piano, which was obscured in one corner of the room under stacks of music and smaller instruments.

"Of course. That's a mechanical piano." He approached it slowly and touched one of the keys. "May I?"

"Go ahead. It's not fragile."

Conn ran his glove over the keys and then searched the tall upright case with his fingers. "How could I have missed this? I'd love to see the mechanism."

Tandra helped him clear the music from the tall upright.

"Play it for me," he said. He uncovered the mechanism to inspect the hammers.

Tandra played a series of chords and was steaming through "Rustle of Spring" when Shawne tottered sleepily into the living room. The two-year-old laughed at the mess Conn had made and decided to present him with her Pooh bear.

Absorbed by the hammers jumping on strings, Conn didn't see her until she tugged insistently at the leg of his isolation suit.

Conn acknowledged the tug, and knelt down to the child's height.

Without a word, she pushed the stuffed toy into his gloves. "Here, asternut. Pooh wants ride to moon."

"Shawne," Conn trilled gently, "are you letting me play with him?"

"You keep 'im. He wants to go in a rock' ship."

Conn looked to Tandra for approval. "All right. He can float around the control panel in my ship. Would you like to take a ride, too?"

"Yes, I'll go in a ship. But you better call 'im Pooh. He eats Kleenex." She giggled, and Conn sat beside her on the floor and animated the toy, making the Pooh talk Elllonian.

Conn knew they were doing the right thing. The baby accepted him without question. And why not? His interest in her was genuine. Ellls loved tads. *Too much. If it hadn't been for the varoks, ages ago . . .*

The varoks had come to Ellason uninvited, soon after discovering the large warm planet coming into perihelion near Neptune, its eccentric orbit a result of some ancient collision in Earth's Oort Cloud. Though the alien varoks nearly incited war between elllonian schools opposed to their interference, the varoks stayed on Ellason and eventually became friends and mentors of the aquatic beings.

Conn sang, misquoting an A. A. Milne poem: "The more it snows (Tiddly pom), How cold my toes (Tiddly pom), And nobody knows How cold my toes (Tiddly pom), Are growing."

Tandra laughed as the elll's lapping tones resounded through the house, then she ran upstairs and came back with a pile of Shawne's books. She handed Conn *The House At Pooh Corner*.

"She loves that one," Tandra said. "One story, then back to bed, Shawne."

"Agreed," said Conn. "You're the wise one here. I'll do my best not to blow this gig."

Tandra set a time for Jesse to pick them up early the next morning. Then she and Conn moved from room to room, scanning everything systematically for Shawne's favorite toys, for items that would be useful in her work, and for artifacts that might interest the ellls.

Gradually, another pile of tools, books, electronics, diapers, and personal care items accumulated in the kitchen by the back door. "Conn, come here and tell me if we can take all this."

"All what?" He came into the kitchen carrying Tandra's portable sewing machine. "That little pile of toothbrushes and dolls? Don't be so conservative. We've got lots of room. I'd like to borrow this, if you don't mind. Junah and Artellian would have good fun with it. It is a sewing machine, isn't it?"

"Yes, but—"

"You don't have to take that microscope or any other lab equipment. Killah will fix up the right lenses for you." He stood thinking for a moment. "We'll talk to him again tonight, so you can compare notes. You may not have to take the dewer of cultures you've collected." He pawed through the pile. "Aren't you going to take anything for yourself?"

"I would miss something to play. May I take my recorders?"

"Bring the guitar, too. I'd like to try it. Bring the harmonica. In fact, I'd like to try everything you've got."

To Conn's disappointment, Tandra ignored his double entendre and went to the living room to get the musical instruments. When she returned, Conn and Shawne were carrying into the kitchen two water-color originals of sailboats on Lake Michigan and a framed print of Picasso's "Don Quixote."

"Do you mind?" Conn asked.

"Of course not. I'd love to have them along." Tandra laughed as she looked at the growing pile. "What are we forgetting?"

"A watch?"

"Do you want me to take a watch? I have one somewhere. Why do I need a watch?"

"I thought human beings always needed watches."

"I refuse to be a slave to anything, especially time." Tandra looked around. "I think I've forgotten something."

"I know what it is, but I'm too much of an ell to remind you. You won't need them anyway."

"Oh. Clothes! What kind of clothes should I take?"

"I'm a poor one to advise you, because I can't stand the things. I'm about to go mad in this isolation suit. But it's warm and humid at base. If you're the modest type, bring a bathing suit."

"I'm not the modest type, but you must be kidding. I'll just bring a change of shirts and jeans." She turned to go to her bedroom and returned with a small duffle bag.

"I almost forgot. Jesse said to bring plenty of tampons. Our ladies don't do that. Their eggs need incubation outside their bodies."

Tandra retreated to the bathroom. "I'll have to stop at a grocery store on the way out of town and improvise something later."

That day and a restful night slipped away quickly, while Conn played with Shawne, and Tandra checked and rechecked her long list of things to do. She asked few questions. The elll decided not to worry about it.

Jesse appeared a few minutes early, and they were soon driving north on I-25. When they reached the San Luis Valley in Colorado, Conn had some fun teasing Shawne about all the UFO trips he had taken there. "Pretty soon you'll get to ride in a UFO, Shawne," he said, "only we call it the *Lurlial*. It's a lovely spaceship with bathtubs to sleep in."

THE UNEXPECTED

Surrounded by tall ponderosas beneath a clear blue sky, the *Lurlial* stood like an oversized vase, visible only to the wild critters that called the San Juan Mountains of Colorado home. The elll Killah waited there for Conn, never bored, usually submerged in the nearby lake watching fish and insects or an occasional beaver go about its business.

Soon, he hoped, Conn and the humans would appear. Perhaps Orram would know when, so he called Moonbase.

The varok answered with a coded negative and thanked Killah for checking in. "But don't take any more chances."

Despite Orram's admonition, Killah talked on in Varokian. "I suspect some humans suspect they're not alone, Orram. What they don't want to know is that they have always shared their sun with us ellls and varoks. Soon the big surprise will be old news. We're neighbors. It's time they treated us to some morning coffee down here."

"Stay quiet and be safe, *aloon*."

"Thanks, Orram." The elll shut down the radio link and stood up. His toe-fins hurt. He was tired of waiting. Maybe he'd have time for another swim.

He clambered out of the spaceship and limped across the deep grass to the small lake bedded deep in a thick forest of spruce and aspen. What he saw drained all the green blood from his face.

"Tallyn, get your mossy green hide out of there. Now!"

The other elll backed up to the beach near the outlet creek and looked into the face of a huge red fur ball rising out of the willow bushes.

– Δ –

Conn rode sidesaddle up the trail to the hidden lake, holding Shawne on his lap. He wasn't sure which was worse, walking this far or getting jostled into pea soup with every step. The only pleasure he took on their long trek uphill was the ride through the thick stands of bright aspen forest on a trail carpeted with leaves of bright gold and yellow.

"How much farther?" Tandra asked. She rode one horse and led another, packed with everything she and Shawne would have for the next six months.

"Here's the creek. The lake lies in a meadow just over this hill," Conn called over his shoulder.

Conn disappeared around a sharp turn in the trail, then appeared on top of the hill. The sky shone dark blue around distant peaks. Tandra's horse came to a stop beside Conn's. The elll assumed she was also admiring the view, but then she slowly raised one hand and held it high, commanding silence.

"Back off into the water!" she called to the lake below, enunciating every word in a voice Conn found unbelievably calm. "Slowly turn away. Let the bear know you're harmless."

Conn's face turned pasty yellow, and he clutched Shawne to his broad chest, crushing the plumes beneath his isolation suit.

A giant cinnamon bear snorted and faced Tallyn as he exited the lake. The bear swung her head back and forth in warning. Two cubs scampered away from the frightened elll, back toward their mother. On the other side of the shore, beyond the bears, Killah stood near what had to be the alien spaceship.

"Is that Killah?" Tandra whispered to Conn.

He nodded.

"Killah," Tandra sang a calming monotone. "Turn away from the bears. Walk. Don't Run. Don't get between the mother bear and her cubs. Other elll—Tallyn?—step back into the lake, move into the water slowly."

Leaving the trail, Conn turned his horse toward the drainage creek, downstream from the bear. He reached into the bushes and broke off a branch. "I know a universal language when I see it." He rode slowly toward the bears a short ways, holding a branch of ripe huckleberries.

Tandra joined him. "No further," she said. "Drop the berries, and we'll retreat across the creek to the ship. Ignore the bears."

The Elllonian tones Conn spoke rolled off his long tongue like the soothing notes of a silken bell. "Have a berry, Dearie." He dropped the berry branch and turned his horse away to circle toward the ship. Tandra followed.

Mother bear stopped harrumphing and looked up, apparently more curious than fearful The cubs ran for the berries, away from the other ellls.

"Okay, Mama," Conn said. "We'll let you be."

The bear snorted and stood tall before moving downstream and away from the lake with her cubs.

While Tandra and Conn led the horses to drink at the lakeshore, Tallyn swam across one corner of the lake and climbed out onto the meadow where the space ship stood ready.

Beyond the lake basin, the spruce trees grew thick. A deep carpet of needles muffled their steps as they gathered for the expected greetings. In their relief from the unexpected terror, all formality disappeared.

"You were lucky," Tandra said. "Mother bears don't think twice if their cubs are threatened."

Conn drew a deep noisy breath. "Remember that, Killah, Tallyn, when you deal with this woman. She, too, is a mother."

On cue, Tandra Grey extended her arms to the ellls in greeting.

Conn stared at her, his wide black orbs larger than the dimming lenses behind his helmet. It was as if his senses had been half asleep during their ten days together, he had been so intensely focused on the child. Or had Tandra's superficial similarity to varoks fooled him?

Her blue sweater rode loosely over her jeans, giving her soft figure an understated warmth, like the plumage of an attractive elll out of water. For the first time he wondered what she looked like without all the clothes. And what would she smell like under water? *Too bad she couldn't school for long.*

Her face moved, surprising him. Her brows—which varoks didn't have—were not set into the frown he expected. They were soft, with a natural arch that said admiration, not challenge. Fascinated, he watched them rise as her eyes moved over the other ellls, exploring, caressing, not probing. And the hair covering her head! It spilled like fine *llaoon* grass onto her shoulders, glinting with dark cool lights.

The human female shifted her weight onto one leg and spoke welcoming messages with her body. *She is nothing like a varok!* Then her business-like words delighted him with their expressive, inviting tone.

"I agree that we should do a thorough study of our microbiota before we attempt contact," she said, "but before I give my approval for contact, I must also confirm what Conn has led me to believe—who you are, why you have been watching Earth for so long, and why you have come forward now."

Conn crossed his long legs and eased down into the grass. "You got a cold beer in your pack? That would help."

"It sure would." Tandra moved across the meadow with Shawne to sit near the aliens on a large rock the bear had turned over earlier. "Do you both have eyes?" she asked. "We humans rely a lot on eye contact to build trust."

"Sorry you have to meet blank faceplates," Killah said, "but that will all change once we are in the ship. That's a promise, Shawne. We will all be your friends. We ellls prefer not to conceal our emotions."

"Right." Tandra smiled. "I look forward to that time, and I promise you honesty in return."

"I am called Tallyn," the other elll said, "and this is your medical colleague, Killah, like Conn, also a native of the planet Ellason. Both traveled to Varok in their youth. I hatched on Varok."

"Let me correct one thing," Killah said. "I am an elll, but nothing

like Conn." He dipped his sonar melons to his faceplate so Shawne
could see them.

She giggled and ran to him.

Conn toyed with the grass to avoid staring at Tandra. "Ignore him,
dear humans, except when he has his gills in a test tube. Let's get to it.
Time to board the *Lurlial* and go to the moon."

OBLITERATION OF DOUBT

"How do you like our ship, Dr. Grey?" Killah asked when they had
finished unloading the horses and transferring the human parapher-
nalia into the ship's sterilization chamber. He picked Shawne up in
his arms.

"It looks like a pregnant bat," Tandra said, "but seriously, is it very
loud? I worry about Shawne's ears."

"It is very quiet for a spaceship, but you and Shawne will wear protective gear once you are inside." He looked carefully at the human
woman, as if he sensed a problem. "Do you need anything, Dr. Grey?"

"Just a minute. I'll be all right." Tandra felt faint, and her palms had
begun to sweat.

Conn finished brushing the horses. "I've repacked all the ropes and
packs. Now what do we do?"

"Jesse said to let them know when we were done," Tandra said. She
sent them down the trail with a sharp clap and the command, "Home."

"Impressive," Killah said, settling Shawne to the ground next to
her adoptive mother. "They're almost like daramonts. Are you feeling
better now?"

"I'll be all right." Killah's concern helped.

"Then I'll go in."

"I'll check with you later, Killah," Tandra said, and he disappeared
into the ship. While she stood with Shawne and Conn under the shadow of the odd silver ship, she found herself trembling. She yearned for

something definite—for guaranteed safety, guaranteed anything. But there was little certainty to be found. *Only faith,* she thought, *faith in life's caring for life, which promises nothing.*

With a gentle touch, Conn ushered Tandra and Shawne into the outer hatch of the ship and gave Tandra instructions for entering the sterilization chamber. He would go inside first. When he had finished and signaled her, she was to enter and close the outer hatch behind her. In the sterilization chamber, she and Shawne were to shower, don isolation suits, shower again, then enter the ship through the inner hatch.

Conn closed the outer hatch, showered, backed through the inner hatch and was gone.

Alone with Shawne just inside the alien space ship, Tandra was possessed by a deep impulse, insisting that she get out to dig her fingers into the soil or grasp the trees before she lost them. How could she know that she would ever stand on Earth again? A wave of nausea sent her reeling. *I can't gamble with Shawne's life this way, walking blindly into such an unknown.*

"No, no. We can't go," she cried, grabbing Shawne by the arm and unlocking the outer hatch. She hurried from the ship, afraid of her feeling of light-headedness, but the baby pulled away and turned back. Conn had placed Shawne's stuffed Pooh on top of something within the forward port.

"Look! Pooh gonna drive," Shawne said. "Want to go with Conn." She ran back toward the ship.

Tandra hesitated, felt a rush of adrenalin, then raced after the child, catching her as she reached the outer hatch.

"Bye-bye to da moon." Shawne thrashed wildly against Tandra's grasp.

"Shawne, we can't go. It may not be safe. As she pulled the child away, she looked up and saw Conn's easy slouch framed in the outer hatchway.

"You can't come alone, Shawne," he said. "I think your mother has changed her mind. I'll try to come see you again sometime." His voice carried the disappointment that lay hidden behind his face-plate. He turned back through the sterilization chamber and brought out Tandra's guitar and the watercolor of sailboats on Lake Michigan.

"I'd like to keep this picture, Tandra. May I? I'll find a way to pay for it later."

"No. No! Take it."

"I'll get your toy Pooh, Shawne."

Once again Shawne escaped from Tandra. She climbed into the ship. "I'm going with my f'end Conn."

As Tandra reached into the outer hatch to retrieve the child, her hand hit a furry spot on the inside of the ship, and several large silver flakes fell off. Startled, she looked above her and saw that rounded stems of a mossy growth had invaded the entrance chamber. Indeed, the walls were covered with a thick growth of the delicate leaf-like structures.

Mirrored in the beautiful plant growing so wildly in that incongruous place, her panic dissolved into laughter. "A moss-covered space ship? You can't be so wrong, can you, Shawne?" *There is nothing but grief on Earth for you now, anyway,* she thought, *nothing but asphalt wastelands and death in greater and greater numbers. Maybe, with the ellls, Shawne would have a glimpse of life appreciated and savored.* "All right," she said. "We'll go. I can't break my promise to Conn and Killah."

She turned around to shut the hatch, but Conn blocked her way. "Be sure, Tandra. If you panic *en route*, the varoks will question my good judgment."

She could see a hint of large dark eyes within the elll's helmet. They were not strange. They searched hers, and seemed filled with a longing she could understand. "We'll see you after we shower," she said.

"Indeed you will, but fair warning. You'll have to put up with me in the raw."

Tandra laughed and pushed him away.

"Time for a shower now, Shawne," Conn said. "Bring your mom into the inner hatch as soon as I'm out."

Tandra noticed again the mossy walls of the outer hatch. They were very soft. Tentatively, she touched an irregular patch of the pleasant growth, then felt the door of the inner hatch that Conn had just slammed shut. It had a neutral, strange, light feel.

As they showered, the walls seemed to close in, and the oddly neutral objects around her mocked her with threats. If only Conn could have waited with them.

"Tandra, are you all right?"

"Dr. Grey?" A new, thick voice came through the ship's intercom.

"Just a little dizzy. It's clearing now. I see the isolation suits. I'll dress Shawne first."

"Yes, do," the new voice said. "It will take you some time to learn fine manipulations with the gloves on."

The heavy, clipped voice continued. "Dr. Grey, I am Generalist in Behavioral Science, Llorkin. When Conn left you in the entry hatch, your eyes grew wide and your movements were like those of an undomesticated, caged animal. If you wish, you may return to your home. You are not obligated to come with us. However, once we leave Earth, it will be very inconvenient for us to return before the agreed upon six months."

His tone was aggravating.

"I am quite all right now, Generalist Llorkin."

"Hurry up and get those suits on, will you?" Conn's voice rang with anticipation. "It's time to celebrate. I've won the trust of a human being! I've worked all my life for this, Tan."

He talked Tandra through setup of the light isolation suits. "Be sure your helmets are locked. Be sure you're getting air through the filters before you come through. The UV lights and disinfecting spray will go on for another minute before the inner hatch opens."

With impatient hands, Tandra dressed Shawne, pulled on her oversized isolation suit, checked their helmets, and suddenly the shower hatch sprang to life. A fine spray emerged at every angle from a hundred obscure fixtures. Tandra counted fifteen seconds, thirty seconds. She tensed with excitement. *Forty-five seconds, fifty-five.* Only a few seconds more and she would be with Conn. *Sixty. Eighty.* The eyes she had just seen, the grin she had seen under water at the spaceport party—it must have been a grin—*one hundred seconds*—was extraordinary, alien beyond doubt. *One hundred twenty. One hundred fifty. One hundred eighty. Conn, this is taking forever! Two hundred. Two hundred and twenty.*

Finally, the spray quit. She held Shawne's hand, and they stood dripping for another interminable minute. Then, at last, the seals on the inner hatch began to turn.

"Conn, you have no sense of time. The shower was on well over—"

The inner hatch flew open, stunning Tandra with a silver-green vision that choked off her words. Within the *Lurlial*'s central passageway—a softly lit cavern lined with thick living mounds of silver moss—stood Conn, tall and slender and magnificent, planted at a relaxed tilt on webbed feet, his body a mosaic of hexagonal tiles of gray-green velvet grouted with pale vibrant chartreuse. His powerful arms reached out to Tandra in welcome, extending delicate prehensile fins tipped with six long, partially webbed fingers.

A pleasant grin gradually spread over his face, accenting the feathered laugh lines that radiated out from brilliant emerald green eyes. His deep brow ridge made a right angle over an elegant nose-like structure, giving him a permanent quizzical expression. Long plumes modestly enclosed his hips like a tunic, and a short, tousled crown of feathery black-green plumes, sprinkled sparsely with dabs of bright red, yellow and iridescent blue, carelessly softened the pointed mounds on top of his head.

Tandra stood transfixed by the vision. Shawne, with a burst of joy, ran to Conn, as if he were a favorite stuffed toy come to life. She shouted, "Dere's Conn. Hi, Conn," as he scooped her up in his arms.

Unconsciously, Tandra followed her, tears of delight and relief streaming beneath her face-plate. Conn put Shawne down and grasped Tandra's gloved hands. "Welcome aboard the *Lurlial*, Dr. Grey," he said, and she buried her head in his wide chest, releasing the accumulated tension of the last few hours in welcome sobs. The elll pressed his free arm around her, frustrated, as any elll would be, with the barrier her isolation suit created between them.

"I'm not that bad, then, am I?"

"You're beautiful, Conn." She pushed him away to arm's length so she could absorb the deep crystal of his emerald eyes and confident strength of his soft features.

"Horr-shit," he laughed. "But I'm glad you don't find me repulsive."

They stood silently enjoying each other, Conn remembering their dance at the spaceport party, impatient for contact in the flesh, relieved that Tandra had found his face pleasant. Tandra remembered the game of stars, anticipating more long stories of life beyond Earth, relieved that the other ellls had left them alone. In Conn's arms, Shawne sleepily toyed with the plumes growing wildly around the elll's face. Tandra turned then to see if they were in fact alone and found a grinning Killah and another elll shifting nervously on wide, webbed feet, watching them.

"Tandra Grey, doctor of microbes, meet Generalist Llorkin," Killah said.

"Our resident head-shrinker," Conn added.

"How do you do, Dr. Grey. Hello, Shawne. I am most pleased to make your acquaintance," Llorkin said. His stilted English emerged thickly and with difficulty, contrasting sharply with Conn's easy slang.

Though obviously an elll, Llorkin did not resemble Conn. He was stubby and irregular, a much lighter green, his plumes obviously clipped. He held himself rigid, twitching in the silence following his greeting. Then he shifted a pencil-shaped object to the hand that clutched a pile of plastic sheets and awkwardly held out his befinned fingers to Tandra. Not knowing what else to do, she shook them.

Conn raised a hand and turned it so that the fins made a fan shape as his fingers spiraled inward. "This is the common varokian greeting, Tandra," he said. "Can you do that, Shawne? Llorkin, there's no need for formality here. Dr. Grey and I have already shared water."

Killah laughed.

Puzzled, Tandra glanced at Conn, but his only answer was a quizzical wrinkle that flashed between his brow lines. She followed his gaze to Llorkin and noted the psychologist's obvious embarrassment.

"Formality may not be required, Generalist Conn, but flippancy is certainly out of place at the moment. I think Dr. Grey should sign this immediately, before we leave Earth."

"Is that really necessary?" Killah said, obviously miffed.

Llorkin's stubby, green fingers held out a thin, dull sheet of plastic to Tandra. It held a short paragraph laboriously hand-printed in English:

> *The undersigned agrees to associate with the designated company, Elll-Varok Science at Observation base, Earth-moon, for a period of six months, and bears said company no responsibility for accidents, unavoidable or natural. He She It enters this agreement and our company in full awareness, under no unnatural persuasion or obligation, and by his her its own free will.*
>
> *Signed _____*
>
> *For the human child Shawne_____*
>
> *Witnesses of other species (please designate):*
> _____
> _____

"Where on Earth did you dig out that ancient trash, Llorkin? We don't need it here." Conn's voice had lost its lilt.

"I believe," Llorkin puffed, glancing at Killah, "it is essential that the human female sign a statement of free will immediately, as is done on Earth. Her behavior has been erratic and emotional. I judge that her actions are unpredictable. Any implication that we have taken her by force is severely detrimental to the establishment of a trusting and effective relationship with Earth in the future. *Uyen l'e advant—*"

Conn's voice flew out of control. "Generalist Llorkin, no more insults to Dr. Grey. Speak English in her presence and when within her audible range." His wide emerald eyes were narrowed to slits.

"Unbelievable, Llorkin. My apologies, Dr. Grey," Killah said.

Tandra stared at Conn, recognizing temper in his formal speech and narrowed eyes. "It's all right, Conn, Killah. I don't mind signing the paper."

Shawne reached up to touch the plumes decorating Conn's sonar melons. "It's okay, Conn." He smiled, and his eyes grew to fill the width of his face, the way the child liked them.

With a nervous half-grin, Llorkin handed Tandra his pen. It was a bit large for her hand, but the conical tip slid easily over the flexible sheet, leaving a dark, reddish mark.

"You may keep the pen if you like, Dr. Grey." Llorkin's tone was condescending now. "You will want to compose some records of your experiences. I apologize that our favorite means of record are synthetic. Wood pulp is a luxury the varoks have not recently afforded themselves. Electronic media is impermanent—"

"And lousy in water," Conn interrupted.

"Thank you very much, Generalist Llorkin," Tandra said. "I intend to keep a diary. I thought it might be electronic. Are there more sheets available or should I use the lab computer?"

"Your choice, Tandra," Killah said. "Let me know if you need anything—anything at all once we're at Moonbase."

"I do enjoy the pleasure of hand-writing."

"Then you've come to the right place," Conn said. "Pleasure is our favorite hobby."

They exchanged a glance that left them feeling open and secure with each other. Llorkin acted as if he didn't know what to make of it, saw he could not share in it, and retreated. *Probably annoyed*, Tandra thought.

"Come on, Shawne, I'll show you my ship." Conn took the child in his arms and Tandra followed.

"I'll return to my study, Tandra," Killah said. "Time is short, and Earth has spawned far too many interesting germs. Enjoy your ride to the moon."

He disappeared into the ship, and Tandra turned to Conn.

"What does 'Generalist' mean? Is it a title I should use when I'm talking to someone?"

"Good grief, no, not unless you want to alert someone to his professional status or butter up some poor, insecure so-and-so like Llorkin. The title indicates educational achievement. After Apprentice, comes Specialist or Generalist. Generalist studies cover an entire field of knowledge, like physics or behavioral science or biology. Masters are experts in their field of knowledge, capable of integrating and using what they know over wide disciplines in the real world, which is annoyingly difficult—"

"Being complex."

"Hence unpredictable more often than not. You get it. They actually deserve their distinction. We have two masters running the base, an elll and a varok. Great people, rare scholars who are beginning to learn a bit about life and reality."

"Conn, tell me about the varoks."

"They're a lot like—I shouldn't prejudice your first impression. For now we'll say they're technocrats of restraint. This ship is a good example of their talents. You will soon meet the varoks. They will mean far more to you than I can."

"I don't think that's possible."

An enormous tear rose like a new sun from the deep green rim of Conn's right eye. "You make me cherish my lonerliness," he said.

"'Lonerliness'? That's the first mistake I've heard—"

"It's no mistake. You'll soon know what I mean."

"You have funny hands, Conn, isn't they?" Shawne lisped. "They're all green."

"They're real good for swimming, Shawne. I'll teach you to swim real fast, okay?"

"Yes, yes."

"Will I be doing nothing but comparative microbiology, Conn? Is that all you want me for?"

"I think you'll be useful to us in many ways. If direct contact proves to be reasonably safe, we can decide then how to make the best use of you—how to carve out the best steaks from your legs, whether your arms should be fried or roasted—"

"Conn!"

"No one knows what you'll be asked to do eventually. There is no clear path. We ellls can look at something for only a short while before we must touch it, know it first hand—even human beings, as repulsive as they may be. All but Shawne, of course." He bounced the child up to his shoulder, where she sat happily inspecting him.

"You're pretty, Conn. You have soft things all over."

"Those are my touch plates," he answered. "You can feel them when you get your suit off. After quarantine we'll snuggle up and look at pictures of some weird friends of mine."

Conn swung the two-year-old around in his arms, pressed his long, straight nose flat against her face-plate, and wrapped his tongue around it, inciting Shawne to screeches of delight. Then he balanced her side-saddle on his hip, and the three friends set off down the *Lurlial*'s passageway, happily aware of the closing ring of emotion pulling them together.

EARLY COMMITMENT

"We will be ready to take off in a few minutes." Conn placed Shawne in Tandra's arms. "I'd better give you a quick tour of the ship and take you to your cabin. We entered the main hatch, which is in the middle of the left underbelly. This is the only passageway, so you can't get lost."

"What is the hull made of?" Tandra asked. "It's not metal."

"The hull and walls use a Varokian low-density polyphase material with a low radar cross-section. The delicious moss trimmings come from Ellason."

Conn walked on down the passageway and absent-mindedly

plucked and nibbled a handful of the silver moss draped haphazardly on the walls. "These doors give access to sleeping cabins, and at the end of the hall down here you can see the entrance to the control room."

Just then another elll passed them, his sharply-muscled body tossing his long tousled head and trunk plumes into a rhythmic swing. He went behind the transparent barrier of the control room, where another elll was seated in a large couch surrounded by panels of controls and readouts. The seated elll turned and grinned at Tandra. She saw his long, pale, golden-tipped plumes framing a face wrinkled by many years of laughter, a strong contrast to the other's knotty, wild appearance, accented by heavily feathered brows.

"That is Aen and Artellian in there. Aen is the thinner one. You'll meet them once we're on our way. We computerize our flights, but we have a full measure of manual option. The nose of the bat surrounds much of this entire area and is nothing but heat shield. Turn around now, and I'll follow you back."

Tandra smiled generously at Aen. He looked so incongruous sitting there like a delighted child in the maze of such stark technology. Varokian ingenuity, she guessed. Yes. Conn had said that only the moss was from Ellason. This was a varokian ship. If the moss was any indication, gray composite and banks of dials were of less inherent interest to ellls.

Conn confirmed her perception as they headed back through the ship. The varoks had built the *Lurlial* as a working vehicle for planetary exploration after consulting with the few ellls interested in its design— hence the moss-lined passageways. Though ellls rarely made the long voyage to Ellason in this ship, they believed in maximizing all experiences and never allowed themselves to suffer unnecessary drought.

Conn rapped his soft knuckles on a door near the control room. "This is Llorkin and Aen's cabin. You and Shawne can sleep there across the hall."

Conn's light touch opened another door across the long corridor, and they entered a room carpeted with something soft, red and alive. The room was furnished with a compact desk near the right wall and two large oblong basins recessed into the floor against the left wall. Tandra leaned over one of them and peered through its translucent cover, admiring the deep red lining, guessing that its design was not varokian.

"Here. Let me retract the seal," Conn said.

As he pushed the cover of the bowl into the wall, Shawne noticed the plumbing. "Mama! A fur bathtub."

"Fur? Where would we get fur? It's a living plant, Shawne, like that in the hall. It not only gives us oxygen, but it is delicious to eat and soft to lie on. Would you prefer hot water or blankets, ladies?"

"We'll take blankets, thank you. You sleep in this, Conn?"

"You'll like it too, even with a blanket and no water. It's called an *uuyvanoon*."

"Tandra tried pronouncing the word. "U...uy...way—I'll call it a sleeping tub."

"'Sleeping tub'? You couldn't think of a less romantic name, could you? And 'pregnant bat' for my beautiful ship. You're obviously not taking things seriously enough around here."

"I'm sor—" Tandra was going to apologize, but Conn put a finger on her face-plate.

"Please don't take things seriously around here."

As if in a gentle dream, Tandra followed Shawne and Conn down the soft gray and silver passageway of the ship, watched while the elll demonstrated the ingenious waste disposal system, and wondered again at his frequent reference to varokian design.

"Conn," she asked, "why don't you tell me more about the varoks?"

"Because they're weird, difficult mutants from a wild, poor excuse for a planet." Conn laughed. "They're even uglier than the human beast. You'll meet one soon enough, no doubt. Don't worry about them. Let's get Shawne to bed now. Then I have to help Tallyn get this ship off Earth."

She followed Conn back to the red room and watched while he placed Shawne into one of the basins and connected her restraints.

"Sleep well, New Life," he said, stroking the baby's back. "*Uleoon*, Tandra. Next stop, EV Moonbase. No more panics allowed. You'll be alone now again. Will you be all right?"

Tandra nodded, but as the elll swung out the door, she sighed deeply to ease the apprehension his absence so quickly generated. She worried that Shawne might be more frightened than had been apparent, but she was asleep already.

Feeling vulnerable and uncertain, Tandra looked around. She found a stack of writing sheets in the small desk, strapped herself into one of the large basins to await lift-off, and decided to describe her first impressions of the ellls. She propped her hand under her helmet and leaned on her elbow, then began to write. She avoided a description of Conn, transcribing, instead, a wave of feeling.

> *I was afraid Shawne would never know a day like yester-*
> *day! The world was bathed in sunlight and crowned with*
> *blue again. No matter how alien, any knowing perception*
> *could have found Earth's beauty. Eyes would have delighted*
> *in the slowly waving, sparkling dance of the pines. Ears*
> *would have captured its endless sigh. Touch would have felt*
> *the gentle, warmed wind. Any sense of smell would have*
> *savored the wind's hint of rich, red earth and sun baked*
> *pine needles.*
>
> *And on such a day Conn came to me! What if I had not*
> *had Shawne to pull me back to him? Until I tried to run*
> *from this ship, I had no idea how deeply my faith in life had*
> *been eroded.*
>
> *I trust him entirely, even love him, but I wish he wouldn't*
> *be so obtuse concerning varoks. Their technological capabil-*
> *ity is awesome—unlike the ellls in many respects. I have to*
> *trust that their purposes with me are as Conn described.*

Tandra became aware of slow steps shuffling through the mossy carpet toward Shawne's sleeping bowl.

"I believe she is a very young child?" a rumbling voice mused. The voice was unmistakably elllonian, but deeper than Conn's. It emerged roughly from the ancient, rotund ell Tandra had seen in the control room. Tandra nodded.

"I am Aen, Specialist in Electronics, one of the old-timers in Earth studies." He moved toward Tandra, his round belly spilling generously over his hip plumes, one wrinkled gray-green hand rolled into a fist. Gently he wrapped her hand around his.

"I came to welcome you more personally to the *Lurlial*, to elllonian friendship," he said. "You don't shrink at our touch. We will not forget that." He turned toward the door with no further comment and nodded at the stocky green figure that had come to stand there. "I believe you know Tallyn," Aen said.

The plumes radiating from Tallyn's eyes pinched together into long arrows. "We leave now, Dr. Grey. I advise reclining in *uuyvanoon* and fasten belts. Normally, we leave fast. Our G-tolerance is much greater than yours. We were delayed by minor problems, so we accelerate near your maximum G."

Abruptly, the ellls disappeared through the door.

Tandra concentrated on breathing, trying to relax. Sooner than she expected she was pressed hard into the sleeping bowl. When the force of the acceleration released her, she was able to look down through the porthole near her bowl. The North American continent floated below like a great brown and green island sugared with the brightness of clouds. She became fascinated with watching Earth fall away into empty space, until at last sleep overtook her sightseeing.

As the *Lurlial* sped between Earth and the moon, Tandra was awakened by the noise of Shawne's laughter. She sat on the floor nearby, working a brightly colored puzzle with Aen. It seemed to be an underwater scene glowing with deep yellow reds and brilliant iridescent greens. Tandra sat up to study the alien scene, but her attention was diverted by a rolling melody coming from the ship's intercom.

Conn's mellow tenor joined Killah's massive throat-bassoon. They sang in sliding, angular Elllonian syllables, which fit like pieces of a puzzle into their tight harmony and haunting rhythm:

> *U aloon, acuh a l'Ran,*
> *Uyan l lea, uyan l leoon, aeyull! Aeyull!*
> *Al Ran oonl adl. Pallte El'sonl?*
> *U aloon, acuh a l'Ran,*
> *Uyan leell, uyan leoo, acuh.*
> *U aloon, acuh a l'Ran.*

Tandra made her way down the hall and braced herself in the weightlessness behind the two ellls as they sang. When they sensed her presence, they began the song again in English, with a musical sound less well integrated with the harder English syllables but still soft and wild:

Go water being, alone to the bright blue star,
Beyond my mating, beyond my love, cry grief! Cry grief!
Are Earth's waters filled with exquisite ellls?
Go water being, alone to the bright blue star,
Beyond mates, beyond good life, alone.
Go water being, alone to Earth.

Tandra placed her hand on Conn's shoulder.

"You see, Killah, old fish!" Conn hooted, pulling Tandra into his lap. "This soft, bright creature is mad for me. She brings out the schooler in me."

"What is this meaning, Conn? Take care."

"Not this elll. I'm swimming deep, and I've got to see where the tide will lead. Did you like our song?" he asked Tandra.

"It had a beautiful sound. Was that Elllonian the first time you sang?"

Killah nodded. "A beautiful language, Tandra. We don't use it often enough. It was developed ages ago when Varoks first discovered Ellason and contacted our ancestors."

"I'll look forward to learning all I can about your history."

Killah retreated to join Aen and Shawne. Tallyn sat silently at the navigation panel, watching Conn and Tandra as they talked.

How can Conn relate so closely to this Tandra Grey? he thought. *How can she bear consciousness, knowing, as she must, that so many on her planet are suffering, their life-joy eroded by the production processes of extravagant cultures?*

In Tallyn's mind, moments of selfless or rational behavior in human history were lost beneath the knowledge of *Homo sapiens'* political and natural atrocities. Tandra was a product of centuries of brutal warfare, of a senseless history of users and manipulators, genocidal maniacs and enslavers, whose progeny believed they had the right to brutalize their planet and use its natural wealth for their immediate convenience or pleasure. Tallyn believed human beings were unspeakably cruel, for they were apparently intelligent enough to save their world's life.

Will they ignore EV Science? he wondered. *Will they suffer as varoks suffered hundreds of thousands of years ago? It looks possible, even probable. Humans plummet blindly toward their "twenty-second" century.*

Tallyn realized he was staring at Tandra, and she had turned to meet his eyes, questioning. Then she smiled.

Tallyn could not feel altogether hostile toward this happy human creature and her child. The baby was a magnificent new life, and her mother had accepted the ellls without question. Any elll would love her for that. But Conn was oddly, personally involved with the woman. Tallyn watched with discomfort. There was something raw, some unreal tone in their relationship.

– Δ –

As they approached Earth's moon, Conn leaned back in the pilot's couch of the *Lurlial* against a cushion of nothing. Annoyed at the persistent weightlessness, he pulled his lap restraint tighter. He closed his eyes, longing for the weight and warmth of deep water, for the constant murmur of pressure-talk against the hexagonal meshwork of his body, for an inviting sonar signal from another elll looking for a game of sound-dodge in the large pool at base. "Tandra, where are you?"

"Just watching the moon go by down there," she said from behind him.

"Is Shawne still asleep?"

"No. Aen is trying to teach her astronomy or elllonian astrology. I'm not sure which."

"Ellls don't do astrology," Conn said. "I love finding imaginative patterns in nature, but if there's no good evidence for a connection to life's random shenanigans, forget it."

"A realist, are you?"

"Just a no-nonsense romantic."

"There are too many infrared stars in your sky that we humans can't see."

"We'll have to compare photos, I guess. Ouch. I must have pulled my backfin trying to dance the rhumba with Shawne last night." He undid his lap restraint and leaned forward to float free of his couch. "You wouldn't want to give a poor old elll one of those famous human backrubs, would you, Tan?"

"I'll try. Tell me if I find the tight spots. I can't feel much through these gloves." Tandra spread her hands on his back and kneaded the firm, deep muscles, realizing only dimly that they hinted at physical strength she couldn't imagine.

"Yes. There. That feels good."

"You just overdid the Latin motion a bit. You do have hips, don't you?"

"Not really. We have other fascinating things, though."

Tandra shook her head. "I'll look at Killah's anatomy books someday."

As he relaxed under Tandra's hands, Conn opened his mind to her, as she had in trusting him. "I've often wondered," he said, "what life on Ellason would be like now if the varoks had not come to aid my planet and us aquatic bipeds when they did—I would guess about 8,000 Earth-years ago. Ellason was just a big water garden at that time, and the ancient ellls lived simple lives. They schooled, enjoying each other's company and the delicious impressions from the deeps of the enormous, warm oceans. Their lives were fulfilled by watching their underwater gardens flourish. They slowly gained some technological know-how, and knowledge accumulated, but what the ancient ellls treasured most was anything that felt good. I think some humans call it being mindful."

"What were the first things they invented?"

"They ignored more inventions than they developed, concentrated production on gardening tools, toys, and musical devices. For the most part, we ellls were simply too busy enjoying our sensuous experience to bother developing time-saving gadgets."

Conn gave an little moan of pleasure. "Could you rub a little further right there? Ah, that's just the spot."

"Sounds like your ancestors had an idyllic life," Tandra said.

"Then things went to pot. Ocean gardens grew huge, crowding out the natural landscapes that provided a critical biodiversity. In some areas, sea-nips infected the monocultures and food supplies dwindled. At the same time the population grew. Schools became large and un-wieldy, showing signs of neurotic stress.

"That's when the varoks first visited and decided to interfere. My amazed green ancestors had considered themselves the only intelli-gent life in their corner of the universe."

The ell stopped talking, and Tandra braced herself into a more com-fortable place behind Conn. "You're a little tight around the backfin."

"Dig it out. Muscles are muscles, ell or human. Oh yes, there."

"So how did your ancient ellls react, once they found a way to com-municate with the varoks?"

"Some understood what the varok Lokan and his elllonian partner were trying to do. Others rebelled. Civil war broke out, and many paid a nasty price, until tragedy opened minds.

"After that, from the varoks' history, we eslls learned of nasty potential disasters we had never imagined. We learned why the varoks remained always guarded and inscrutable. In ancient Varokian history, they had reached a crisis of their own, choking on their own cultural excrement. Their rampant procreation had suddenly outstripped their intelligence and adaptability. Sound familiar, Tandra?"

"Oh yes," she said.

"Big difference. Human genes are more . . . sensibly adaptable. The varoks treated themselves to the wrenching horror of mutation after hideous mutation, until the species lost its familiar identity. They call it the Mutilation. The more fortunate millions quickly went mad or starved or died in infancy. But, finally, nature carved an efficient, though fragile, being that could survive in the wastes of Varok.

"Apparently, the ancient varoks really freaked when they saw Ellason treading the same disastrous path they had taken. After Lokan's tragedy, the ancient eslls saw their problems, and we eslls never knew the terror of near-extinction. We . . . never even . . ."

Conn was nearly lulled to sleep by Tandra's attentions, when Tallyn interrupted. "Be secured now, please. We are near moon landing."

Conn sat up. "Okay, I'll be sure the humans are strapped in," he said. "Please take the *Lurlial* in with Aen, Tallyn, so I can remain with them. Let's head back and strap in, Tan. Let's wake Shawne so she can watch."

As the ship swung around the moon, Conn pointed out places the EV team at base had explored by land to check equipment and take rock samples. There were rolling hills and stark boulder piles of singular beauty, selenological formations that had fed fascinating numerical food into the varoks' data banks, and an assortment of craters adding visual interest for elllonian painters.

"We're over the Ocean of Storms right now, coming up on what your human geologists call the d'Alembert Mountains. They're looking dry and miserable as usual," Conn said. "We'll be braking into lunar orbit in a few minutes and dropping beneath the mountains. Buried in those dusty crags is a lush oasis waiting warm and wet for us."

His voice cracked, and he wasn't sure how to go on, wasn't sure if he should go on. "I just wish we didn't have to wait so long before sharing the pool. I don't understand why I'm so drawn to you. It's as if I need to know you in water, as an elll."

Conn felt himself reaching out to the woman with a longing his soul had never known before. "Tandra, have you ever had a dog?"

"I think I understand. Yes, I have had three, though I have always regarded them as persons to respect, in their own right."

"I was just wishing I had a tail to wag," he said. "I'm a little frightened of myself. I need you as my sponsor—what would you say? My sister, my cousin? Something like ellls find in the school."

Tandra smoothed his disorderly plumes with a gentle hand, as if he were a treasured pet. "I seem to need you in the same way, Conn. We're sharing something . . . universal. I can't help but love you."

They were silent as they watched the moon. "We're coming in now, Tan. We might be able to see the base from your port soon."

At the approach of the *Lurlial*, a hidden entrance yawned open to receive the ship. After some minutes of settling and maneuvering, landing and docking were accomplished, and the ship lay at rest in the warm red glow of an enormous pressurized hangar beneath the dry rugged wastes of the d'Alembert Mountains, on the western edge of the moon as viewed from Earth.

II. FIRST REAL CONTACT

Conn's home planet Ellason could have been a normal planet, if it hadn't been clobbered. In its early days the planet sailed around the young sun in a perfectly reasonable oval orbit, scooping up icy planetesimals rich in uranium. At the same time, huge Jupiter was sucking up leftover hydrogen and kicking nearby icy planetesimals out to the young Oort Cloud. One icy body, kicked too hard by the Jovian gravity, collided with Ellason, breaking off a few large pieces and throwing the smaller planet off course. No longer in the orbital plane of its fellows, Ellason careened through the embryonic solar system. It sped away from the outer planets. Just as it passed beyond the Kuiper Belt at 1100 astronomical units, the sun's gravity took over. Ellason reached aphelion and looped back toward the sun to begin its first 12,000-year orbit. Its broken pieces continued to orbit their mother planet and slowly gathered into thirty moons.

BEHIND THE WINDOW

Tandra stepped out of the *Lurlial* into the steamy red glow of the hangar at Elll-Varok Science's Earth Moonbase. She shuddered involuntarily with the sensation of being swallowed by a cavernous mouth. The hangar's high, arched palate loomed ominously behind giant braces. The *Lurlial* and the other vehicles—a long, interplanetary cruiser and a smaller rover—glowed ruddy silver and brown against the walls like irregular teeth. It was clear that the hangar was of varokian design.

Conn followed her, with Shawne perched on his hip. They hurried toward an entrance panel inscribed in Varokian, beneath which hung a strip carefully lettered "Quarantine."

"Nice touch," Tandra remarked.

Conn grimaced, which made his nasal gills contract. "I wish it weren't necessary, Tan. Promise to tell me if you need anything. Tell me if you've got hiccups and need a beer. Anything." He held Shawne close. "When all is safe, we'll go swimming, Shawne. It's real fun in this low gravity."

"It's okay, Conn," she said, picking up on his mood.

Tandra took the child in her arms, and Conn opened the entry to the quarantine unit.

"You can take your isolation suits off in the outer shower chamber and leave them there, my dears. We'll unload your things and send them through the decontaminating zapper. When you feel presentable, you can open the panels on the opposite wall and meet the school. If you need to sleep, leave them closed. No doubt Killah will want to start pumping you full of vaccines right away."

The elll tried to look through Tandra's face-plate for a clue to her quiet stiffness. "Hey!" he whispered. "Not another panic. Come here." He pulled Tandra and Shawne into his arms, molding his body to theirs. The hug gave Tandra the reassurance she needed.

"There will be walls between us for a long time," she said. "Stay near us, Conn."

"Don't worry. I'll stay as close and as long as I can. You can't understand yet what you mean to me."

A new voice spoke. "You are welcome here as one of us, Dr. Grey."

Tandra turned from Conn and looked into the huge eyes of a dark green elll, a solid figure of quiet dignity. His bulk was accented by plumes turned to muted gold with age. "I am Artellian, Moonbase director." His voice was firm and resonant. "Tallyn, good trip." He nodded to the grim engineer as he approached. "The school is ready for your return adjustment as soon as Dr. Grey is settled."

"We'll keep you informed as we receive Jesse Mendleton's news from Earth." Artellian gave her a winning, apologetic smile, then ushered her and Shawne into the quarantine room shower.

Conn faced the master elll, and his fin spiraled up in greeting. Now that Tandra was out of audible range, he reverted to Elllonian, the ellls' throat language. The soft syllables tumbled over each other as he explained to Artellian that all had gone well. He foresaw no problems in communication or cooperation with the human microbiologist.

"Apparently," Artellian grinned, "if I know anything about human response."

Tallyn's brow deepened as he stood by and listened to Conn's cool report. Conn saw he was about to make a blunt comment, when Llorkin came rolling and steaming down the hall toward them.

"Director Artellian, the human being has signed the release papers. However, I would suggest that you post a competent watch, certainly not Generalist Conn, on the quarantine chambers. I regard Dr. Grey as a psychological risk."

Conn answered Artellian's quizzical glance with a shrug. "Generalist Llorkin and I don't agree on Tandra's stability. She is adaptable, tolerant, and thoroughly capable of her assignment here. I'll take responsibility for problems she might have."

"You leave out most of story, Conn." Tallyn spoke in English.

Conn's eyes narrowed with annoyance. "I have been able to establish significant rapport with Dr. Grey. Other members of this crew could exercise more tolerance, until we all know her better. She'll integrate quite well."

"Integrate?" Artellian nodded, his lips wide with an understanding smile. "Then she is willing to school? To speak the true language of ellls? I don't think that is possible, Conn."

"Trust me," he said, not willing to reveal all that had transpired between himself and the woman.

Artellian let it drop, respecting, as he always did, the young loner's idiosyncrasies.

"Let's wait a moment longer. Aen is coming," the elder said. "He wants to be present to welcome Dr. Grey when she opens the panels of the quarantine room. Ah yes, here he comes with the others."

– Δ –

Shawne responded with curiosity and delight, but Tandra's first vision from the quarantine room almost unnerved her. A window full of tall, be-plumed, green beings glanced at her and concentrated on Shawne.

Tandra searched frantically for Conn. With considerable relief, she found his loving, crooked grin. Thanks to his witty introductions, she soon lost her self-consciousness at being viewed like a specimen in a cage. She didn't completely relax, however, until she felt with her hands the tough, transparent composite that walled her away from the ellls. Then smiling Killah appeared, and she began to enjoy meeting the two dozen ebullient, irrepressible characters. Some of the feather-like fronds were long, some short, some blue, some green, tousled over the sonar melons that rose like twin peaks over their wide faces.

When Killah stepped forward, Tandra noted that he was not as tall, not as thin, not as un-glued as Conn. His array of crown plumes framed his sharp features like neatly trimmed bangs.

"You know our medical practitioner, Tan," Conn said with mock formality, "a quack by nature, but an artist of considerable talent, Killah, Generalist of the Pathological Life Sciences. He won't waste time on amenities."

"I see no point in it, Dr. Grey," Killah said. "You must be as eager as we are to have the formalities done so that we can begin serious study together."

"It's encouraging to hear you call these immunizations formalities."

"I hope that's all they are. Most of your pathogens, like ours, are highly specialized organisms, designed to parasitize only certain species. Our germs have become increasingly benign, but yours have not."

"Resistance to antibiotics is a problem that won't go away if continue to be used irresponsibly."

"However, I doubt if either of our germs can conquer whole new biochemical systems."

As Killah talked, peering at Tandra through the glass with a cocked half-grin, a warm professional congeniality grew between them.

Conn interrupted. "You'll have lots of time to talk bugs later," he said. Tandra looked at him. He was watching a blue-plumed elll approach.

"Dr. Grey," Killah said, "this is Ellalon, Apprentice of Pathological Sciences."

The smaller elll joining Killah gave Tandra a bright smile. Her delicately chiseled green features were accented by long, pale blue crown plumes meticulously clipped and shaped into a smooth downward curve. Tandra decided that this elll, like all the others sporting blue plumes, was subtly but definitely female—though her sex, shrouded in a stylishly clipped bikini of the curious, soft elllonian plumes, was betrayed only by wide hips.

Again, Conn interceded. "Shawnoon, this is my dear friend, Ellalon."

"Hello, Shawne," Ellalon called. "Come here. I've got something for you."

Through the ultraviolet hatch, she pushed a small plush model of a Varokian *kaehl*—a squat little animal, hairy and pink, with black eyes, a large red nose, and a flabby pocket containing soft pink eggs.

Shawne ran to pick it up and hug it close.

With visible delight, the crowd of ellls watched Shawne mother the soft toy. Then abruptly they turned their attention to one another, as if they had remembered something they wanted to do.

"After the adjustment, our work will begin, Dr. Grey," Killah called. "Ellalon, do not neglect Conn. See to his adjustment."

The Killah and Ellalon laughed heartily, and unceremoniously hurried down the hall after Conn.

Tandra was perplexed at finding herself alone so suddenly. Were ellls always so erratic and abrupt? If she were here for a serious purpose, the result of much planning, as presumably she was, why had they left her alone? Were they all as unserious as Conn? And where were the varoks? Why had she not met one? Was the ellls' appearance of technical and intellectual competence an illusion? Perhaps they were just the lap dogs of the varoks—whatever varoks were.

"Shawne, where are you?"

The child was engrossed in showing the toy *kaehl* some pictures she had found on a low shelf.

"Look, Mommy," Shawne laughed. "They glow funny."

Tandra spent some time looking at the pictures with Shawne, and then, together, they explored the quarantine room where they would spend their first six weeks with the aliens. The floor was covered with two deep red, shaggy rugs. An overstuffed chair stood near a lofty bed-pad on the wall opposite the curtained access window. Both bed and chair were covered with an incredibly soft, oddly tough, beige material. A desk and a closet occupied the left wall. Both were fitted with compartments and shelves of all sizes and shapes. Next to the desk stood a small bed for Shawne covered with three climb-in pillows shaped like elegant flowers. The wall behind the desk held shelves covered with books and a control panel which, Tandra saw from its carefully lettered English labels, allowed quarantined human visitors access to the base's intercom, its long-distance communications, and its entertainment.

The ellls had gone to some trouble to make the humans comfortable, welcomed as respected guests.

Beneath the window and along the right wall stood long workbenches and cabinets with what Tandra guessed to be an incubator, a small sterilizer and a telephone-booth-sized complex of fine instruments for which the word 'microscope' was hardly adequate. Apparently, Killah expected her to do some real work.

Shawne crawled into her flowery pillows with her new stuffed toy, and Tandra tried out her bed. Both were soon asleep.

When Tandra awoke, refreshened from a short nap, she searched the shelves for volumes that might tell her more about the varoks, and one title caught her attention. She picked up Rikh's *Mutilation: Price of Survival*.

As she began to look through the book, Aen tapped on the large window of the quarantine room. Shawne awoke and ran to the window. "You would like this, Shawne?" He uncovered a small model of an elllonian girl. Long blue plumes framed the delicate face, giving the doll character with delightful laugh lines and exaggerated large emerald eyes. "This should stand a good bath, Tandra."

He pushed the doll into the narrow tank of disinfectant that formed a bridge between the base and the quarantine room, along with the UV hatch. He watched with child-like excitement as Shawne scooped it up and settled down on the floor to groom and dry it.

Tallyn approached the window as Aen hurried off. "I see you reading," Tallyn said, glancing at the book Tandra held in her hand. "What?"

"The title intrigued me," Tandra said.

"Rikh's book. Yes, you must read. Carefully. And learn. You ruin Earth for all. Resources, then life gone at once. Why choose so much death?"

"Because natural disasters, so-called, make good scapegoats. Humans don't see what they don't want to see. Now it is too late even for the most unpopular decisions."

"Too late years ago. We heard talk. Too much talk. Many species already gone. Who cares? Every day. And who cares? Can see no change in wasteful living."

"You're entirely right, Tallyn. Not enough care."

"Is human race worth saving? Man earned right to survive? Agh. Read history, eh? Read your history. And, if continue with Conn..."

The English words momentarily failed him. "If know what you do to Earth, don't read Rikh. Read of ellls. Learn of Conn. He is elll. Learn of Ellason and ellls. Do not destroy him. Do not lead him to yourself so."

He turned quickly away.

What had she done to anger Tallyn? Tandra unpacked, arranged and rearranged her few things, wondering what Tallyn meant.

She was relieved when he left and Killah appeared. "Now then, Dr. Grey," he said, "are you ready to begin work? Do you or the baby have allergic reactions?"

"Yes. We should be very cautious with Shawne."

Shawne continued playing with her new toy, and Tandra and Killah set to work. They decided to try some scratch tests before proceeding with the more hazardous intradermal and intramuscular inoculations.

Killah pushed through the ultraviolet hatch a small box containing a set of sterile packets. In each packet were two small needles filled with a nonviable elllonian biota.

"There is a marking pen in the tool drawer to your right," Killah said. "Mark squares however you like, and I'll keep a diagram of where you apply each vaccine."

Tandra found the pen and drew a grid on her left forearm, then on Shawne's.

"There are gloves and sterile tongs available," Killah said. "All used contaminated items go into the trap door on your left. It opens with a foot pedal."

Tandra found the tools she needed, set them out, and opened the first packet. Carefully, she scratched the alien antigen into the top layers of her skin, within the upper left square drawn on her forearm. Killah marked the corresponding square on his diagram: "Sonarplate Apraxia—elll. RNA agent," and repeated the label in elllonian box letters.

"Double-check the labels, Dr. Grey," he said. "Can you read my writing through the window?"

"Yes, I see it." She looked down at her arm and waited.

"There are no known human toxins in any of these vaccines, Tandra," Killah said, perceiving her concern. "We've checked chemical structures and modified those few that were even remotely similar to molecules toxic to humans."

"I don't mind experimenting on myself. It's Shawne."

"Yes, why don't you wait? Test Shawne after you've done all the scratch tests on yourself."

Tandra agreed and applied the other eight vaccines to her arm.

"We'll watch you for a few moments and then take readings every four hours," Killah said.

"Fine. If I have no reactions to these tests, we might as well do the intradermal vaccinations and then re-check for sensitization."

They agreed, and Tandra began her work with the elll. The days that followed were so full she soon forgot Tallyn's anger. She and Killah isolated, cultured, counted, and tested innumerable bacterial and viral strains, looking for loopholes in their concerted effort to avoid biological catastrophe. It was soon evident that they needed the facilities of a large institute and an army of bacteriologists to do the work they outlined for her six-month stay.

Tandra's frustration was considerable. Ideally, each alien organism's chemical and biological reaction to all known Earthly organisms should be thoroughly studied. However, alien contact by just one organism could be more than one man's life work. She and Killah would be able to make only the grossest first approximations with the more dangerous pathogens of human beings, ellls, and varoks. The enterprise was overwhelming, as was the responsibility it implied, but Tandra relished the latter for the secure feeling of usefulness it gave her.

After her initial concern, Tandra continued to wonder about the varoks, their unspoken presence in the fabric of Moonbase, its routine, and their strange absence from her window.

While the work at base continued and the ellls eagerly anticipated Tandra's release from quarantine, an occasional three-centimeter radio signal leaped from the Moonbase and rode through space for forty minutes on its way to boost Conn's hero ratings on Varok, then sped on for hours more, past the outer planets into the black void where Ellason lurked. There it stirred up in the ellls only a mild interest in their cousin's experiences with the human being. A brief message of encouragement and approval returned—inadvertently exciting, for a moment, a few radio astronomers on Earth. The ellls at base read and re-read these messages from their home planet. They grew homesick and found solace in their sleeping bowls or in the large pool deep inside the base.

Conn ate all of his meals with Tandra and Shawne at the window of the quarantine room. At first the dinner hour stretched into extensive periods that almost overlapped, as Conn surprised Tandra by trying to talk about himself.

"I've had a strange new feeling, Tan. It came on when you first talked with Killah. You seemed to get along so well. The talk came so easily. You humans need to talk a lot, don't you?"

"I suppose, but not really, Conn. I don't need—"

"But I do need to connect better—like Killah. I don't want to lose . . . how we danced."

"We won't lose that Conn, but I must work with Killah."

"It was like schooling."

"And working with Killah is work."

"I'm sorry to admit it, but I'm worried that we ellls are just as capable of fooling ourselves as humans are. At least, I am."

"I don't think we were fooling ourselves, Conn. We connected. I feel that we both need a hug right now, but talk will have to do."

Through the long days, both Tandra and Conn endured with impatience the impenetrable wall of clear synthetic that separated them.

Conn talked for many hours of warm deep Ellason enclosed by the swirling colorful mists of Alahranon. He described ellls he had known and told Tandra of things that he loved: the touch of *llaoon* grass on his plumes; the gentle thumping of pressure signals from every direction as the ellls schooled, each telling a different story or carrying a different message; the shrill chatter of the tads as they experimented in social integration and learned to school; the cool, living touch of moss when he donned a wet-sweater over his water-starved body too long exposed to air; the intense, climactic moments of adjustment when an ell returned after being absent from the school. During adjustment, he told Tandra, the pressure signals mounted and joined with the sonar chorus to finally drown each individual awareness in the overwhelming presence of the school.

"I wonder," Conn said, "what it is about you that makes me talk so much."

Tandra enjoyed listening to him, always with an unquestioning devotion. She didn't say much, except when Conn showed some willingness to pursue larger philosophical questions or, better yet, to discuss the pitiful dilemma of the planet Earth and her rapacious species, *Homo sapiens*. Then her eyes would flash and her dark hair would fly with frustration.

To the observant Killah, these exchanges were a waste of energy and time. Why didn't she and Conn wait until they could mingle and understand each other, not just throw words back and forth?

Time seemed to slip away too quickly, even while it dragged along with heavy feet. Tandra couldn't find minutes enough to keep a diary of her impressions between the endless rows of cultures and microscopic samples and twenty-eight garrulous ellls eager for her attention.

Three weeks in quarantine passed before she was able to add to the little writing she had done on the *Lurlial*:

> *I have grown to love the ellls very much—all of them—*
> *even poor, bumbling, obnoxious Llorkin. They are such*
> *open, accepting beings. I feel that I know them already—a*
> *good thing, for I spend what little time I have reading*
> *varokian books.*

She started to write more about the ellls, or at least Conn, but her pen stopped. There seemed to be no words for them or for him. They were soft with a warm muted-green understanding that eased her mind and gave her pleasure. And Conn was like an intimate extension of herself, like a home of unquestioning acceptance.

When her pen moved again, it strayed into words she usually did not allow herself to say:

> *The magnificent EV microscope (I have finally mastered it) must have been manufactured by varoks. The inscription on its base is in a flowing script quite different from the boxy Elllonian symbols. I am very curious to know more about the varoks. Though they are "hideous mutants" (to quote Killah), they must have remarkable skills and possess a good measure of intelligence, perhaps beyond the human. Killah says they will be pleased with our results, but I wonder. What do they really want with me? And why do they watch Earth at such expense? What are they waiting for? With their technological capability they could do much to help if they wanted to. Is help what they intend?*

What if they assume control of the lives of other beings, as men do, Tandra thought. *Would they wait until the great masses of humans died off so that they could more easily take Earth for themselves?* The varoks were unquestionably brilliant enough to betray the ellls and use them for such devious purposes. It was too much to hope that another intelligent species besides ellls should be so unlike human beings as to forego the power they must possess.

She was marshalling her thoughts to continue writing, when Conn tapped on the window. He was there, as usual, to spend some time with her.

"Hi, Love. What are you writing?"

"Just some notes to myself." She got up and pressed her hands against the window. The gesture had become a habit. The window substituted for the security Conn's touch had given her at first. She loved Conn no less; it was just good to feel the window there, knowing it held out everything that threatened her: the germs still unstudied, the varoks, the ellls. *No. Certainly not the ellls.* She looked at Conn and hesitated before she spoke again. "Why haven't I met any varoks yet?"

Conn choked loudly with a burst of amusement. "Finally you ask! Tandra, you're the strangest enigma. How can you be so competent with those bugs of yours and so blind and assuming about so many other things? I thought you would never ask about the varoks. Most of them are out on expedition. Orram is with them. That's why Llorkin was able to insist that you meet no varoks, so he could sort out your psychological response to ellls first. Personally, I think that your reaction to varoks will be infinitely more interesting.

"I should tell you about Orram sometime—Master Oran Ramahlak, director of Scientific Operations. He would have been here to greet you, in spite of Llorkin, but the crew had trouble with their landcraft. The *Arlaht* is an old moon car—been working almost a century—and she can hover or clamber around anywhere without leaving a messy trail to upset your moon watchers, but she's got a neurotic power package. They should have taken the *Nalkah*. I'm afraid they won't be back until after you leave quarantine."

Tandra said nothing, hating to admit she felt some relief.

Varoks

The master varok, Oran Ramahlak, turned away from the controls of the landcraft *Arlaht* as it ambled through the lunar dust, and spoke to the young varok behind him. "Vohn, when the geophonic probes are planted, call base. Tell Director Artellian that we should reach base three cycles prior to our last estimate."

Orram left his couch and motioned to Vohn as he continued to speak without sound. *I will take some rest now, Vohn.*

Yes, you look tired M. Ramahlak. Vohn answered in mind, then spoke in Varokian. "I will guide the rover from Shröter's Valley and then call Erah to the controls. We will complete the navigation to base so that you may remain with Junah."

"You misread me, Vohn, My time with Junah will be brief. I will return to the controls after I have rested. Call me if any new indication of trouble develops."

Orram made his way back to a small cabin as the craft continued to maneuver through the rocky lunar terrain.

Junah was waiting for him. She was entirely composed, as one might expect a varok to be, but a bit less decided than most. Her eyes were not firm, but they were even more beautiful for their dreaming quality.

"Thank you for being here, Junah," Orram said.

"Your touch is welcome."

"As is yours. It will help me sleep. I have worked too long in the sun. My exposure suit was barely adequate. But our work is finished now, and we will arrive at base within fifty-two hours unless more trouble develops. Are you satisfied with the samples we have taken?"

Junah was chief geologist at Moonbase, and, though a generalist of planetary earth sciences, she preferred to confine her studies to mineralogy. "The samples are adequate for a detailed analysis of the Aristarchus Complex," she said, as she extended her forearm to Orram.

He smiled at her, but took a step back. "You understand that I need only to relax."

"Yes, M. Ramahlak. Your mind is your own." He clasped her to his feverish body and, after the first shock of contact, enjoyed its soothing effect, but a persistent longing reached out to him from the varokian female and disturbed him, for he could not satisfy it.

– Δ –

Shortly before her quarantine ended, Tandra made one more entry in her diary. It was to be her last.

> *The period of quarantine has been hardest on Shawne. She soon learned that she could not leave this room, nor could she follow her favorite friend, Conn, when he disappeared down the hall. Shawne cries to go play with the ells, and her assortment of toys has grown at an alarming rate. Our elllonian friends belong to a species that shamelessly pampers and adores their children. They have continued to bring her bright ingenious building toys and elegant dolls.*

> *At first Killah carefully supervised the sterilization of the toys, but as the time approached to introduce us to the microorganisms that constitute the normal bodily flora of*

*the ellls and varoks, he relaxed his vigilance. Finally, we
both approved Aen's gift of a jumping mossy lohn bird as
an appropriately humorous first contact between the life
forms of Earth and Ellason. Killah said that our constitution
is much too alkaline for his poor bugs to survive in, on, or
under. None of the alien normal flora or fauna has shown
any interest in us at all.*

*Yesterday he asked me to look over the last of our initial
findings. He said, 'Two more days to verify your good health
under the onslaught of two weeks of filthy toys and rotten
food, and we can let you out of there to meet us in the flesh."*

*"In the flesh." Why are those such fearful words?
Sometimes I wish I could stay here, observing the ellls from
behind glass. I must be afraid that they will evaporate into
a dream, and I will wake up too soon. But more likely I am
simply afraid of direct exposure to potential pathogens.*

*As for the varoks, I am plagued by the vision of them as
blank-eyed, organic protozoan forms endowed with a men-
tality equal to that of man at his worst.*

She couldn't deny that she was afraid of the varoks, of power and
intelligence in an unknown, perhaps hideous, form—afraid of their
unspoken purposes with her.

*In any case I wish they would return while I still have
the window.*

Suddenly she felt something watching her, a presence she had not
experienced before. It was very near. She looked up in terror and her
vision became insanely narrow. All she saw were two brilliant blue
eyes, deep and demanding, fixing her with an intense awareness.

She drew back. The eyes were set into a face of smooth, angled
planes, as if chiseled from granite, unlined by the wear imposed by
emotion. The countenance was firm but kind. Her terror subsided,
though she was still conscious of nothing but this new presence.

As she stared, her vision cleared and broadened. With difficulty, her perception left the eyes and moved down the dark figure. As tall and lean as Conn. Dressed. Trim and brown, apparently human—exquisitely human. *Then I am not the ellls' first human visitor,* she thought.

"Orram, you bastard," Conn hollered, as he ran up the hall toward them. "You're six weeks too late."

Tandra, holding her breath, watched the seamless face crack slightly into what had to be a smile.

"I thought I was just in time," she heard the face say, in careful rasping tones and precise English. The dark granite figure turned toward Conn, and Tandra saw a distinctively non-human organ, a disk-shaped patch, lying behind and below its ear. Orram, Oran Ramahlak, the master varok.

His resemblance to humans was shattering! Conn suddenly looked naked and bestial standing next to the fully clothed figure. As she watched the man-like being, a more profound fear than her fantasies of protozoan monsters possessed her. The varok resembled man too closely.

"Dr. Grey, you and Killah have done a thorough job. I am perfectly satisfied with your results. Are you willing to risk direct contact with us?"

Was the varok speaking to her? She answered, uncertain. "I believe the risks are very small, Master Ramahlak."

"Call him Orram," Conn chuckled, "and relax. You look as if you've seen the proverbial ghost. Normally, Orram, this human specimen radiates somewhere near medium warm, like one might call luscious tan—not the frightened cold darkness apparent right now, like what you might call toilet-bowl white, Tan. It sets off your blood-shot eyeballs though. Come on, let's get you out of there so I can feel you again."

He approached the sealed double doors of the quarantine room and pulled them open. "Llorkin's going to split a gasket when he learns that he missed this scene."

He reached for Tandra's hand and must have found it trembling, so he pressed it against his chest. She felt the excited movement of his primary blood chamber as he led her out of the room.

With a cautious smile decorating his face, Orram watched as Conn explored Tandra's delicately exotic face with an affectionate, becalming touch. The varok was obviously fascinated by the elll's sensitivity to her. Her breathing became difficult. She was afraid Orram would realize that she felt as vulnerable as a raw wound.

Slowly, the feeling of exposure left her. She ran her fingers over the traces of feathery down on the back of Conn's hand onto the thin, partial webs between his fingers. Then, very briefly, she absorbed the feel of the mossy, tiled green skin on his arm.

Conn presented her hand to Orram, and she chilled at the contrasting feel of the varok's bony, humanoid grasp.

At that moment Shawne discovered that the door to her prison was open. Racing against her expectation that it would shut her in again, she bounced, jello-fashion in the mild gravity, out of the quarantine room, past the three adults and down the hall.

The burst of exuberance left the varok smiling broadly and the human being and the elll laughing. They turned to follow the child. As they passed an intercom, Orram hesitated for a moment, said, "We are coming," and then walked on beside Conn and Tandra.

"Already?" Conn asked, ignoring Tandra's curiosity.

"Why not?" Orram said.

– Δ –

Conn's velvety green body flashed with its hexagonal patterns and dabs of color as he strode loosely beside Tandra, one long arm balanced on her shoulder. Orram felt the elll's easiness as a contrast to his own straight, brown figure.

"Wait for us, Shawne," Tandra called and walked swiftly after the toddler.

Orram found Tandra's smooth control and serenity to be a pleasant surprise. He·had expected the human female to be more talkative and jumpy. He slowed his step very slightly, so he could watch the red glow from the hallway's hidden lights dance in the sheen of her long, black hair. His eyes moved slowly over her light frame. Well worn dark bodysock, jeans and plain white shirt. Good. Comfortable. She was probably not concerned with form and trappings. Thoroughly self-restrained, yet she allowed her body to swing in an unconscious, sensual way that no varokian woman could effect. Little wonder the ellls loved her. *It seems we have here a mix*, he thought, *a compromise between the wild extremes of elllonian indulgence and the equally wild extremes of varokian denial.*

Just then, Llorkin came storming down the hall toward them. Before the enraged psychologist could speak, Orram raised a hand to stop him. "I have authorized both Dr. Grey's release and our meeting," he said in a cool, rough monotone. "I regret that the circumstances were unfavorable for your observation, but you will have a complete written report of our first contact from Conn, Dr. Grey, and myself within two light cycles. Now, won't you join us? Dinner is served around the pool tonight."

The excitable elll stamped and fluttered for a moment, but there was nothing he could do or say in the wake of the director's pronouncement. "Well, yes, thank you. Thank you for your—help. Yes. Thank you. I will eat now, too. Thank you." He laughed musically at his own befuddlement.

REFLECTIONS IN RUBY WATER

Tandra wondered if it were possible to dislike an elll for any length of time.

As they turned toward the large swinging doors on their left, Conn and Orram stepped aside for a boisterous gang of young ellls who scooped Shawne up, swinging her gently by her hands. The child screeched with delight, and the ellls set her on Conn's shoulders, then disappeared into the large room ahead, which erupted with a billow of steam as they entered. Conn placed Tandra's arm in his, and Orram ceremoniously opened wide the swinging doors for them.

Tandra stood in the doorway, enthralled by a misty red vision of twenty-eight gray-green figures lounging around a large moss-lined pool of clear, deep, ruby water. A few silver-crowned varoks stood like sentries against the walls.

A soft deck covered with fine random patterns of maroon and pink moss surrounded the pool. Apparently the moss was the same edible plant that graced the *lohn* bird toy and the sleeping bowls of the *Lurlial*. A high, light, rose-hued ceiling, walls hung with brown robes and blue moss wet-sweaters on hooks, a shower stall on one end, and several large low tables set around the pool gave the steamy room the appearance of a luxurious bath house.

The sight dispelled any sense of foreboding Tandra had. "It smells wonderful in here, Conn," she said, "like a rich, dense jungle." She took Shawne's hand as the child bounced happily on Conn's shoulders.

When they approached the pool, the ellls burst into a cacophony of whistles and shouts that gradually ordered itself into a wild, rhythmic song:

> *Bayoon kahla! Bayoon! Bayoon!*
> *Va ya lel be. Leoo be. Leoon be.*
> *Bayoon kahla! Bayoon! Bayoon!*
> *Can sensoe. Vabrin vano eyahka.*
> *Leoo be. Leoon be. Va ya lel be.*
> *Yao ba lel be. Leoon be. Leoo be.*
> *Ssro ek savolla sava be.*
> *Bayon akl. Leoo lel lak lokbe.*
> *Vabrin senseo. Bak can eyah o.*
> *Yav ne be ba lel yavalla.*
> *Leoo k fahno k broon yavalla.*
> *Bayoon! Bayoon! Bayoon! Bayoon!*
> *Ssro ek savolla save be.*
> *Savoll uom be akl yavalla.*
> *Leoo k leoon be. Yavt ba lel be.*
> *Bayoon! Bayoon! Bayoon! Bayoon!*

Orram translated line by line:

> *Welcome stranger! Welcome! Welcome!*
> *Come to life now. Live now. Love now.*
> *Welcome strangers! Welcome! Welcome!*
> *Work will wait. Science knows forever.*
> *Live now. Love now. Come to life now.*
> *Join in life now. Love now. Live now.*

Strip the strangerness away now.
Welcome friends! Live life full rich now.
Science waits. Let work itself do.
Join us now in life together.
Live and breathe and sound together.
Welcome! Welcome! Welcome! Welcome!
Strip the strangerness away now.
Stranger gone! Now friends together.
Live and love now. Joined in life now.
Welcome! Welcome! Welcome! Welcome!

Conn set Shawne down, and the ellls tried to coax her to themselves as they sang.

"Two-year-olds and water don't mix, Conn," Tandra hollered. "Shawne can't swim, you know."

"She will, soon," Orram said.

Tandra tried to explain that human babies might have no innate water sense, but no one seemed to understand her. It was all she could do to keep the toddler with her, away from the inviting ellls and their watery play.

Orram made a point of taking both Tandra's and Shawne's hands, as he and Conn introduced them to the enthusiastic crew. Slowly they circled the large pool, greeting each ell and varok in turn as the song went on. On the far side of the room Conn placed Shawne in Aen's lap, and soon the elder ell had her clapping heartily on and off the driving beat. Finally, the song drifted into a chant of welcome, steady and insistent: *"Bayoon! Bayoon!"*

"Expect to get wet," Orram shouted to Tandra. Conn had taken her by the elbows and was firmly pushing her toward the water.

"Conn, stop. What are you doing? I need to stay with Shawne."

"Initiation into elllonian friendship. Aen will take care of Shawne. We love you, Tan. I know it's mutual, so in we go. *Adjustment*, we call it."

The ellls hollered with delight as Conn clamped his arms around her waist and took her into the wine-red water. Tandra came up smiling, hesitated a moment, then released herself to spontaneity, while the ellls cheered her on. She was no longer subject to the rules and customs of men; she would be the natural animal she was meant to be, just as the ellls were. Their absolute lack of self-consciousness gave her that gift.

With little hesitation, Tandra threw her shoes, jeans, and sweater out of the pool, then swam through the clean, deep-lighted water while Conn dove under and over her, occasionally mimicking her stroke. Winded at last, she paused, and the entire elllonian crew dove in to roll and tumble and leap through the water like intoxicated porpoises. All but Aen.

She saw that Aen had carefully lowered himself into the pool with Shawne on his shoulders. He swam slowly about, keeping her face well above the slow-motion waves generated by his friends.

Tandra took no more chances, staying close to Shawne and Aen in the water. Soon it became obvious the child was in no danger, and she relaxed enough to look around.

Outside the general commotion, the five varoks of the crew had stepped out of their simple clothes and more sedately joined the watery fracas. They stayed apart, and the ellls gave them wide berth. They stayed in water for only a short time, so Tandra was able to study them from her vantage point at the side of the pool.

Beneath their outer clothing of light pullovers and loin wraps, the two varokian females wore plain tank suits that revealed mammaloid forms. The three males wore firm shorts of a brown so close in color to their skin that at first Tandra thought they were naked. A gentle hump suggested genitals, in striking contrast to the smooth neuter appearance of the ellls, dressed in plume tunics. The skin of the varoks was a delicate brown, and their hair covered only their scalps. It trailed long or short, as their whim dictated, in frosted streaks of red-brown and silver, neatly framing the conspicuous round plates behind their ears.

As she watched them, Tandra began to imagine the power they must possess. What did they intend? They were too self-assured, too purposeful a people to leave Earth entirely to herself. Where did she really fit into their plans? The blood drained from her face, as her fears took hold.

"It's all right, Tandra. We will make no plans without your approval. We are sworn to your protection." Orram was beside her in the water, close, not touching.

He smiled, and smiled again when the expression didn't surprise her, as it would an elll. "We might even protect you from yourself."

REFLECTIONS IN RUBY WATER

His presence was warm, reassuring, safe, no longer strange.

Suddenly Conn rose from the bottom of the pool, dragged Tandra away from Orram, and tossed her high into the air. She came down with a hoot and dove deep into the water in search of Conn's long legs. Her hands locked on his ankles, but his strong webbed feet thrashed easily, pulling her along underwater with exhilarating speed. Finally, she let him go. She rose for a breath and saw, extended along his back, a long narrow fin rippling with powerful strokes.

"No wonder you swim like a fish," Tandra laughed when Conn surfaced with her. "I didn't know you were so well equipped."

"Equipped?"

"I didn't know you had a dorsal fin."

"It's hydraulically engineered. Can't stand dry air. I wish you would read about us ellls in more detail, Tan."

"I will. I promise. I'll take some time now. Top priority: elllonian physiology and," she emphasized with a smile, "psychology."

"Hah!" Conn blew water into the air. "You'll head right back to the varokian shelves."

Just then the small, blue-green figure of Ellalon brushed past Conn and turned, grabbing his shoulders and forcing him deep under the surface. When he didn't return, Tandra worked her way through the playful mob in the pool until she found Aen. He was alone. Shawne was nowhere in sight.

"Easy there, Mom. No one is going to let her drown," a passing elll said.

Aen whistled, and a bright blue elll leapt out of the water with Shawne in her arms.

"She's doing very well underwater already," the blue elll said. "A few more lessons and she'll be on her own here."

Shawne threw herself out of the elll's arms into the watery melee. The child came up, sputtered, laughed, and disappeared again, while Aen hovered nearby, and the blue elll swam beneath her.

"She already schools like an elll," Aen said, offering Tandra a calming smile.

Again Orram was close to her in the water. "Watch," he said quietly. "Watch the miracle of ellls connecting with all that is good and natural in your precocious child. Ellls love tads more than anything else. Shawne is safe with them. There are no better teachers in water."

Tandra heard him. She watched, then relaxed and rejoiced.

Soon the baby had enough of watery play. Aen lifted her onto the mossy deck and showed her how to nibble its tiny end fruits.

Tandra came out of the pool to give her a congratulatory hug, and Orram brought them both tunics made of a thick, absorbent brown material.

"Come, talk with the other varoks," Orram said. "Aen, we will take Shawne now."

He led them first to the communications engineer, a young varok with a pleasant face set with competence. Orram gestured to the male varok. "This is Erah, a hydrologist with a passion for moons."

"You are most welcome here," Erah said in a deliberate, softly roughened voice.

The varokian astronomer, Ahl, his face deep brown with age and his hair turned entirely to silver, approached them with hands held poised at his sides. "Welcome," he said. "Come spend some time at the telescope. No clouds to obscure vision. Marvelous."

"Thank you," Tandra murmured. She didn't know what to say. Their precise mannerisms and lightly accented English left her feeling awkward. They seemed to confirm her fears. She stopped herself. She wasn't being fair. Resolutely, she took Orram's arm.

He startled, but a glint of kindness narrowed his eyes. "Let us take our places at the table," he said. "Master Artellian is leaving the pool."

As they turned toward the tables, a second varokian woman came toward them. A look, long and intense, focused on Tandra's hand on Orram's arm. "May I join your table, Master Ramahlak?"

Tandra noted a hint of surprise in Orram's eyes, but his tone betrayed nothing but bland acceptance. "Of course," he said. "Dr. Grey, this is Generalist Junah, our chief geologist."

From deep within a placid face framed with smooth, silver and blond hair, Junah looked at Tandra, then shifted her search to Orram's expression. Tandra followed her quiet gaze and felt a tense, ill-defined questioning surge between the three of them. As quickly as it had come, the tension dissipated, leaving questions unanswered.

When the golden-fringed Artellian left the pool, his crew gradually followed his example, laughing and teasing merrily as they tossed their heads and shook their hips, sending droplets flying in all directions from their plumes. Some took moss wet-sweaters from the wall hooks and pulled them over their heads before finding their seats on the deck around the low tables.

Soon the gentle, rolling chatter of the ellls filled the room, and the surface of the pool quieted until, with a boiling roll, the water was thrown back by two young ellls. They emerged, squealed loudly when they discovered that everyone was gathered around the tables. They clambered quickly to their seats amidst hoots of joy, which rose to a new crescendo when Conn, too, broke the surface. Ellalon immediately followed him, and sat happily at a far table with the varoks.

"Conn, where you been?" shouted Tallyn. "We have dessert already."

"No place that you haven't been, wise guy," Conn retorted.

"Well, least I know what to do once there. You don't get practice enough to know which end is up."

The ellls whistled and laughed like rowdy boys, but Conn only shrugged, cocked his brow good-naturedly, and sauntered over to the wall to don a blue wet-sweater.

"Hey, you don't need sweater, *aloon*," Tallyn heckled. "Must you drive all girls mad?"

"I would if I could." Everyone hooted as he sank to the moss carpet between Tandra and Shawne, who was busy scolding Aen and trying to dry his head plumes.

Tandra couldn't restrain her curiosity, though she knew better than to expect an answer from Conn. "What in the world is going on?"

She was surprised at the serious tone in his voice. "You should have been doing some elllonian homework, Tan. We're not 'in the world.' Remember?"

"All right. I've already promised."

"Keep that promise. Please." He smiled. "Now try some of this. I think you'll find dried *oeln* fish more tasty than the sterilized *brilln* brains you've been eating."

They ate with relish the savory elllonian food and simple varokian staples, laughing and enjoying their new companionship, talking more for pleasure than for information. Shawne got the most attention.

Junah sat quietly beside Orram and said nothing. Tandra wondered if the varokian woman's silence annoyed him. He showed no indication of either accepting or rejecting her presence.

For a long while the meal continued at a leisurely tempo, accompanied by the musical voices of the ellls and the sparse, rasping talk of the varoks. Slowly savoring the continual barrage of elegant tastes, all three species nibbled down the heaps of *arl* and *brilln* and *challall* weeds on their tables until there were none left. Occasionally some of the crew were prodded and teased until they made a second, then a third, trip to the food center to refill the pitchers and trays, and time forgot its race with life beside the steamy, red, crystal pool.

"C'mere," Conn mumbled through his last mouthful, "let's go make vibrations, Tan."

"I will take Shawne to her bed when she is tired," Aen said. "She will not be left alone."

Conn pulled a reluctant Tandra to her feet, towed her to a bank of controls set into the far wall, and pushed several switches. Soon a familiar melody drifted diffusely into the room. As the volume increased she felt engulfed in sound; the beat throbbed in her bones.

"Give an elll a complex, hard beat and a good melody, and he'll go anywhere, even in this light gravity," Conn hollered "Let's see what we can do."

He threw himself with abandon into a syncopated dance that tossed his body slowly and oddly back and forth in the moon's easy grasp. It made Tandra laugh, and she followed his example, until both were lost in the joy of sound and floating movement. Many ellls joined them, until a complex of rhythmical body patterns filled the room, in and out of the water.

– Δ –

Orram sat watching Tandra and Conn, keeping track of Shawne and talking sparsely with the other varoks, according to their custom. He was not surprised when his patch found a call from Junah.

The human being looks very much like us, doesn't she, Junah? he asked. *Is it disturbing for you to see elllonian qualities in her, too? I am fascinated, but you must develop your own relationship with her. We varoks make her uncomfortable, I believe. You may ignore her if you choose.*

I want to know her with you, Orram.

The varok met her gaze and searched her mood. No emotion crossed his face, as he replied in thought, *It is not possible, Junah. I am driven alone.*

You have not judged her suitable, M. Ramahlak, for all the tasks in mind? Junah said, searching for contact with a different approach.

Not yet. I do not want to offend her, but I cannot trust her with too much responsibility until we are sure of her attitudes and her qualifications. Meanwhile, there are many unanswered biological questions that she can help us answer.

The varoks were silent in voice and thought then, as they watched the dancers. The beat of the music changed and continued and changed again, and the ells stopped dancing to re-dampen their dry throats with red punch. Finally, a polka emerged from the walls and threw them wildly in and around the pool. When it ended, Killah mercifully changed the music and bathed the exhausted dancers in a flowing varokian melody.

"Oh Conn, Conn, my marvelous big lizard," Tandra gasped, sprawling beside him on the deck. "I'd forgotten what it's like to dance with you. What a glorious sensation! Tell me what you did to my music to make it sound like that. It's penetrating."

"I'm surprised you noticed much difference. Hey, get off my flipper. Our audible range doesn't extend downward very far, so we miss much of that great beat. Stop it, woman! Electronically speaking, we tore the band apart and rechanneled the bass notes—Dr. Grey, for shame—and the most rhythmic parts into a sonar generator. There." He pinned her down with his legs, putting an end to her teasing. "Then it's terrific under water, though we can still pick up the sound in air."

He released her and she enclosed his broad chest in her hands and stroked his sides, burying her face under his chin. Here was not only home, but joy-in-life personified. She was oblivious to everything but him.

Gently, Conn pushed her hands away and eased her head down further on his chest. "There," he said. "Homework, my little beast. Old Conn can't take too much all at once. I'm loaded with hedonic glands along my sides and under my chin, and I do tend to be a bit modest with so many varoks watching."

Tandra sat up with a start, sending the room spinning around her for a moment. "O-o-o-o, I drank too much punch. It tasted much too good to be healthy. Hedonic glands! And lots of them! I think you should be my pet lizard."

Conn grinned. "I'll be your pet lizard, Tan, but not right now." He touched her lips with his as he got up. "Not a bad sign of affection, but I prefer a nudge under the chin. I'm leaving you, in self-defense."

He joined Ellalon and a group of astronomers who were playing a slow-motion version of volleyball, using the edge of the pool as a net or goal, Tandra couldn't tell which. Shawne was merrily trying to chase the ball when it went astray of the game, and the ellls urged her on with warm enthusiasm, laughing pleasantly at her antics in the moon's light gravity.

Tandra drank in the scene around her: energetic gray-green bodies splashing and running, silver-brown images of varoks mingling again with their green colleagues, red water, pink ceiling; Orram's black moccasins walking toward her on red plush moss. Where would they walk on Earth? And to what purpose? She shivered.

"Aen will put Shawne into bed soon," Orram said. "It looks as if she is now going after more Ellasonian moths and varokian sweet cakes. Let us say goodnight to Shawne and go to the garden. The party will end soon. It is late."

As Tandra and Orram followed Aen toward the kitchen, Junah watched from a distance. Tandra saw the varokian woman's brow crease into a piercing question when Orram gave Shawne a tender kiss goodnight, following Tandra's example.

The garden occupied the full length of the underground compound along the innermost wall of the base immediately in back of the pool-room. Orram led Tandra between rows of feathery moss beds and tall, succulent plants. Deep tanks were filled with tufts and strings of angular shapes growing under the warm, red glow of infrared light sources. *Ahlrialka* and other Varokian trees sported brilliant oval fruits: some large and purple, some tiny and fresh blue, others plump and pale and furry. On one wall stood a large tank containing leafy blue aquatic plants and large, flat, iridescent pink creatures that stared with bright green eyes set decoratively around their periphery. Next to the tank was a tall moth colony, vibrating with color, and above all was a maze of reflecting devices designed to trap just enough sunlight for maximum growth of the varokian plants.

"You don't grow all of your food, do you?" Tandra asked.

"Yes we do, but only because Ellasonian mosses supply most of our food requirements. Ellason specializes in moss the same way your planet specializes in insects. Our stores of preserved food last a very long time. Space vehicles travel rarely from Varok. And, of course, we must always maintain a reserve for evacuation."

"You are such a Spartan people. Yet you don't deny the ellls the comfort of so much water. It can't all come from Colorado lakes. I don't know whether to ask how you do it or why."

"The *how* is not difficult. Little moisture is lost in this sealed den of ours; it is continually reprocessed. And the *why*—perhaps it is a symbiotic relationship we varoks have with ellls, as they have with the moss that cushions and feeds them."

Orram turned to a door near the far end of the garden. "We will call this the *recreation lounge* in English, though such a term has no real meaning to either ellls or varoks."

The room was a comfortable place, softly lit and furnished with smaller, sprawling versions of the *Lurlial*'s sleeping bowls. Storage shelves and working space covered the walls not occupied by a variety of boxy shapes Tandra decided were books or recorded information of some type. Three intricately marked and pocketed game tables were strategically placed in corners about the room, and on a work bench in the fourth corner, surrounded by piles of Conn's wires, rectifiers, transistors and speakers, were Tandra's watercolor of boats on Lake Michigan and Shawne's Pooh bear. On the far side of the room, wide curving stairs led upward and out of sight.

"Those stairs lead to the observation deck," Orram said. "Solitude is respected there. Even some of the ellls need to be alone at times. It is not occupied now. Come and see. It is about time for bright Earthlight."

Tandra followed Orram through the recreation room and up the stairs. She came upon a large transparent wall framing a view of the moon's entangled pits and craters, throwing long shadows over each other in the knobby terrain. Beyond the bowls of dust, the irregular mounded peaks of the d'Alembert Mountains lay silhouetted on the rim of Earth.

"How can I thank you for bringing me here, for letting me know the ellls." Tandra sat beside Orram on one of the long couches facing the window. She concentrated on the view, trying to burn it into her mind so that she could carry it with her always—a precious but fragile painting, so very plain and harsh a painting, so very dead, stark and lonely, like the varok, smooth and dangerous, too unweird, too ungreen.

When Tandra's head rolled against his shoulder, Orram looked down at her face and watched the glow of her smooth brown skin accent the bridge of her small nose and the easy turn of her chin. Daring to lower the gate of his being, so that he might know this human being better than his nature would normally let him, he slumped into the couch and eased her body against his. Though disturbed by her closeness, he cherished it and was amazed at himself. Then he too slept.

Who Speaks for Homo Sapiens?

As the moon turned slowly away from the sun, and the d'Alembert Mountains grew dimmer, the sun-filter in the large window of the observation deck gradually started to clear, and the lights in the garden began their two-weeks' work.

Tandra stirred and reached over her head to clutch her pillow, but she missed the expected softness and came awake with the realization that her head was cradled in Orram's lap. He did not move. Apparently he was asleep. She stared out of the window at the horizon, visible as a bright sliver beyond the darkly silhouetted mountains. Then slowly, so as not to wake the varok, she turned her face upwards and dared to look into his eyes.

Her gaze met his. "I must have slept for some time. Why didn't you wake me? I must go to Shawne."

"Aen came in to say that she was eating a good breakfast and would be in the nursery until she asked for you."

Tandra sat up and looked at the short silver and auburn hair framing his hard, brown face. "Your hair is very beautiful," she said uneasily.

A smile shone deeply from within Orram's eyes. Impulsively, Tandra touched the patches behind his ears and the varok's smile spread slowly across his face. Tandra watched the rare phenomenon with delight, and when their eyes finally met again, she and Orram laughed aloud together.

"M. Ramahlak," Tandra said, "Except for those patches behind your ears, you would easily be taken for a man anywhere on Earth. How are you different from us? Are the patches sensory organs of some kind?"

"Yes, but we rarely talk about them. Their function is a personal one for us. At very short range, they detect and amplify low frequency electromagnetic signals. I can't explain the patches to you in any detail, for their full potential has been ruled off-limits to human beings for now. I think you'd agree this sense could be easily misunderstood and evoke unnecessary fear in those who do not possess it or understand its limitations. You are correct in assuming that it is the most obvious difference between our species, except for some . . . biochemistry."

He paused and searched Tandra's face. "Your eyes are very beautiful, and your body language is quite easy to read. If only I could understand myself so well. It is strange that I am not repulsed by your touch."

"I understand."

"You do? Dr. Grey, we anticipated problems in relating effectively with you. But I am afraid our real problems could lie in the other direction. I am glad that you have not yet studied varokian psychology. Your ignorance may have saved us both from useless and time-consuming precautions."

"But I have studied varokian psychology, M. Ramahlak."

"You seem not to understand the varokian aversion to touch."

"I think I understand it. A series of mutations occurred during the period of stressful overcrowding on Varok, which resulted in the appearance of highly sensitive tactile organs in some of your ancestors. Those mutants could not stand the constant jostling and super-stimulation of your urban centers, so they moved out to the wastes and eventually learned to survive independently there. As a result, they and their offspring avoided the plagues and famines of Varok; they were the ones who saved your species from extinction, when they recognized sexual consummation as normal—as well as the natural expression of a mind-link—and defined family as a committed economic unit. Before that they had gone to great unnatural extremes to avoid contact with others. Am I right?"

"You have learned your history well. But what of us now?"

"Your avoidance of touch cannot be as great as most, Orram. You took my hand when we first met."

"You needed reassurance."

"And I assumed that you would let me know if I overstepped the bounds of your sensitivity."

"Then you lay the responsibility on me?"

"Yes. Forgive me, but I wanted to touch you. I need to touch you, to know you are real and alien. Conn learned this about me when we first met."

"Ellls are very aware beings, Tandra, usually more intensely aware than you or I could possibly be. Awareness gives birth to caring. Ellls go to extremes to avoid intruding on our varokian tactile senses, even though their own similar senses contribute enormously to their awareness. They value them equally with life itself."

"I have always been something of a bulldozer, Orram. Most people would be more sensitive."

"But not so adaptable, so accepting, as you. I promise to be honest with you, Tandra. I find your combination of physical aggressiveness and mental passivity quite appealing."

The varok stood up before the panorama of the moon. Then he turned to face Tandra again. "Why don't we continue our tour of base? Then we can pick up Shawne and go to breakfast."

They stepped down from the observation deck, passed through the recreation lounge, and entered the hall leading to the quarantine facility. After turning into another short hallway on their left, they glanced into Artellian's office (a small, comfortably pillowed, circular room lined with maps and diagrams and moss wet-sweaters) and the food center (which was almost always occupied with nibbling ellls). Then they walked through the biomedical labs, the health examination area, and the isolation room. The latter three were ingeniously grouped together on the other side of the hall. Soon they came to a wider, longer hallway. Like the others, it was draped with silver moss that glowed with a dim sheen.

The peace of a mellow fall dominates this place, Tandra thought. Everything seemed full of life and its living. She recognized the large doors to the pool on her left, followed Orram to the right, and watched him open the sealed panels of the genealogy and chemistry studies. There her impressions were not only confirmed but enhanced. The studies were rich, comfortable rooms dominated by plump couches and soft mushroom stools and a thick growth of moss. Buried here and there in the cushiony elegance were crystal sculptures, transparent tangles of glass and rock, evidence of some ellls' tinkering with moon dust.

Reluctantly, Tandra turned away and followed Orram down the hall. Beyond the studies, next to the hangar, was a small observatory, and beside it perched the centrifuge room, a simple mossy cylinder fitted with body-molding exercise devices.

"At Killah's insistence," Orram explained, "the ellls take turns sleeping and exercising here." He stepped back over the threshold and looked down the hallway. Shawne had emerged from the room nearest the entrance to the pool and was happily bouncing toward them. Orram caught her as she leaped carelessly at him.

"It's funny to run here," Shawne told the varok.

"But you must learn not to get ahead of yourself, little one. Go more slowly." He turned to Tandra and set the child down. "You should see one of the apartments. They are all on the other side of this hall. The nursery is right here. The ellls would not be happy without raising a few children, so they have put six adults into one room and left part of the end apartment free for an incubator and elllonian-style cribs. You have seen the boy, Da-oon, run past the quarantine window now and then, haven't you? He is almost four Earth-years old now. He should be a good companion for Shawne. She will want to play here most of the time."

They turned toward the open room, but Conn suddenly appeared and stopped them at the door.

"No need to check here, Tandra. Everything is okay."

"I'm sure it is. But I'd still like to see it. Shawne will be in there most of the day."

"Ellalon will be with them, and Aen takes over later. There are some good toys there—nothing that can hurt Shawne."

Tandra bristled. "Why don't you want me to see the nursery, Conn?"

"I'm sorry, but I've got reasons."

"Then I had better know them before I send Shawne there."

"You've got to find out some things for yourself first."

"Conn, I am stubborn about very few things, but one of them is Shawne. I want to know where she will be and what she will be doing when she's not with me."

Conn looked at Orram. "Alright," he grumbled, "come on then."

He ushered Tandra and Shawne into the room, glanced quickly at two large tanks built into one wall, and invited Shawne to sit with him on the warm mossy floor near a pile of three-dimensional puzzle pieces and a small elll busily sorting them out.

"You know Da-oon, don't you Shawne?" Conn said.

The baby buried her face in Conn's side before she ventured to smirk at the small elll studiously ignoring her. Then a large moving model of a *kaehl* caught her eye. She ran to the toy and was carefully removing the eggs from its soft pouch when Da-oon, excited by the promise of fun on his own terms, began gathering up the generous supply of ell-lonian plumes that were scattered among the toys. Together then they began to build a nest for the toy *kaehl* and her eggs.

Abruptly Tandra stood up and smiled at Conn. "I'm perfectly satisfied. It's quite safe here. I don't know what I wasn't supposed to see, but I see nothing that can hurt Shawne. Those tanks are too high for her to fall into, and the toys look wonderful. Lots of building blocks to fortify hand-brain learning."

"You are finished, then, with the nursery?" Orram asked.

"This isn't the first time I've trusted Conn." Tandra saw a prolonged, worried gaze travel between Conn and Orram. Her imagination flew wild again. What did they really want with her? What would happen to Shawne? Had Conn used her romantic tendencies to win her confidence? The thought repulsed her. She erased it from her mind. She relaxed again as she watched Shawne and Da-oon playing happily in the pleasant nursery.

"Artellian should be awake," Orram said. "I will show you the room I share with him."

Conn followed Orram and Tandra back down the large hallway. They entered the last room on the right, next to the poolroom. Like the rest of the base, it glowed warm and humid with a plush, lived-in elegance. Tandra wandered into the apartment's chaotic maze between two bed-pads and two sleeping basins, all invitingly rich with soft, blue moss. Behind Orram's meticulously ordered bed-pad was a great heap of Artellian's books, pens, clean synthetic paper, a terminal, and belabored manuscripts set on broad working spaces.

From deep within a small niche above her head, Tandra saw a purple stone figure staring down at her. Its one large black eye glared menacingly from a fine, high brow. The face merged indiscriminately with a pitiful, bony abdomen and great bulbous legs, cruelly pitted and stained, which twisted into uselessness.

"What is that, Orram?" Tandra asked, running her fingers over the rough stone figure. "It is no Varokian beast."

"Its name is Gurahn," Orram said. He stepped over the literary heaps on the floor and took the purple monstrosity from its niche in the wall. "It is the personification of Varok's history, an interpretive sculpture made by the *ll-leyoolianl*, a species of great-fish who inhabit the deeps of Ellason. They convey their ideas through three-dimensional images."

"Through three-dimensional images? How can you know that your interpretation is correct?"

"They have developed the art of their communication to a high degree. One cannot miss the meaning in one's own context."

Conn nodded.

"Does this ugly figure really tell you something significant, Orram?" Tandra's voice was no longer hesitant; it had an edge of disdain. Apparently the varoks were enough like men to be plagued by human-like pretensions. "I think you have fallen victim to a contemporary human fallacy."

"What do you mean, Tandra?" Orram said. "You . . . seem cynical. About art? Or symbols?"

"Maybe symbolic art," she said. "Ah! See the eight-by-ten-foot masterpiece: One giant splash of paint, elegantly framed! The empty canvas conveys the hopeless void of existence that surrounds us. The rough edges of the paint trail here and there in the emptiness: souls stretching out for truer knowledge, for fuller consciousness. But they end too soon, fallen in despair."

"Okay. So how would *you* describe such a painting?" Conn asked.

Tandra disliked her own cynicism but she went on. "I think the true meaning lies closer to the fact that the artist drew an ordinary paintbrush across a piece of canvas and horn-swaggled someone into paying thousands of dollars for it."

"I see your objection," Orram said. "But how would you describe our Gurahn figure?"

Tandra felt Orram's challenge and took a moment to search deeper. "It's ugliness suggests that something terrible has happened to it."

"Yes. The Gurahn represents Varok's history."

"Of course, the Mutilation. I'm sorry, but it's difficult for me to believe that a huge aquatic fish could formulate such a far-reaching world view."

"So you're suggesting that our Ellasonian great-fish has learned to dab mud into weird shapes that have triggered the ellls' imaginations and appealed to some varoks' hungry search for meaning?"

"Not really. I believe that we . . . verbal creatures need to be realistic in how we assess the intelligence of other life. Some people would ask, 'What else have these fish done? Designed any tools, written any dictionaries?' How do you know they are intelligent enough to represent abstract ideas, Orram?"

For a moment Orram looked puzzled. "I see. But do you insist on equating technological prowess with intelligence?"

"No, of course not, but I do equate it with higher abstract thinking. And you are the proof."

"And the great-fish, like Earth's whales, are proof to the contrary. Their expression is entirely different from ours; they are brilliant and inventive in the ways they perceive and communicate." The varok spoke pensively, quietly, with nothing but kindness in his voice.

"Okay. I can understand that. All living species on Earth have had just as much time to evolve as humans." She looked at Orram with new respect and less fear. "It disgusts me that humans can't get past the assumption that our intelligence is some kind of unique phenomenon in this universe. Even I can't seem to admit to the existence of an entirely different form of intelligence. I think you're wise to avoid open contact with Earth. Humans are not ready to relate compassionately with similar species, especially not to a completely alien intelligence like the great-fish."

"You are human, Tandra. Are you ready to relate rationally to alien intelligence?" Conn asked.

"I hope so. Some of us humans respect animal intelligence and their consciousness, their sentience, now. It has been only a hundred years since the behaviorists have been able to publish studies of animal emotion. Some aquatic mammals are still killed for meat."

As Tandra spoke, the sparse shadows grew deeper in Orram's face. "Come sit down, Tandra."

He cleared space on the workbench, and the three huddled together. "You know that we have taken elaborate precautions to avoid accidental encounter with your species."

"That was very wise. You might not be welcomed kindly. I saw the disintegration guns in Conn's isolation suit."

"We have a healthy respect for humans' potential fear of aliens. Someday we hope to exert some influence in helping your planet find a stable condition, much as we advised the ellls, but we see no way to introduce ourselves effectively to Earth yet. The ellls were a docile, schooling people, capable of denying for themselves inventions of convenience, if their manufacture proved costly or disruptive to their beloved oceans. I doubt that men are so capable, but we won't attempt to force solutions."

"What solutions would you force? What could you force? Almost anything, I suspect." She tensed and looked up.

"Quite the contrary," Orram said. "We could force very little, and I'm afraid we may also impact very little."

Tandra looked up to see Tallyn and Killah standing in the doorway listening. Tallyn's rough, powerful torso was balanced skeptically, his eyes narrowed behind agitated crown plumes. Finally, he spoke. "Earth was once most beautiful diverse living planet by this sun. Is now losing many species quickly."

"Tallyn, I know. It's my planet."

"Is it now?" Killah asked.

"I care more for the life of Earth than for the lives of all mankind, that's why it is mine."

"Tandra, surely not," Conn said.

"You came too late to know, Conn. How I wish you could have seen Earth decades ago. The trees grew in huge forests and jungles. You could still see deer in some areas. Have you ever seen a deer, Tallyn? Your water birds are exotic and lovely, but no alien creature I have yet seen can compare with the delicate beauty of a doe or the majesty of her buck. I cannot honestly defend the human animal, Tallyn."

"You can't deny yourself, Tan," Conn said.

"The human animal is an integral part of the planet Earth," Orram added. "Your concern for any part must of necessity concern the whole."

"When a pathogen infects a body," Tandra replied, "the whole is endangered until all the pathogens are destroyed."

"Your duty is with the human race," Conn said. "You are one of them whether you like it or not."

"It's not a comfortable feeling, Conn. Surely you understand my deep . . . disappointment with human failure."

"About some of this you are right, Tandra," Killah said. "The state of your planet's life will continue to deteriorate until *Homo sapiens sapiens* decides to contain itself. Earth is a closed test tube, eh? But perhaps humans are adaptable germs and will learn to survive on excrement, become *Homo effluetus*."

The elll ran his webbed hand slowly over his crown plumes. "More likely you will simply learn to ignore it all—become *Homo insipidus*. You are an adaptable species, too adaptable, capable of extraordinary repression. Well, we cannot know yet. I would like to see your best potential realized myself."

"Since eight decades," Tallyn broke in with a rising crescendo, "when ecology is a common word on Earth, humans still-always misuse Earth's life and resources with destruction and rebuilding, not repair. You still burn fossil fuels, never walking, wasting food when one billion are hungry. What insanity is this?"

"Tallyn," Orram said quietly, "Tandra knows all this."

But the gruff elll raged on. "You do all you can, eh?"

"No, no, of course I don't," Tandra cried. "But would it help for me— one person in nearly ten billion—to forego electricity?"

"You are blind hypocrite," Tallyn insisted in a deep elllonian roll. "You do nothing! You see proud animal here, this varok? He is vastly more than wise you or I. Do know how he lives? Has he told you what is home?"

Further words failed him, and Killah picked up the point. "Master Oran Ramahlak lives in his ancestors' house, formed from whatever his land on Varok offers, recycling all water, using little grid power, only some to communicate, some if he needs more light. Varoks take the train, share wheels, or ride daramonts, more often walk or stay home. He has one child, a replacement, and he knows Varok is secure for ages. No life need fear him, except when he must eat."

Tallyn shouted, "Do you know that? Does no life fear you?"

"How can you accuse me, you ellls, living in this base the way you do?" Tandra asked. "How much energy did it take to keep that pool full of water? You go to Earth for some of it. Sleeping bowls are everywhere, to coddle the ellls. You are the hypocrites, Tallyn." She looked to Conn for support.

Conn's face had crumpled, hating the exchange. "Probably, in one way or another. Life costs."

"Everything on this base calculated for maximum efficient," Tallyn grumbled. "*Uuvanoonl* increase surface area for moss to grow. Ellls need water and play. Pool was necessary. Energy required is less than staffing with all varoks. All is known. All is accounted for. Do you know that?"

Tandra rose abruptly to pace the room, tears crashing hot on her cheeks. "I account as best I can. No life need fear me," she cried, shaking with fear and rage. "I try to maintain my integrity. I am not all people. Don't you see? I agree with you. Human integrity exists in human minds as doublethink so they can survive. I do what I can, but I must find a way to live first. We have too few trains and no daramonts. Horses are fragile by comparison. I must use a car to get to work, even to eat."

Tandra saw that Orram read clearly the profound frustration she felt, that his empathy reached the depths of his felt emotion. He rose from the bed-pad and caught Tandra in a sympathetic embrace.

The varok's close physical contact with the woman jolted Tallyn into silence.

"You know that Tandra is right in questioning this base, Tallyn," Orram said. "It was an enormous expenditure and required a moral compromise to build. We try to be self-sustaining here, but our maintenance requires continual justification. The study of Earth is still thought to be worth the price."

Tandra found little comfort in Orram's embrace or his words. Questions boiled through her mind, and she felt utterly alone: the ellls and Conn couldn't or wouldn't understand, and the varoks were in absolute control.

"Tallyn," Orram continued, "human beings are not like ellls. They have no innate sense of cooperative self-denial for their common causes such as you have. Their genetic makeup tells them to react quickly, to secure the present for the self, not for some future benefit for all."

At first Tandra was afraid that he was talking about her; then she knew he was. She denied it and tried to justify her denial with all the passion of self-assurance. Human civilization was an entity apart from her. Yet she felt degraded and shamed.

Tandra's feelings of humiliation grieved Orram, and he was profoundly moved. Her intense aloneness was also clear, as was her apprehension and distrust. But where was the focus of her mind? Was she trying to invent her own comfortable reality? If so, she was having some success; he must break the invention or she would be of no use to them later.

Conn, no less than Orram, seemed to sense her distress, for he had immediately taken the varok's place, holding close the shaking human. He turned Tandra away from the others and tried to give her the support she needed.

Tallyn's eyes widened with sympathy when he saw Tandra's warm response to Conn's attention. "Forgive me, Tandra, little *kaehloid*," he said softly, "M. Ramahlak, I not seen you touch anyone so before. And Conn—now I see how much is this schooling with Tandra. I would not if you! Human love is difficult, too much one elll to carry alone."

Identity and Comparison

In the weeks that followed, Tandra focused on her microbiological studies. She and Killah grew cultures of throat swabbings and fecal and blood samples from all the crew in order to watch for an exchange of normal flora between the species. Their relationship blossomed, business-like and comfortable. She enjoyed Killah's habit of making biological observations with a philosophical bent. It kept him at an entertaining distance.

Conn, however, pressed closer. Tandra's work provided her with a handy escape from his hovering. During her first days in the lab, he had not intruded. But, now, because her work left him too little of her time, he occasionally interrupted her there.

One day, after Tandra had worked several hours at her desk, she suddenly realized that Conn was standing behind her. "Yes," she said, looking up from her microscope.

The cold in her eyes was obvious. "What did I do?" Conn asked.

Tandra smiled nervously. "I'm sorry, Conn. I'm just irritable today. I'm glad you came. I'd really rather talk than work."

"All right." Conn sat down in a moss chair by her lab desk.

"All right what?"

"Go ahead, talk."

"I can't just go ahead and talk."

"So ask me a question," Conn ventured. "Sometimes I wish you wouldn't accept so much so blandly—ask more questions or something."

"All right. Try this one again. And really tell me this time. Don't play it off," Tandra pleaded. "What does it feel like to be an elll?"

"You've got to be kidding. That's a TV interview cliché."

"Answer me."

"It feels good, sometimes real good."

"Stop it, Conn. I asked you a serious question."

"Why do you think I'm not serious? I gave you a good answer. It feels good to be elll. I feel good. We feel good. What more can I say? I don't know how you feel to me. Yet."

"You see why I don't ask questions?"

In spite of their problem, they talked amiably for a short while before he left, but he didn't try to intrude on her work again.

As time passed, Tandra tried but could not shake herself free of her apprehension about varoks. They moved through their daily routine like zombies, always courteous, never offering more than they were asked. Fantasies of fear burned in her mind only when she was alone, for the warm rasp of Orram's voice snuffed them out, leaving her feeling that she had been paranoid.

Spontaneously, after just such an incident, she mentioned the problem to Killah. "Intellectually, I know it's foolish," she said, "because the varoks are absolutely forthright in their manner, but I can't rid myself of the idea that they are sinister and devious—supermen in the worst sense."

His response was a hearty laugh. "There is nothing so dull as a varok, Tandra. You have read something about them, but not enough. Put aside some time and study them thoroughly. You will soon see why I laugh at your fears."

When Orram passed by their lab and disappeared into Artellian's office, she said, "Killah, please, I need to know that he is really not human. The patch organ is the only significant difference I can see."

Killah shook his head. "Crisis of identity, Tandra? What is it to be human, eh? If it is troublesome for you to be so much like the varoks, you had better do a subjective comparison, and I mean subjective.

Orram wouldn't mind. Look him over. In fact, he asked me what I thought of the idea."

"Oh?" Tandra's mouth dropped open just a little.

Killah's brow plumes came together. "What are you afraid of? Varoks need more than physical cues—" The elll grinned. "Oh, I see. You're afraid of—how do you say?—being attracted to him."

"M-m-m." Tandra couldn't deny it.

"Oh my. You humans. Well, Tandra, do remember, we are all merely collections of molecules—hormones and what-have-you—sharing the gift of consciousness, complex blobs of obvious relevancy in an incomprehensible universe. So what do they matter, our attractions and intellectualizations, even our grand philosophies? We share cognizance and are grateful. That should be enough."

She smiled. "Thank you, Killah."

Tandra acted on Killah's advice then and began studying in more detail Orram and his species. It was like entering a strange, guarded room of hidden switches. She devoured all the information the varoks provided, but knew they withheld much, for security, they said. She did not dare to ask the difficult questions: Why were they really here on Earth's moon? And why had they chosen her? For what, beyond the obvious biological studies?

The answers lay within Orram, just beyond reach. When the varok again sensed Tandra's uncertainty, he told her he had been too cautious, too passive. "We need to establish a comfortable pattern of encounters," he said, and she agreed.

After the long, congenial dinner hours, when the lights had dimmed to a soft ruddy hue, they would meet at the pool to swim lazy circles or to play floating slow motion games invented to test each other's physical stamina and reflexes. Then they would retire to the observation deck for long conversations.

One evening while the ellls were gathered in the food center to choose their meals and to tease and push and chat companionably before they drifted off to the pool, Tandra noticed that Orram was alone, eating more hurriedly than usual, standing at a serving counter. Though she could find no clue in his expressionless face, an ill-defined uneasiness was apparent.

When he had finished eating and started to leave, she cut her own meal short and, following her intuition, linked her arm in his.

He looked down at her, his face still blank, then led her gaze with his own toward Junah, who was watching them from across the room. Junah disappeared into the hallway when she met Orram's glance, and Orram moved with Tandra toward the observation deck.

"I was going to spend my time alone with my thoughts this evening," he said. "Now I would rather not. You noticed Junah leave the room when you came over to me in the food center?"

"Yes. I noticed and felt sorry. She doesn't like me to touch you, does she?"

"No, she does not."

"And you? Be honest, please, Orram. You don't have to tolerate my thoughtless human habits."

"They surprise me," he said, pausing to think, "but I welcome them, which surprises me even more."

The woman and the varok climbed the stairs to the observation deck and relaxed into lounging chairs before the window.

"Tell me about Varok, Orram," Tandra said.

"What can I tell you that you do not already know? Our security restrictions are a nuisance. I would like to tell you more than I may."

"Tell me what it is like to be a varok on Varok. What the Mutilation means to you."

Orram stretched his long legs over the couch, and gradually submitted the control of his elegant form to its comforting hold. Then he began to talk in mild, silken tones.

"When our first space ships left Varok for extended exploration, an aging astronomer, Llorain Analahk, wrote poetry and songs that expressed what you want to know. I should remember something of his."

The varok's warm, thought-filled voice slowed and paused, then moved on into a leisurely rambling lyric as he translated the poem to English.

> *Arise great orb, and moons sink low.*
> *These lands float free in mist*
> *Where color spins on ethereal webs.*
> *Come home to this great swirling mass.*
> *Come home where lands float free beneath the moons,*
> *Where color spins.*

Beneath the danger-veil, behind the storm,
Below the freezing crystal tones,
Come home to hues forever changing, color spinning.
Come home to mist, to warmth beneath the moons.
Come home where color spins,
Where lands float free.

Great orb arise and hide the moons.
Find shadows nowhere when you move.
Obscure the mist and pale the hues.
Become the sky itself.
Come home to mists retreating wildly,
Come home to colors maddened by the shade.
Come home to this great orb
Where color spins and lands float free in mist.

"You must have been magnificent creatures before the Mutilation," Tandra said quietly.

"Perhaps," he said, smiling with the word *before*. "We were tall humanoids with a wingspread of three or four meters. The historical reference Mutilation refers, not to the mutants who died in infancy or left infertile offspring, but to the gradual altering of the entire population—the degeneration of the wings and the loss of flight, the increasing inability to function rationally under emotional stress, and the tension between casual relations and the sexual imperatives generated by the mind-link. It is as if nature had to force us to mate again more frequently after the major die-offs.

"As you have seen all too well, Tandra, the Mutilation left deep psychological and sociological scars upon us. Emotional involvement of any kind, and especially sexual involvement, still cost us a great price. Reason cannot co-exist with emotional motivation in the varokian mind, unless a mind-link is established. We must seem extremely stolid to you."

Tandra shifted uneasily. "And yet you are OK with my touch?"

"Don't let Conn worry you about that. The ellls respect too much this tendency of ours to avoid touch. They see us varoks as hopelessly cold because their lives are fueled by their senses, especially their sense of touch. Ours are ruled by physiology; extreme emotion can cause irrationality.

"Do you understand, Tandra? We varoks cannot will our reason to take control, once intense emotion takes over. If we allow ourselves to feel joy or anger or even grief at the loss of a friend, the emotion will rapidly overcome our entire minds, until we are thrown into an irrational fit. Sometimes it is days before we recover some conscious control. That is why we must never allow ourselves to be driven into emotionally untenable positions. I have a problem to deal with now—"

"Junah?"

"Yes. She is imagining a relationship with me that goes beyond our original agreement to mate casually. I may have to terminate that relationship. I could not consummate a marriage with her, but she continues to look for signs of marital contact from me. You understand our customs—and our compulsions—in this regard, don't you, Tandra?"

"Incompletely. I know that consummation of marriage is a merging of identities that involves the patch organ in a way I cannot know. Varoks in consummation can lean on each other psychologically and experience some emotion rationally. This is called release."

In spite of, or because of, their alien biology, Tandra knew, the varoks usually remained with one mate for life, once the mind-link was established. "Do I have it right, Orram?"

"I believe so. You can understand that Junah has been a recent casual choice for me, but I realize now that her emotional desire for a mind-link with me is greater than my response. I'm afraid it will take long, careful months of clear indifference to undo her increasing desire for me as consummate mate."

They sat quietly for a moment, watching the moon landscape.

"I think you would find Varok quietly beautiful, Tandra," Orram said, frankly changing the conversation. "It is an unhurried place. True peace of mind can be found there, and creative wills such as yours are quite free. We have learned to value life—to savor the quality of moments above all else, as the ellls do."

"Some humans have also learned that," Tandra said, "but too many focus on material wealth. We have paid a huge price in human lives and wasted resources for the belief that economic growth is essential."

"You grew up in an age when fossil fuels made continual growth possible on Earth."

"But even when resource limits became obvious, economists and politicians didn't understand that the costs of economic growth out-weighed its benefits."

"We noted some decades ago that humans do not understand the unpredictable nature of economies as complex systems." Orram's gaze focused on Tandra.

"Are you suggesting something about my role here, Orram? Does EV Science have plans to trigger something that may be unpredictable?"

"We can't know what will happen if we contact Earth. We are too alike, superficially, we ellls and varoks and humans. It would be easy to make damaging assumptions, for we are each driven by totally dif-ferent biological imperatives."

Tandra flushed. "Maybe that is what I have sensed. I need to know just how we are different."

"It's quite simple really. Humans—I should say Earthlings—and ellls are driven by reproductive hormones. Varoks are not. That makes us more alien than we appear."

"In what ways? What are you implying, Orram? Are you trying to warn me? My imagination tells me that you are something I can't know, or you have motives I couldn't guess."

Orram sat up, and a dark crease formed between his brows. "So that is why you have feared us," he said. "Do you assume that we have a hidden agenda of some kind?" He smiled and locked his gaze into her eyes, until she returned the searching look. "I think . . . that your imagination has given us varoks too much credit. Perhaps you must learn at a deeper level that we are not human."

Tandra hesitated before she answered. "Yes, I wish I could see you as some kind of natural creature. I have begun to learn Varokian, but that hasn't helped much."

"We varoks have an extra sense or two, and our technology may be a bit more advanced than yours, but we have serious flaws in our na-ture. The ellls don't normally indulge in technological games, but they have far superior biological equipment for absorbing and interpreting sensual stimuli than either you or I have. The great-fish—whose skills you questioned—have neither language nor tools, but they have an enormous talent for conceptualizing experience and communicating their ideas with great clarity."

"Even more than the ellls?"

"The elllonian mind is continuously subjected to an enormous sensory input. If their minds were computers, you would say that their bit-rate has a broadband-width and a high frequency. Lots of data coming in all the time. Much more than ours. We have fewer senses, hence fewer signals to sort out and interpret. On the other hand, the great-fish probably don't perceive bits of information at all. They simply understand what they perceive."

"And how would they talk to Conn about our problems?"

"They would school with him."

"You're serious."

"I'm rarely capable of any other mood." Orram almost smiled. "The great-fish are a respected species. They are more often correct than not and are looked to for counsel by many species, not just ellls and varoks. But more important than the great-fish, do you understand what I have said about ellls?"

"Many impressions all the time, little integration. It fits. Immediate experience is what they are made of. Killah and Conn have both said that to them awareness is life. And I do know, Orram, that there are many measures of life besides so-called intelligence."

"I am sure that you do, Tandra." The varok searched the woman's eyes carefully. "I think that you are almost ready to trust me. Tell me now what you need to know about varoks."

"I need to know what you intend to do about Earth. Why do you watch and wait and do nothing?"

"We can do nothing but watch and learn. The reminders we see of our past mistakes are invaluable, Tandra, but extremely painful. We are not masochistic. Indeed, the reminders are doubly painful because we are so helpless."

"That can't be true. There must be something you can do."

"That's the irony in it all. We could probably help relieve some suffering by sharing what we know, but any help we give will result in even greater suffering later. The simplistic example—if we feed the hungry now, there will soon be twice as many to feed. It is well known that partial solutions only postpone and magnify such crises. There is no way we can impose solutions on human society; they must come from collective resolve on Earth. Emergent phenomena can self-organize rapidly. If we can trigger human resolve, I believe there might still be time to avert total collapse."

"You must try, Orram. Try anything. There is no predicting the world's reaction to alien contact. You might have great influence."

"Or none at all. We can say nothing new, and we cannot open closed minds or change those who prefer profit and expediency to the difficult answers."

A profound sadness settled over Tandra and the varok. He took her in his arms, as he had before, and throughout the night they remained together sharing thoughts and resting and searching for answers.

– Δ –

When the next day's light cycle had been established, Orram searched Tandra's mood and found no apprehension left. "You are still too much in awe of me, Tandra," he said, "but at least your fears are eased. Come now. Explore me thoroughly." With a few quick motions he undressed and stood nude before her on the observation deck. "Convince yourself that I am alien."

Tandra backed away and studied his taut brown body. Except for the lack of body hair, he was not obviously alien. She stepped closer and moved her hands slowly along his arms, over his elbows to the broad tips of his fingers, and down his regular, firm sides. "No hedonic glands here, I hope," she said, in an effort at humor. He did not smile.

She moved her hands quickly over his hips. His testicles were smooth and oddly bare; and the lack of pubic hair made what must have been his penis seem raw and vulnerable. As she moved her hands on down his legs she missed the expected feel of coarse hair. She looked at his feet, counted his toes, then stood up; and her gaze was drawn into the deep blueness of his eyes.

For a moment she savored the good feeling their openness now gave her. Then she explored with her fingers Orram's silver and red hair, his high cheekbones and deep brows, his straight long nose, and his chin, smooth from lack of beard and shaving.

Once again she stepped back, and slipped out of the robe that she had worn to dinner the night before.

"Surely you are not done," he said before she could remove her bodysuit.

"Yes, I am done."

Orram's face was grave. "But you have avoided the two areas of my body that are most unlike your own."

"I did avoid the patches."

"I thought you were anxious to establish my alienness."

"I was. There doesn't seem to be any alienness to establish."

"Sometimes our deepest fears find us when we least expect them. Examine my arms and the patch organs behind my ears, and you will know that I am not human."

Again Tandra ran her hands over Orram's long arms; she noticed nothing unusual. She started to reach toward his patches when he grabbed her hands.

"You refuse to see, Tandra. You must learn now. You must know without doubt that I am not human. I am alien to Earth! We share many biochemicals, but no DNA codes. My home is a floating oasis entrapped by a hostile, gigantic mass millions and millions of miles from here." He turned his hands outward and spread his fingers. "Run your hand along the inside on my arm and between my fingers."

Tandra obeyed, and the faint line of heavy tissue that had seemed like a scar loomed in her mind as an obvious vestige of an ancient structure. She traced the line downward to the tip of Orram's fifth finger, which was slightly longer than the others. Then she followed it toward his body and could see that it flared into a tough thin web for a short distance under his arm.

"My legs now," he commanded.

Tandra knelt and encircled his knee with her hands. "I see on both sides of your legs similar vestiges of what must have been extensive tissue. Killah said that your ancestors had been magnificent aerial creatures. I thought that they might have had wings, but these vestiges could be the remains of something like the alar membranes of bats."

"Indeed they are. Before the Mutilation, our ancestors were built very much like your extinct flying reptiles, the pterodactyls. The large wings extended from elongated little fingers, down both arms and legs. The remaining four fingers were used for manipulation, as they are now. An additional membrane extended between the legs and a short tail. Now examine my breast. Isn't it broader than a human male's?"

"Yes," Tandra said, probing firmly with her fingers, "and there is a short ridge running down its center. I can barely feel it beneath your muscles."

"A keel, really," Orram said, "very much like the keel on the breast-plate of birds. It served as an anchor for the large flight muscles that extended into the wings." He looked at her with anticipation. "And now what do you think of me?"

"You are varok. It is resolved. You are also—" She stopped speaking, afraid of her thoughts, *also male*, she said to herself. But the meaning did not escape the varok's patches.

"Now touch the patch organs, Tandra. They are not fragile. They are sensitive only to electromagnetic signals related to mood and direct thought."

She placed her hands behind his ears and felt the raised discs of tissue. Orram bent his head down so that she could examine them closely. They were textured very finely with tiny slits and membranes, but no other details were obvious.

She finished undressing then, and stood before the large wall which framed the lunar sunset, her long, dark hair spilling over her smooth shoulders onto her breasts and touching the fine, straight arms that contrasted gracefully with the muscled tension in her modeled legs.

Orram touched her chin. "You are a very beautiful woman, Tandra. I, too, am disturbed. Only your behavior tells me that you are most decidedly not varokian." His fingers brushed her temples, stroked the smooth skin behind her ears where there were no patch organs, and moved systematically over her entire body.

When his touch left her, Tandra pulled her head back, searching his stony face with bewilderment. "You belie everything that I have read about varoks, Orram. Your touch is sensitive, but you savor it, as if you didn't have to fight a feeling of repulsion."

"You are no more surprised than I am. In some way that I do not understand, you have made me forget my varokian inhibitions. I will stop now, Tandra. I need some time to consider my observations. Shall we relax and swim?"

Carrying their clothes, they descended the stairs into the recreation lounge, passed Conn, who was absorbed in tinkering with a solar concentrator. As they entered the pool room, they saw Killah with the ell-lonian girl Tllan.

"Well, well, *kaehloids* in the flesh," Killah said. "Going to enjoy your swim for a change, Ramahlak?"

"I just might surprise you, Killah."

"I hope so," the elll grinned.

"What did you call us, Killah? *Kaehloids*?"

"In effect, this rude elll is calling us furry little beasts," Orram said.

"Ha!" Tandra came at Killah with curved fingers and a glare in her eyes.

"*Aeo-o!* Tandra Jekyll becomes Miss Hyde," Killah screamed. He backed away from her, leading her toward the pool. Orram circled behind her. Suddenly Killah lunged. Tandra pulled out of his grasp into Orram's arms, and managed to pull all three of them into the water.

Tllan jumped in after them with an unearthly whoop, and the noise of their rough play brought Conn into the pool room. With wide, unbelieving eyes, he watched the game grow from hesitant chasing to unrestrained wrestling. They were handling Orram as one of them.

With sudden anger Conn dove into the fracas, found Tandra, and towed her to the center of the pool.

Her eyes glistened expectantly.

"You've read about varoks," Conn said. "You know that they hate being touched."

"Sometimes they don't," she answered firmly.

"Hardly ever. You and I can wallow in physical contact and enjoy it, take it, or leave it. But a touch is like an electric shock to a varok. Unless there is some very basic meaning behind a touch, they avoid it. I know Orram well. You don't. And you can't tell when he's had enough."

Tandra smiled. "All right, my big lizard. But I think you exaggerate."

To her surprise, he was stern, almost angry. "I don't exaggerate, in *Harrahn*. Orram is like a . . . a brother to me; I know him. You could break him. Leave him alone." His deep emerald eyes narrowed slightly, emphasizing his annoyance. "And *frog*, Tandra, *big frog* is more accurate."

III. ALIENATION

In the days of their first contact, the varoks taught ells how sulfur
compounds had powered early life in the warmer waters of Ellason,
as it had on Earth. Polyenes (biochemicals with alternating double
and single bonds) jostled for reaction space beside the hot veins of
molten volcanic and tectonic rock that laced Ellason's oceans.

Other chemicals with strong infrared absorption bands captured light
in well-placed nooks near the surface of the planet. Their reactions,
selected and enhanced by oxygen, formed primitive cells, which
then cooperated to survive as symbionts, until plant-like beings
evolved in Ellason's calmer watery crannies.

Soon the more venturesome organisms tested the dry shores. Some
covered the land as moss-like plants, glowing with a light of their
own. Oxygen began to accumulate in the atmosphere.

Ellason's gravity (1.4 Earth's) proved too much for some organisms;
many gave up their dry land venture to continue their evolution in
water. Thus, near the warmest spots in the vast oceans, oxygen
breathers like great-fish joined the race for life.

Much later, clever swimmers with prehensile fins, stereoscopic infrared vision and frontal gills—Conn's ancestors—found temporary
refuge from predators upon verdant shorelands. As their ultrasonic
bio-equipment and optional lungs rapidly evolved, more oxygen contributed to their ever-growing awareness and inventiveness. Their
fins extended into powerful limbs that withstood Ellason's gravity.
The tips of their upper appendages became ever more dexterous as
the creatures escaped and foraged on the gentle land. As aquatic
bipeds, they also met the challenge of farming in warm sea currents.
Thus, over a span of six and a half billion years, life-loving ellls
came into being and named their planet Ellason.

THE GREEN VEIL

There was probably nothing Conn loved better than floating suspended deep within the pool with Ellalon, indulging his elllonian nature while he waited for Tandra or Orram—with whom he indulged his loner's needs.

Sometimes, after working hours, Tandra appeared first, and they would create good moments recording their beloved sound-pictures. Now, as the weeks passed, neither would admit that their music was becoming a crutch between them. Conn retreated more often to the sensuous comfort of Ellalon's soft body and to the more remote emotions he shared as part of his school—purely abstract sensual pleasure, little personal pride or desire, and an overriding collective joy in living that all but negated individual consciousness.

He also sought retreat in Orram's friendship. More often now, when the day's work was done, the varok's distinctive swimming stroke called him to the surface of the pool and they cautiously experimented with the breaking of old taboos, searching more actively to secure the bond that had grown between them when they were very young on Varok. The elll wondered if he shouldn't try schooling with the varok; and the varok pried more words from Conn, relying less on his patches to better know the elll.

Orram discovered that Conn had been as drawn to Tandra as she to him on their first meeting. It was not surprising. They both valued the experience of life above all else. Apparently they had reveled in a simple-minded awareness together, enjoying stars and pianos and dancing with no murky thought between them. Now it was clear, that time had passed. Something had broken the original troth.

Orram probed into the deductive channels and vacillating emotions of the elll and finally unearthed in Conn a surprisingly deep disturbance that centered on his complaints against Tandra. Since she had left quarantine, their conversations had become two-sided, one side at a time. Conn had found little to say in answer to Tandra's probing for truths she could generalize; and she had grown tired of his obsession with the sensuous experience, refusing to understand what it meant to be part of a non-verbal, schooling species.

In spite of himself, Conn had continued to try to satisfy Tandra's insistence on an intense level of verbal exchange, but it seemed that the harder he tried to project himself verbally, the more foolish he sounded. It was certain that Tandra didn't respond to his efforts. Nor did she appreciate them. He knew his anger toward her was not fair. But neither was it fair for her to expect him to be so human. If only he could get her to study elllonian biology. She knew nothing of ellls yet. They were supposed to know each other now—use their favorite sense, touch, to aid in the verbalization process. Why did she seem more distant since she got out of quarantine?

He asked Orram. "It's got to be a two-way exchange," Conn said. "I'm finding this problem hard to verbalize. The point is, I can't hack the words without some more meaningful input from her."

"Perhaps you should help her with her Varokian. or try a combination of sensual and verbal contacts," Orram suggested. "Isn't that how you first met? And be patient, Conn. Killah and she invent more projects for themselves than they can complete, and Tandra is still trying to sort out varoks and men. She is very tired. The number of new impressions she has to absorb must seem overwhelming at times."

So Conn stubbornly worked at placing tags of meaning on the words he forced from his mind.

It didn't help Tandra. She became more remote. "Give it up, Conn," she said one day. "There's just not much we need to talk about. I can accept that now. I don't love you any less for it."

Untrue. There was too much to talk about. Or ought to be. Where was her curiosity? "I wish she'd vomited when she first saw me," Conn grumbled to Orram. "It would make more sense. I can't stand this indifference." But *indifference* wasn't the right word.

– Δ –

As the Earth rolled toward a bleak, dry April, Tandra continued to study the varoks—and she grew to idealize Orram. She spent less and less time with Conn.

"You won't take time for me," he complained, "unless I drag you into the rec lounge with a new sound."

One day she refused all his suggestions, and his exasperation drove him into a fury. He had to have it out with her. He followed her to her room. She was alone, sprawled comfortably on her bed pad with pen and synthetic paper in hand, her computer neglected. Conn stretched out close to her and wrapped a long leg around hers.

"Go away, Conn," Tandra snapped. "Can't you ever stop playing? I'd like to try writing some Varokian—"

"Let's do something that's worth writing down," Conn said, pulling her closer.

His eyes succeeded in capturing hers, and she was drawn into the crystal depths of brilliant emerald, down toward the unknown mind of the elll. But something there was more than frightening—it was almost horrible. Tandra jerked her gaze away, and shuddered.

Conn sat up, feeling lost.

Tandra busied herself picking up the writing sheets. Then with growing irritation she stopped and stared at him. "Why did you come here—like that? What do you think I am?"

"You're probably soft and warm. I've forgotten," Conn mumbled.

"Is that all I am to you? Something soft to feel?"

"You should be something old and homey and familiar to feel by now. It's been a long time since you got out of quarantine. I want to know you now the only real way I can, Tandra. We've talked ourselves out, or at least I have. Now I need to touch you, to feel your heat when you think of all that philosophy you love to toss around in your mind."

Tandra recoiled and got off the bed pad. "My philosophy doesn't put out heat waves."

"I'll bet it does, the way you care. It must. Let's try." He grabbed her leg and pulled her back to the bed.

"Let me go!"

Conn flinched, but he let her go and tried words. "*Aeyull*, Tandra, we ellls can't talk the way you do. We don't even experience emotions in a human way, individual to individual—we school. Our whole culture—everything we are—is geared for collective emotion. Yet I feel longing, and it must be like yours. We both still look to our first hours together. Please understand that I need to learn, to explore. I'm a loner, Tan. Even I can't know what to expect of myself, but you might be able to learn for me. At least, you could do some reading about ellls."

"I don't need to read about you."

"Why not? You don't know a thing about us, and you're wasting your time studying a species you'll never have a chance of relating to."

"You talk to me about relating? You've only memorized the word from some psychology text. You don't relate to me. None of you ellls do. All Tallyn does is gripe at me, and Llorkin scribbles down everything I say. Killah does his work and then looks for something to joke about, just as you look for something to try your slang on. You don't seem to care about what I really feel, what I think. You won't talk about our lives, why we're here, the miracle of our existing together, what your idea of God is, anything at all that matters."

"God? Whatever made us also made beauty and love. That's good enough for me."

"That's just what I mean. All you care about it is how to enjoy life."

"Isn't that important?" demanded a voice. Orram stood by them, his uncompromising gaze once again making Tandra flush with shame.

Conn stared at her, then left the room.

– Δ –

As Tandra became more and more distant from elllonian reality, Conn became ever more tied to the human female. Her musical, accepting, life-loving personality kindled in him a deeply satisfying but, for an elll, strange love, directed as it was toward an individual. Her rejection initiated a longing for personal acceptance and a rudimentary anger based on special pride. Her arrogant capacity for bitterness and repression fostered a dislike directed both at her and at himself—the latter because he feared the judicial self-righteousness he saw in himself. All of these feelings were new to him. They were new to ellls.

It was with great difficulty that Conn continued his work, monitoring events on Earth. He floundered more and more, until even Orram became entangled in the subjective chaos of Conn's emotions. Tandra's simple, friendly touching of the varok nurtured a feeling of inferiority in Conn; her growing mental contact with Orram exaggerated his frustration at his own species' limitations; and the time she spent with Orram kindled his latent jealousy.

As Conn watched Tandra and Orram's friendship deepen and his once-fulfilling open contact with the woman become shallow and misplaced, his elllonian store of explosive emotions began to overheat. In desperation, he decided to talk to Llorkin. But all Llorkin could tell him was that Tandra had a "belligerent" temperament. "She is bound to show us that *she*, not *we*, can touch varoks—and that she needn't touch us, we who live by touch." It was no help.

In his increasing dismay, Conn found it difficult to work and impossible to study. He took to walking the halls, muttering to himself angrily. He was doing this one day when he felt a small, smooth, chubby hand work its way into his. Tiny fingers explored the five fins between his fingers. "Where goin', Conn?" Shawne asked, rolling her enormous blue eyes up at him.

"Hey there, fat stuff, you're supposed to be in the nursery, aren't you?"

"I don't like that Lorka. He's got big, mushy green eyes."

Conn knelt down and set the toddler down on his knee. "He wears the same kind of contacts I do, Shawne," he said, rounding his lids affectionately.

The child laughed and poked a finger at his face. "No, no, no. You got marbles. Like glass." She snuggled into his arms and rubbed her fingers over the soft hexagonal tiles of his skin. "Can I have a 'flume? Just one, okay, Conn?"

"What color do you want? You pick one out."

"M-m-m. blue. Where are your blue?"

"I don't have any. Only the girls. Try again."

"Then I have—green!"

"Ouch! Hey, you've got to remember to ask before you yank. That one wasn't quite ripe."

Shawne hugged him generously and said, "I sorry, Conn. Goodbye." Then she raced back to the nursery shouting, "Take me swim, Conn."

"Sure. After dinner." The elll stood watching her, longing for the same kind of acceptance from her mother.

– Δ –

Early one evening in the pool room, Conn and Tandra finished selecting the bass tones of a richly rhythmic varokian study for translation into the ellls' ultrasonic range. Conn seemed totally absorbed with his sound engineering, so Tandra settled down with a book of

Analahk's poetry and some varokian music she had not yet heard.

Soon she was completely immersed in an older world of word images and wrapped in the misty veil of the music. The words and the sound became one—sometimes strange, sometimes beautiful, often incomprehensible-and she imagined that she was on Varok, sharing the essence of what it meant to be varokian. She floated, ecstatic, searching, until Conn's insistent tugging brought her back to the moment.

"Tan, I've got it! This is the best we've done yet."

"Wait a minute, Conn. Don't disturb me now."

"Come on, let's try it out in the water."

"Later." She started to read again. The music continued arrhythmic, haunting. Conn shut it off.

"Conn!"

"Tandra, you owe me some time. You've been putting me off too much. You'd spend all your time here, all six months, on the varoks if I let you."

"I'll hear the sound you've done later—"

"If Orram walked in here and wanted to swim, you'd be in the pool before I could get the switch flicked."

"The switch flicked!? Conn—" She laughed.

"Tan, I'm trying to tell you something."

"Well, tell me then."

"You wouldn't hear me. You're tuned in on the varoks, and you won't even touch me. You know touch means everything to me—to us ellls. Yet you don't touch me, you touch Orram. You know varoks are supposed to hate it, yet you keep communicating with him the way you ought to be talking to me."

"I'm relaxed enough with Orram to be myself with him—like I am with you—or used to be before you started complaining so much about elll this, elll that. Be patient. I love you like—like my own brother."

"That's part of the problem. I'm not your brother. I'm more like a neglected pet."

"Oh, Conn," she sighed, exasperated. "A figure of speech, that's all."

"No. No. It's a lot more than that. I won't roll over and sit up for biscuits, Tan. We loners need something beyond the school, but not at that price."

"What are you talking about? If I'm as mixed up as you seem to think I am, you'd better have Llorkin shrink me."

"That might not be a bad idea."

He left the room, sure that he would be a target for her shoe, then disappointed that he wasn't, and finally bitterly depressed.

He dove carelessly into the pool and let the full force of his pressure signals convey distress through the water.

From deep within the pool, Ellalon and Artellian, as if drawn by a powerful magnet, responded by converging on the source of distress.

"Let's try schooling with Tandra," Conn pleaded. "I'm losing her. She won't accept me on any level now."

"I will get her," Ellalon said. "I have wanted to know her as you do Conn, but it has not been possible. I don't understand why." She glided to the edge of the pool, disappeared into the recreation lounge, and soon emerged with Tandra. The human woman was annoyed, more than reluctant.

"I don't want to swim now, Ellalon. I'm having a wonderful experience with Analahk's poetry and some varokian music."

"We need you, Tandra. You are fading away from us, and we want to stop it. Try knowing us in the school. Conn is in pain. Please help us. Come into the water."

"No, I really don't care to, Ellalon. Can't we talk here on the deck?"

Ellalon looked at Conn with a darkened, bewildered knit in her blue-trimmed brow.

"Tan," Conn sighed, extending his hand to her, "come in just for a moment."

"I told you I don't want to swim. I can talk more easily from here." She sat down on the deck and waited, immovable.

"All right, Tandra," Artellian said as he climbed onto the deck, "we can try to talk here, dry, in your manner."

"Damn it," Conn railed in English, "we can get along fine on your terms, but if I ask some respect for elllonian needs, you back off. You can't force me to it, Tan. I won't take the leash."

"Is that your fear, Conn?" Artellian asked. "I don't think it could happen. The varokian theorists say that the loner needs special personal contacts beyond the school, not masters."

"I just want Tandra to love me as she did at first. I am not some kind of fearsome, fairy-frog turned prince."

Tandra didn't laugh.

"I am elll. And you don't know what that means."

"I think Conn needs the assurance that you love him as elllonian, not as pseudo-human," Artellian suggested.

Tandra looked blankly into the broad open face of the older elll. "Of course," she said.

Artellian extended his golden-tinged hand, rolled in submission, hoping that the matter was settled; but Tandra turned away and ignored his gesture.

Ellalon's eyes widened in horror at Tandra's cool, blatant rejection. "I think Artellian is right," she gasped. "You have never accepted us, and you can't face your own intolerance. You have always regarded Conn as human. No wonder Llorkin was surprised that you adjusted to our differences so easily." With a sudden agitated thrust of her soft blue-green frame, she stood up, but there was no anger in her eyes. "We took you in that first night after quarantine as one of us. But now you have lost us. Now we know that you never loved us at all; you loved only your own image of us. You are much more alien to us than we realized." She lowered herself into the pool.

Artellian finally dropped his hand, reluctant for so long to accept her rejection, and the three ellls swam slowly away.

SELF-DOUBT AND KNOWING

An hour passed. The water lay deserted. Talk at the food center rose to a crescendo then gradually fell to an occasional murmur. Tandra sat by the pool. She clutched her knees and pressed her face into them, numbed by the tangle of confusion and self-doubt that spun unanswerable questions in her mind. Certainly she understood the ellls: mild, capable, colorful people, enjoying life like uninhibited children, intending harm to no one and no thing. She loved them.

What was missing? How had she lost Conn? Was Ellalon right? Had she been avoiding Conn's touch? Artellian's? *Yes, Artellian's.* Why? What was it that she wasn't letting herself see? How does one become unblind? She lost track of time, while her mind timidly approached and retreated from a set of new visions and untested concepts.

She realized that the lights had dimmed and grown brighter again; another artificial day had begun. There were no sounds coming from the food center now. The morning meal was done; yet no one had come near her. She understood then that her presence might have kept the ellls away from their beloved pool. The thought sickened her. A deep quivering frown embedded itself on her face.

When she saw Conn, she wondered if he had been watching her for some time, apparently determined not to approach her, perhaps hoping she would seek him out. She looked up at him and nearly broke down, and he hurried to her without further thought, pressing his arms firmly about her, ignoring the tremor that shook her body.

"Look at me, Tan. It's only me, Conn."

"I'm afraid, Conn. What am I afraid of?" She looked into the dark green lenses that covered his eyes and found only their crystal beauty. "You are still there, aren't you, Conn? Was Ellalon right? No one came to the pool, Conn. I want you all back. I'll read the books. I must apologize to Artellian. I—"

"Books and apologies, Tan?" He gently lifted her face.

"I didn't think you would ever see me—come to me again."

"Daramonts know, I shouldn't have," Conn sighed. "It's your turn, many times over. Take a cue from Shawne. You trusted her natural judgment when you came to the *Lurlial*. Watch her now, Tan. Forget the books and apologies."

"Ellalon said I had lost you."

"Lost today, found tomorrow," Aen grumbled. He came across the deck to stand close beside them. "Right today, wrong tomorrow. Ellls react when we react because that's how we must react when we're reacting."

The crushed-velvet figure of the aging elll stood over her, refusing to be ignored. "So we are in trouble," he said, as she glanced up at him. "It will soon pass. Come talk with us. I have spent all my time these past weeks with Shawne and have neglected you."

Ellalon and Tllan joined them then, and the four ellls made a tight circle on the deck around Tandra.

Conn said little at first, then he began to grumble. "I'm not sure I like this attempt to reassure Tandra. The reassurance is being done

solely on Tandra's terms, through words. I don't like to see you all con-
descend to her this way. She can analyze herself verbally with remarkable dexterity. But this will change nothing. You're actually making
Tandra feel comfortable."

He left in disgust. Walking into the food center, he noisily vented
his anger on an innocent raw egg that had the misfortune of being left
out on the counter.

Soon after, Ellalon and Tllan said they were tired of the talk and left
Aen and Tandra alone by the pool.

"Your mind enjoys exercise, I think, Tandra, like old Llowellian."
Aen said. "I would like to take you to Ellason to meet her."

"Tell me about her, Aen," Tandra said.

"You would love her, Tandra," he said. "She has a universal outlook,
a tolerant acceptance, a faith in life like yours, as well as a wisdom
acquired the hard way. But she is very old now—over two hundred
Earth-years I would say.

"She was born with no sonar capability, no sonar organ at all. And
her chemical sensitivity was somehow impaired, too. In our environment on Ellason, without her sonar, she was as good as deaf, dumb,
and blind. As a tad, a young elll, she worked hard to overcome her
handicap with what senses she had, and eventually, she was even able
to mate, quite successfully, I might add. Several times I was able to find
her and to love her in the deeps."

He smiled as fond memories flooded his aging brain. "Hm-m,
makes me—how do you say? Horny? Delightful word. From the deer,
eh? Yes, just thinking of that warm, dear one makes me very horny. I
must go find Ellalon. She did not have Conn and Killah yesterday and,
of course, last night none of us—but do not worry, Tandra. We will survive one evening without the pool. Should I apologize for talking like
this? We have tried to respect human custom. Now, of course, Conn realizes it's not been wise. Not quite honest from your point of view, eh?
Well, off I go. Very horny. Yes. Delightful word. *Uleoon*." He grinned
with an enormous flash of white teeth and hurried off.

Tandra stared after Aen. Decorated generously with long gold-
fringed plumes, as if dressed in a tunic, he did look attractive. There
was nothing so serious for an elll that joy would not soon take over.
A smile found its way onto her face, and, almost simultaneously, her
mouth went dry, and a gripping pain tore through her stomach. Vivid

images rose in her mind of ellls leering at each other, of ellls rolling together in the slimy mud of a lake bottom, of ellls laughing vulgarly at her naiveté. She slammed her hand down hard on the mossy deck. Then she looked down and saw the imprint she had left. She had crushed the life from the moss. Its plump, tough leaves lay ragged and empty. For a panicky moment, she worked furiously to pull the life back into the tiny, intricate structures, but there was no restoring them nor what they represented. Her vision of the ellls was gone. Only a faint green blur remained.

– Δ –

"I need to talk," Conn said as he entered Orram's room. He carefully placed a hand on the varok's shoulder, and Orram laid his hand over the prehensile fin.

"Tandra?"

"I had a glimpse of something—" He couldn't continue. Silence tore between them for a moment, then Conn dropped all regard for their differences. "It's no good. I can't talk, Orram, I need you in the pool."

He threw himself past the varok, too steeped in himself to hear Orram's quiet response, "I'll try."

They slipped into the ruby water, and Orram watched Conn glide around him, trembling and beating out pressure signals and electro-pulses with the outpouring of his frustration. His grief covered the varok like a pulsing blanket of agony in the warm water. Orram felt as if his every nerve was stripped raw by the insistent drumming. The intensity of the pressure signals rose, throbbing and tearing. *Too much, Conn!* Piercing pain!! He couldn't stand it. *Too much.*

Suddenly it subsided. Orram looked for Conn and found him contentedly throwing himself high out of the water and falling haphazardly back in. Before long he swam to the shaken varok.

"Schooling with a disturbed elll is certainly an experience no varok should miss. I am honored—intellectually and spiritually honored. Emotionally and physically, however—"

"Should I get Killah?" Conn asked.

"No. Just float still for a moment. Don't make any waves. I must be bleeding from every pore."

"What made me bring you here?"

"I have a mind of my own, usually."

"You also usually don't give a *kaehl* egg for yourself. Why did you get in my water, Orram?"

"You needed me here, Conn."

"I wanted Tandra here, so I took it out on you. That's a rotten price—you won't have to pay it again. I've tried all the talk I can. It's her turn to learn some elll-talk."

"As I just experienced?"

Impulsively—perhaps to avoid Orram's patch contact—Conn dove to the bottom of the pool, where the weighty blanket of water did much to calm him.

Through the following days, since nothing seemed to work between Conn and Tandra, Orram suggested that they keep strictly to their music. Reluctantly, Tandra joined Conn each day, and gradually they became engrossed in comparing the styles of Earth's classical and modern composers. They enjoyed reshaping them with Ellasonian and Varokian music. More often than not, elllonian rhythm was high above Tandra's audible range, since it was written to stimulate the ellls' sonar receptors. Conn reversed the operation that he had performed on Tandra's grandfather's CDs and devised a system that generated low driving tones from the ultrasonic beats. The resulting sound was wild and rich in harmonies, scattered between tones western civilization calls notes. Tandra moved her body to the rhythm as if she loved it.

Conn danced, laughing as the music began to pull them together again. But when he begged her to teach him classical western harmony, all her efforts failed.

"I just don't see what's so special about combining sounds with frequencies of 261.63, 329.63, and 391.995," Conn said.

"I'm sure I don't know," Tandra admitted. "Just call it a C major chord and let it go at that. Doesn't it sound—well . . . happy—or solid or finished to you?" she said. "If I had a piano I could show you what I mean. Remember the arpeggios I played for you at my house?"

"Happily, but no, I didn't hear anything solid in those frequencies, either."

"Conn, you have no real sound appreciation. Only half of it goes in your ears—"

The elll interrupted her, suddenly very serious. "You have done a subjective physical comparison with Orram, and you know he is truly alien. Right?"

"Yes."

"Do one with me. Now."

"It's not necessary. You're obviously alien."

"Am I?"

"Not too many Earthlings run around in green feathers and velvet hexagons, Conn."

"Nevertheless, I want to do a formal study." He led her toward the pool.

Tandra hesitated. "If you insist." She followed him, undressed, and closed her eyes while Conn moved his hands slowly over her body and through her hair. He smelled like ripe green grass. His touch stopped on her cheeks, and she felt the soft, dry tip of his tongue on her eyelids.

"Look at me, Tan. Please, see who I am."

"I do know you, Conn. I don't like set-ups like this."

"Feel me all over with your eyes open, the way I felt you." Conn's breathing became shallow, and his eyes started to narrow.

"Don't order me around that way, Conn. I won't."

"You will! By Harrahn's teeth, Tandra, you will know me as elllonian!"

The emerald lights of his eyes dimmed and went out, and his mood reversed. "At least you'll swim in the same pool with me. Right? Into the water, landlubber." He lifted her in his arms, ran to the pool, and flung her in. Then he somersaulted after her and disappeared beneath the surface of the wine-red water.

Tandra clung to the side of the pool and waited for him to resurface. She waited a long time, knowing that ellls could remain underwater for several minutes. She waited ten minutes more before she became anxious. She searched her mind. How long had she seen them stay under? Could Conn have hit his head when he dived in? Probably not. The pool was over twenty feet deep. She swam quickly to the spot where Conn had disappeared and dove toward the bottom. She saw nothing but the deep red of the pool's mossy lining. She surfaced, and her stomach tightened in alarm. More than twenty minutes must have passed since Conn dove in. His lung capacity couldn't be that great.

She climbed out of the pool and searched the clear water for Conn's dark form. There. But he wasn't moving. He seemed to be floating upside down. Fear gripped her as she entered the pool again. She swam until she spotted Conn's long body lying motionless on the bottom.

She filled her lungs and dove, determined to ignore her fear of the dense liquid ruby water. It was beautiful, rich with reflected light. She found Conn's shoulders and managed to cross her left arm over his neck and under his right arm. Then she kicked furiously, her free arm pulling hard toward the surface. Slowly she rose, and finally, with a gasp, surfaced with her burden and began to move toward the pool's edge. She was making good progress when she realized that Conn was slowly kicking, and smiling into her strained face. He clasped her in his arms and rolled underneath her, supporting her in the water.

"Conn, you devil!" she gasped, struggling to free her arms for an angry strike at him. But in the warmth of the water, he was too quick for her. Pinning her arms behind her back and winding his legs around hers—his central backfin erect and undulating rapidly—he supported Tandra's body above water and floated her slowly across the pool. The elll's velvet belly rippled with the concealed effort of firm muscles, and his feathered loin pressed provocatively against her. For a moment she relaxed into his tender strength.

"At last you're ready to talk my language, Tan. Now you will know elll's as no varok can."

The probe of his sexual organ grew more obvious, then insistent and undeniable.

"Conn, stop. I can't—we can't do this."

"We can," Conn murmured, pressing her closer. "I've checked the geometry. It should be a good fit."

"No!" she cried, struggling against his embrace. "Don't, Conn. This is ridiculous."

"No it's not. You've wanted us to communicate better. Now we'll talk my way for a change." He encased her in long arms and took her deeper into the crystal red warmth of the pool.

Conn!" Orram's voice reverberated above the water. "You are needed in the hangar."

Tandra tore out of Conn's arms, and the elll glided toward the edge of the pool where Orram was standing. "I'm not on duty now, Orram," he said. He climbed out of the pool and stood before his varokian friend, a half-smile on his lips, a furious expression in his eyes, and his male organ thrust out from among his groin plumes.

Orram studied Conn's eyes for a moment before he slowly and deliberately moved his glance over the elll's flushed body and erect organ. "What is the meaning of this challenge, Conn? Ellls don't display themselves."

"What is the meaning of your challenge?"

"Why were you here alone with Tandra?"

"Why not?" The quizzical ridge deepened on Conn's brow. He waited, belligerent, his eyes narrowing.

Panic began to strangle the bewildered varok. Why couldn't he reach Conn? Why now a price on honesty? And what feeling was this in himself? Fear? Yes. And anger, too. Both emotions were alive within him, and he was not able to rationalize them into either understanding or repression.

Ellls care nothing for the social implications of sex, he thought. *Conn's belligerent display makes no sense. Yet he has come to the pool alone with Tandra. This is no simple teasing. This is—what? What is this? Conn cannot prove anything this way. It's too much like what humans call rape. He will push Tandra completely out of reach. She is not ready for this. It will not work. I care. Why? Pushing Tandra too hard . . . I care too much!* Suddenly the varok's emotions crashed over him and possessed his mind.

"You will get nowhere this way. It's mindless bestiality!" he raged, his clenched fist slashing toward Conn's disappearing organ.

The elll blocked the attack with a powerful sideways thrust of his joined arms, jumping to one side into a crouch.

"You've lost control, Orram. Shake it off. You've got to help me. I must make Tandra know me. I am too alone."

The desperation in his voice sent the varok back to reason. Orram trembled inwardly, badly shaken by the sudden thrust into emotion and out again. "I thought I was strong enough for you. Perhaps I am not. But leave Tandra to me. You are not helping her. You are only deepening the dream."

"You're wrong, Orram," Tandra said. "I am not dreaming. I see clearly now. I love you both as dear friends. I would have submitted to Conn if you had not come in when you did. He is not a beast to me, and neither are you."

With a cry of protest, Conn caught Tandra by the shoulders. "No, Tan, no. I am beast—alien to you. I am elll! It's not sex as humans understand it. You miss the whole point."

SEACHING FOR ANSWERS

"Orram, I would like to go with you on this next expedition," Junah said.

"That is a strange request," he said. "There is no need for you to go."

"There is need in it, for us." She probed deeply, trying to contact him beyond mood. But he resisted her probe, denied her entrance to his mind, and warned her that logic must deny her desire.

"We have no need for time together," he said quietly, turning away.

The invisible pull of yearning, buried and denied, distorted the pale light in Junah's eyes, though her face displayed no expression.

Tandra, working in Killah's lab, saw the exchange, and thought she understood why the varokian woman seemed so upset. The pain of rejection, the desperation to fix what couldn't be fixed, was too much to bear.

She resumed her work. She took culture tubes, inoculated forty-eight hours previously, out of the incubator and set them on the work-bench. She selected a turbid reddish growth marked with an elll's name. Her little finger and side of her hand automatically uncapped the tube under the sterilizing cone, as her thumb and forefinger manipulated a long narrow probe with a small loop on the end. The culture was viscous and ropy with a common elllonian organism usually found at the back of the ellls' long tongues. The tangled masses in the culture would have to be avoided if Tandra were to isolate the other bacteria.

When her probe became entangled in a sticky string of the teem-ing life, she pulled it from the tube and let the heat and radiation of the sterilizing cone destroy it. Then she reinserted the probe into the tube and trapped a drop of turbidity. Quickly she recapped the tube, carefully opened a large, flat octagonal disk of gelatinous nutrient, and made several streaks on the surface with the bacteria-laden probe.

She sterilized the probe and crossed the end of her first streaks three times, dragging fewer of the millions of bacteria out across the nutrient. She sterilized the probe and crossed the last three streaks again, and repeated the process five more times, then carefully closed the flat dish. The process diluted the bacteria by spreading, and separated them by friction. With luck, a few individuals would land on spots isolated enough so that with proper incubation they would

multiply undisturbed. In a few hours a distinctive colony of geneti-
cally identical individuals would grow to visible dimensions with
identifiable characteristics.

Tandra repeated the process four times for each culture tube; there
were two culture tubes for each member of the crew. Hours later she
finished the two hundred and forty streak plates, labeled them, organized them into their trays, set them with some difficulty into the varokian autoclave, waited while the pressure mounted, set the timer—
and then remembered that they should have gone into the incubator,
not the sterilizer. She stood staring at the autoclave in dismay. Most
of the organisms, so meticulously separated for cultivation, would already be dead.

There was no point in trying to work. Her mind was preoccupied,
struggling to free itself from an entangling green veil. She must try to
find the ellls again.

She wandered about Killah's lab searching absently for something
to write on. She picked up a sheet of synthetic and stared at it. It was
very empty. She tried to concentrate on Conn. Nothing. His features:
straight nose (yes, she was sure of that); short, tousled plumes (they
looked so much like hair); brow line cocked at a permanently amused
tilt (eyebrows? No. Must be tiny plumes there); long legs (taut with wiry
muscles, powerful yet soft, firm yet gently grasping, sensual); wide,
smooth, muscular chest. When she had finished a detailed description
of Conn, she hurried to find Orram.

Artellian stopped her in the hallway. "Are you all right, Tandra?"
he asked.

"Yes. No," she stammered. "I must find Orram."

"He's in the hangar. Go slowly, Tandra. There is time for everything."

She smiled gratefully at the master elll, but his green alien countenance no longer seemed fatherly, just strange and bestial. She shuddered, and hurried down the hall.

When she reached the hangar she strode directly to Orram, who
was standing beside the plump gray-brown vehicle, *Arlaht*, with Junah
and two ellls.

Slowly Orram's face turned away from the landcraft toward Tandra.
Before she spoke, she watched the varok's face return to its usual placid
veneer as Orram locked away a look of frustration.

"Orram, please read this."

He took the synthetic sheet, read it, and handed it back with a grim look on his face. "This is no elll you have described, Tandra. It could be a human or a varok. Where are the pressure plates and sonar lines and melons, the backfin, the nasal gills, the lack of ears, the webbed extremities, the large eyes covered with dimming lenses?" He led her away from the others and chose his words carefully. "Have you confronted the fact that you may find the ellls unacceptable, even abhorrent, now?"

"After loving Conn so well . . ." Tandra paused. "I'm obsessed with a vision of his as a green blur, wallowing in the mud with whomever comes along."

"What is it that you love about Conn? Try to define that," Orram said.

"I loved his easiness and wit, his directness, his competence, his modesty, his beauty."

"And what has destroyed all of that for you?" He paused. "Why do you fear knowing more about the ellls?"

Suddenly Tandra was shaken with an insight that seemed to come from outside herself. "Can you read anything that is in my mind? Even thoughts before they have formed into words?" she asked. "Is that what the patch organs do?"

For a moment Orram stared searchingly at her, his brow heightened in surprise. "No. Nothing that specific," he said. The dim caution in his face lifted, and he spoke lightly, with a touch of excitement in his voice. "Tandra, come with us on the expedition to the lunar pole. There are things we must discuss. I will assist you in your adjustment to the ellls. You will have a fresh perspective after two weeks away from Conn. Come over here. Take a look at the lunar map."

She followed him to the map built into the *Arlaht*'s control panel. "We will go to the lunar north pole, swing back toward base on the side facing Earth, and stop briefly before we make the southern loop. This is an old, well-worn route for us. It was scouted in orbit from the *Lurlial* before we tried it on land, so we know the rough area northwest of here quite well.

"We regulate our speed to take advantage of the more moderate temperatures and better light within the terminator. It should be an interesting trip for you, Tandra. We will gather data, take samples and perform maintenance on the experimental probes and communication web along the route. We should have long periods of time to talk."

Tandra listened with rising excitement. "When can we leave?"

"I agree," he said in answer to her unspoken thought, "the sooner the better."

Within forty hours, Tandra and Orram boarded the comfortable rover, *Arlaht*, accompanied by Aen and Ellalon. Within minutes the pressure lock of EV base swung open and deposited the vehicle and its passengers onto the moon's surface.

The *Arlaht* was a versatile hyrogen-powered craft, designed to travel as efficiently as possible to make good use of solar exposure when available—and, as Conn once said, hover, galumph, or tip-toe if necessary over any terrain. It contained all the equipment one might expect. There was a complete life support system for four oxygen breathers, including storage tanks for water, oxygen, and dried food. Most of the rear compartments of the vehicle were crammed with sampling equipment, repair tools, and life support suits for lunar exposure. Ellalon and Aen made frequent use of them in order to collect data, to catalogue samples electronically, and to repair faulty equipment at the EV experimental lunar substations.

The vehicle also was designed to maximize the pleasure of its passengers. The interior was draped with the tastiest of Ellasonian mosses, and the couches were spacious and carefully contoured.

Tandra and Orram spent most of the time relaxed into the large couches of the resting cabin in the rear of the vehicle. There they talked about Varok and Earth and themselves, while they watched the lunar terrain slowly move by. When it was Orram's turn to take the controls, Tandra moved up to the control deck with him, and the ellls always gave her their seat without question.

Tandra was as fascinated with Orram, and the strange depths within him, as she was captivated by the harsh panorama of the moon's tortured surface. For many days neither mentioned Conn. She realized Orram knew she was avoiding Aen and Ellalon. Thankfully, he said nothing.

On the tenth day of their journey, after Tandra had been watching Orram maneuver the *Arlaht* for almost an hour, he suddenly stopped the vehicle and stood up, motioning for her to take his place. "It is quite simple, simpler than driving an automobile in traffic, I would guess. You want to give it a try, don't you?"

"I've been longing to, but I see you're not about to take any chances."

Tandra laughed, for he had stopped more than a mile into the flat wastes of the Sea of Cold, where she could hardly do any damage to the vehicle if she tried.

She slid into the driver's couch and reviewed the controls. Then carefully she eased her knee against the velocity bar, testing the *Arlaht*'s response.

"Aen, we have a fourth driver," Orram called over his shoulder.

"Could not resist any longer, eh?" Aen said. He moved up to the control deck and patted Tandra on the shoulder. She recoiled, and he shook his head slightly. "I wonder how Shawne is doing alone at base with all the aliens?" he asked, watching Tandra's expression.

"I have no worries about Shawne," Tandra said. "Conn promised to watch over her carefully. She didn't even want to come with us."

Aen shrugged and turned away.

"Tandra, you are a master of selective repression," Orram said abruptly. "You are seeing Aen as smoked, green glass, and you will not rediscover Conn when we return to base unless you face your intolerance squarely."

"I am not intolerant."

"You do not accept the ellls as they are. Nonacceptance is the child of intolerance."

"Orram—"

"Tandra, what would it mean—" He stopped talking, then his words emerged gradually, as if he were experimenting with them. "What does it mean that our biochemical differences are not as significant as we first thought? What if our two species were interfertile?"

"Not much." Tandra laughed, relieved by the diversion. "We are too calloused to new realities, even to the bizarre, these days, given the extremes we invent as entertainment."

"'We' you say. The loss of human uniqueness would have no significance? No influence?"

"I suppose human pride might be damaged."

"Human pride would be threatened by interfertility? Uniqueness disproved? Anything else? Tandra, what would it mean to you?"

"It would also upset a few atheists. Such complete biological convergence might imply direction in universal evolutionary processes."

"I am not sure about that, but I am sure you are evading my last question."

"I'm—yes, I was, wasn't I?" she said, feeling foolish. Why was she trying to protect herself from Orram? Because she was trying to be more than she was? "Certainly love is more important than biochemistry. I keep thinking that it shouldn't matter that you—or Conn for that matter—touch me for a moment. If love motivated the act, isn't consent justified?"

"We agree then, that consent is essential."

"When you confronted Conn I assumed you did not approve of interspecific sex," Tandra said.

Orram smiled. "I have no opinion, really. I do not care to make such generalizations."

"Am I making cultural judgments without realizing it?"

"Decidedly, but your eyes are opening, Tandra. My question was foolish; we have better things to worry about. I think we all agree that love—hormonal or not—is more important than its particular expression."

"Most human beings would not agree. Most attach some kind of cosmic significance to all human acts, even sex play. Ridiculous, but it's true. And yet what are we? Our existence must mean something. We may be tiny blobs of pompous protoplasm in terms of geologic time and space, but at least we are capable of love."

Orram offered his hand to her. "I believe that you and I and Conn can agree that love is an integral, shared force capable of binding the cosmos together. Ask the questions that we all share: why have formless gases and minute particles come together in the enormities of space to invent complex, unique organisms capable of cognizance? Why have molecules molded themselves into forms of beauty? Why have they become self-conscious? Why have they learned to love?

"You almost took Conn's sexual touch as a natural extension of his friendship, for you know that he needs sensual expression. I see that now. I think you can love him for what he is—to accept, to appreciate, and finally to cherish those elements that make him different from you."

"You must be wrong, Orram. I can't face the ellls now that my daydream has been denied. I am too human, too insecure. We humans look to differences too easily. We look for an excuse to hate and to reinforce our tribal instincts."

"If that is true, then you will have to go beyond your human ideas, your species or cultural identity, if you are ever to know Conn as he really is."

– Δ –

The *Arlaht* picked its way south across the Sea of Cold, skirted the rim of the crater Plato, and dove between the Straight Range and the Teneriffe Mountains into the Sea of Rains. Ellalon watched with interest the growing bond between Orram and the human female. She was keenly disappointed when Tandra consistently avoided her, which was no easy feat in the close quarters of the lurching, crawling vehicle they shared.

Eventually, Ellalon learned that Aen, too, was searching for ways to awaken Tandra's awareness of himself. The ellls' instinctive pull toward shared experience made them ignore Tandra's coolness and continually probe her defenses to find chinks into which they could stuff bits of humor and easy comment and some honest affection.

One twilight time, after they had swung toward base in their looping course around the moon, Tandra drove the *Arlaht* through the lowlands around the Lansberg craters toward the gray-brown wastes of the Ocean of Storms so Aen and Orram could check maintenance data taken from the experimental station near Copernicus.

Ellalon awoke from a restless sleep. Seeing that Tandra was alone and trapped by her duty at the controls, the delicate blue-green elll slipped quietly into the other couch before the control panel and stared for a moment through the window to the endless craters that surrounded them. Then, without warning, she spoke: "Tandra, if you can't let yourself know us, then at least let us know you the way Conn has."

The blood drained from Tandra's face. "I'm sorry," she said, meaning it. "I can't face you, Ellalon. When I look at you, at any elll, I feel as if, as if I'm drowning in—I can't say. I feel this even while I admire your beauty. And, it sounds ridiculous, but with you, I'm jealous. I didn't know until recently that you were Conn's mate."

"Jealous?" Ellalon asked with a shake of her long, blue plumes. "I'm not sure what it means. Something to do with possessing a person—or wanting to? But Conn is not here now, and I am not his only mate. He mates with many ellls at base, though not as often as we would like."

"I suppose he does," Tandra said. "Jealousy may be the wrong word, Ellalon. I didn't expect to monopolize Conn. No, I think my problem with you is more like a moral confusion."

"Moral confusion? Oh, Tandra, I don't understand you at all." She laughed. "I thought we were talking about mating with Conn. How could our morals confuse you? They are quite simple. We insist on honesty and hate physical violence. We abhor anything that dulls consciousness and life-joy. That's all. Morals have nothing much to do with mating."

"Nothing much?"

"Only when we choose fertile eggs to hatch. We have no words in our languages that translate the English words *bigamy, premarital sex, adultery, jealousy.*"

Tandra laughed, and a wave of affection for the elll washed through her. "You mean so much to me," she said. She reached for Ellalon's arm, but before her hand touched the green, mossy skin, the elllonian female grabbed for the controls and threw the *Arlaht* out of the path of a large boulder that was bounding lazily down on them from its precarious position high on the wall of crater Grimaldi. The boulder skidded past them, but it brought behind it a slow motion cascade of smaller rocks. Rapidly they engulfed the *Arlaht*, bringing it to a halt.

"Well," Ellalon grinned. "Let's go throw rocks at each other."

Tandra laughed with her. The warm regard was there again. Now if only she could clear the blurred vision.

Orram was at the back of the craft with a lunar exposure suit already pulled over his legs.

"It will save time if we all help repair the road," Ellalon said. "Tandra and I need some exercise and a good stretch. Aen, are you coming?"

"Wouldn't miss the chance. I'll do some exploring while you three do all the work."

They helped each other into the exposure suits. The *Arlaht* was depressurized, and they disembarked to scramble about the boulders that blocked their path. Aen tossed a few small rocks away from the *Arlaht* and clambered up the hill leading to the bowl of the crater Grimaldi.

"I don't see any loose rocks," he said into his communicator.

"Look around some more," Orram answered.

Aen climbed higher, while Orram and Ellalon and Tandra quickly cleared the path. They were moving the last of the boulders when

Aen carefully turned on the steep slope above them and started back. Blinded by the brightness of the sun at the horizon, he stumbled into a depression. He grasped at a large boulder as he fell, but it tore out of his hands, then rolled slowly down the hillside, ricocheted suddenly off another precipitous outcropping, and before it hit the path, mindlessly crushed the life from Ellalon.

The Sound of Grief

No sound told the tale. Tandra thought she heard Aen grunt and mumble into his communicator as he made his way down the rock slide, but she didn't realize that anything else had happened, until she turned away from the *Arlaht* and saw Aen roughly drag Ellalon's limp body to the side of the path and strip off its space suit.

Tandra cried out and ran to him, tugging desperately at his hands doing their gruesome work. "What happened? What are you doing?" she cried.

He looked at her blankly. No sign of grief, no indication of care or regret showed behind his helmet. "Go to the *Arlaht* and fill an injector with disintegrating compound," he said calmly. "I fell, and this was in the path of the boulder I knocked loose."

Horror grew within Tandra. "This! This? Aen!"

"Do not excite yourself. There is nothing more to do. There is no more to Ellalon."

Orram came from the *Arlaht* carrying an injector. He picked up Ellalon's delicate green arm, probed its vein, and waited quietly while the powerful chemical found the elll's blood pools and quickly converted her back to organic molecules.

"Pea soup," Aen said, and he smiled with warmth at Tandra.

Incredulous, she broke into wild, angry sobs. Orram pulled her to her feet and urged her toward the *Arlaht*. "We must continue our trip."

"Even you," she sobbed, "even you will just leave her here."

"I have no choice." His voice was very tight. "I must get us back into the *Arlaht* safely. Then I can allow the grief to break me apart. Remember, Tandra, I am varok. I cannot function rationally and feel an emotion like grief at the same time."

"But kind Aen—how can he do this?" Tandra shook uncontrollably, her mind a fierce tangle of emotions.

Orram held her firmly. "Please, please, Tandra. I need you to be calm. Ellls have no grief. Ellalon no longer exists in Aen's mind, as she does not exist in fact. The school has changed its composition; that is all. There is no human counterpart for what Aen feels now. This is a real difference. Ellalon would want you to understand. Accept it. The ellls will miss her in their own way, for they will have to adjust to her absence from the school; but they will not grieve. They will not curse fate and storm against what is unchangeable. But I shall.

"When it is safe and when I am somewhere where the risk will not be too great, I shall release the grief that is within me. It will be much like yours. I shall grieve for the loss of a gentle friend—a selfish emotion really. I want what I clearly cannot have. I want Ellalon to be alive. Is there more to grief? Ellalon does not need our tears. She needs nothing. The ellls know this better than we. I shall grieve as you do, Tandra, but when I do, that will be all I shall be able to do."

Aen offered Orram physical support. "We had better continue into the highlands immediately," he said.

Tandra followed them into the *Arlaht*. Aen sealed it against the moon's vacuum, and they took off their exposure suits. Orram started the drives and guided the vehicle down the rough path, leaving Ellalon's tragedy to itself.

Somehow Tandra managed to do what had to be done. Then she found a couch and sat frozen, unmoving, her eyes fixed in a glassy stare. She was only dimly aware when Aen took the controls from Orram with a kindly insistence.

"You had a friend named Ellalon who was like a daughter to you, Orram. You must have grief to release."

The varok nodded. Already the smoldering pain of his grief threatened to burn the tethers of his reason.

"There is no need to wait," Aen said. "I will take the *Arlaht* to base. We are only twenty hours away."

Orram moved slowly toward Tandra and sat heavily beside her.

"Forgive me, Tandra," he said. "Aen is right. I wanted to spare you from my grief, but I should not wait. Twenty hours is too long to contain this pain."

His straight, invincible body bowed and crumpled with great heaves that left him helpless, lost to reason, his consciousness nothing but incoherent fragments, his mind shattered by the impact of his grief.

Tandra took his head in her lap, smoothing his silver brown hair. The books had not exaggerated. The threshold was crossed; Orram would not be rational for hours, perhaps days. She longed to give him what human strength she could. "You can live and know and feel such pain too, Orram," she whispered. "Pain is a warning. It need not kill."

Aen stopped the *Arlaht*, moved quickly to the resting cabin, and tried to pull Orram away from Tandra. Angrily, she resisted his pull and clasped Orram even closer.

"Tandra, he must do this alone," Aen said. "He must maintain his own way back, or he will go too far. You may not be strong enough to hold him."

Aen had worked with varoks during most of his long life, and even Orram, who was no ordinary varok, rarely surprised him. Now, however, he drew back amazed, for Orram straightened and took Aen's arm, sitting up on the couch next to Tandra. "She is strong enough," he said, and he gathered her hands to his forehead. Tandra looked at Aen questioningly, but he could only shrug in bewilderment.

"Orram, are you out of your grief?" he asked.

In silence they waited for his answer. When he spoke, the words came slowly, with considerable effort. "No," he said. "I am neither out nor in. I am held somewhere between reason and emotion by what I receive from Tandra. I am aware, and controlled, and still full of pain. How odd to know both at once. I will be back in control before we reach base, Aen. Continue, please."

"So you were right, Tandra," Aen said with a worried smile. "But you must be very strong now. You are taking Orram along an unknown path." He returned to the controls, and the small, gray craft bumped and turned and groveled its way through the highlands at a painfully slow pace.

Orram did not move for hours nor did he say anything, until they were well into the d'Alembert Mountains. Then he rose silently, found three packets of food and drink, and took one to Aen. When the elll had eaten, Orram returned to Tandra and offered her one. Then he sat again on the couch and ate.

"We are only three hours from base. I have reported the accident," Aen called over his shoulder.

"Then I will put away this grief. Aen, come and rest. I will return the *Arlaht* to base."

The elll stopped the craft. "Are you really able, Orram? So soon? Yes, I see you are quite out of your grief. Perhaps the human element has introduced another factor into varokian existence, eh?"

"Decidedly, Aen," Orram said. "Stay with Tandra now. She is in a limbo even stranger than mine."

During the rest of their trip, Aen spoke continuously to Tandra, with all the understanding and gentleness that his kind soul possessed. But the state of death meant nothing to him, so he could offer little relief for her shock. The mindless glint that formed in her eyes when she looked at him told him that she could not focus on him, that she barely heard him. But still he talked. He talked of Shawne and the tad Da-oon; love of children they could share.

Finally, Orram drove the *Arlaht* over the rim of a small crater that lay in partial blackness near the crater Schlüter and guided the land-craft across its floor to the sealed entrance of the base.

THE VALUE OF EGGS

Conn waited in the hangar for the *Arlaht*'s arrival. He started to insert his light-limiting contact lenses so that he could turn the lights back up to the brightness required for the varoks, then hesitated. Until Tandra had left on this trip, the lights had not been dimmed, as a courtesy to her. Now, Conn decided, the lights would remain at Ellasonian levels. He put his contacts back into their case on his wrist and reset the elllonian-light-only warning system.

Finally the *Arlaht* entered the dark hangar and settled to a halt, and its passengers climbed out of the hatch. A dim red light reflected like fire in Conn's enormous black pupils as he searched Aen's face. In response, the elder elll glanced at Tandra and shook his head slowly, but then he suddenly brightened: "Look here, Conn, Orram is already out of grief," he said.

Conn clapped the varok heartily on the shoulder. "In and out? That must be some kind of varokian speed record."

Bitter tears rose in Tandra's eyes. "How can you joke? Ellalon is dead. Her blue plumes are all that are left, smeared with her mashed green. Your mate, Conn, she's dead. Crushed! Care, Conn. You must care."

For a moment Conn's eyes narrowed with anger. "Yes, I care—because the school will have to go through adjustment, when it is already small. I have lost no mating. There are plenty of others."

A wave of nausea swept over Tandra. Conn's voice was hard, and his appearance was shadowy, unfamiliar in the dark red Ellasonian light. "Conn?"

He relaxed and grew easy again. "I respect your grief, Tandra," he said gently. "And I thank everything Harrahn represents that Orram is out of his so easily. Respect *me* now. Anger is not what I need from you." He placed his hand-like fins under her chin and waited.

Tandra stood with her eyes averted, understanding what he wanted and fearing it. Finally, her determination crystallized, and she raised her eyes to his. "You are elll," she murmured. She searched, but she saw nothing—nothing but her own reflection and a glittering she hadn't seen before in the great black circles of his eyes without dimming lenses. She turned away from the vision and ran blindly toward the door to the labs, where Orram found her.

"Tandra, the *Arlaht* is proceeding to the south pole, with Conn in charge. Will you go? You are well qualified now to navigate."

"Aren't you going?"

"No. I will stay here and consolidate our data for transmission to Varok."

"I don't want to go with Conn now," she said. "I need time to find my way out of this wilderness." Her consciousness was centered in Orram. He was the key to reality, a stable reference to play her fears against. "I cannot go."

The elll had joined them. He nodded curtly and walked back toward the *Arlaht*.

Orram called after him, "I shall send Erah and Tllan to fill out your crew."

"Erah can't go," Conn said. "She is still in grief from the news of Ellalon's death. Junah never went into grief. Send her. Tell her we'll eat before we leave."

Orram took Tandra's arm and turned her firmly toward him. "Go help feed Conn and the others."

"Orram, please, I want to see Shawne."

"The vision must be cleared, Tandra. Do it now. With delay it will only become more difficult."

They left the hangar, and while Orram continued down the hall to Junah's room, Tandra turned into the food center. Moving mechanically and with difficulty in the dim red light, she selected some leathery Ellasonian fruits, cut them into squares, and was adding black Varokian *hoats* when Conn entered the room.

"We'll just eat a few raw eggs," he said crisply and set four large blue eggs on the central table.

Tandra spoke without much awareness of what she said. "The eggs are very large. Where did they come from?"

Conn looked at her in disbelief. "They're ours, Tandra," he said.

"Yours?"

"Certainly you know—no, you don't, do you?" He grabbed her shoulders, his desperation rising. "Tan," he said slowly, "our females produce several eggs every six weeks or so."

"They do? These? These are your eggs? You are eating your own eggs? You are eating your own—"

Suddenly then she saw him, stark and real—alien, denuded of fantasy: high, green cheekbones on a hollow, straight visage, and a mouth too broad. She could not tolerate the new strangeness of his face, once so familiar and loved. "It's like eating your own children."

"They're eggs, Tandra, not ellls."

She answered as if in a daze. "All potential life should have a chance for continued existence." An angry alien image wavering over her, a dim black-green shadow, mocking her.

"That's semantic nonsense. I'm not talking about a carefully nurtured, incubated egg or a quickened fetus that awakes love in its mother. I'm talking about the first bit of tissue that has no awareness, no knowledge of pain or joy—not even in its mother's mind."

"There is meaning in potential life," Tandra said. Where were his eyes? Black, hollow, gaping holes, looming huge and empty—

"*Potential* meaning, Tandra, for the developing individual—and potential horror for the real individuals who must make room when there is no more room."

"But where is your respect for life?" Strange, branched hairs waving stiffly, grotesquely, planted at odd angles all over his head. "The right to life is more fundamental than the right to happiness."

"Happiness? Happiness? Freedom from starvation is ecstasy, if it can be found on your miserable planet. You can't mean to place the rights of an insensate, organic growth above the rights of a conscious, feeling being."

"What is there to value, if we don't value all of life, Conn? I thought that's what eIlls value most." Vile, inhuman, long tongue. Ears gone. Slimy, black green mouth, so broad! How could she stop him speaking, make him go away?

"Yes, we value life above all else—life that feels soft touches and knows love, life that sees the stars and knows the wonder of eternity, life that tastes the bitter, poisoned gruel called pain and knows the terrorizing degradation of eating garbage in order to survive. Tandra! Tandra! You human beings can't continue to define conscious life as less meaningful than the potential in fertile eggs."

"It doesn't have to be that way, Conn," Tandra whispered. Great cloacal lips, emerging eggs, closed probe, wet and smeared with feces. Vomit rose in her throat.

"It-is-that-way!" Conn screamed. "It-is-already-that-way, Tandra. It-has-been-that-way-for-decades on Earth! Go mad for lack of living space! Watch the boils of hunger rise in Shawne's mouth! All for the sake of eggs!" Violently he smashed an *el* egg, and, in a furious rage born of true elllonian grief, threw Tandra into its slippery remains and left her sobbing on the floor.

"Orram! Oran Ramahlak!" Junah called. An unusual tightness in her voice betrayed some urgency as she hurried down the hall. She found Orram in the nursery with Shawne. "Come to the food center," she said in Varokian. "Dr. Grey is very ill."

With his usual calming tone, Orram told Shawne that he would soon return, but when he reached the hallway, he broke into a full run. He composed himself before entering the food center. Tandra was sitting on the floor with her head bowed between heaving shoulders.

"What is it, Tandra?" he said, kneeling beside her.

She shook her head slowly, fighting for composure. "Conn," she said, "Conn." Words tumbled from her dry throat. "Conn! Killah! Hollow eyes. Swamp things. Eggs and waste and sperm—all from one—all from the cloaca. And they mate all the time, underwater, with anything."

Orram's face darkened. "Yes," he said.

She grasped him with cold hands. "Conn said hedonic glands and a spermatophore. They're alien, Orram. They're like amphibians. They're not even remotely human. They have no mothers."

"If I could only reach you, Tandra." Slowly, with gentle assurance, he lay his hands on hers, while his mind reached toward her, concentrating on ellls, their love of life, his love for them.

Gradually, in his secure hands, Tandra began to relax. The revulsion subsided, and the shock dissipated. She knew, somehow, that Orram was showing her a view of the ellls that she had not seen before. Her mind began to focus clearly on them again: *Killah—handsomest of the green, aquatic frogmen. Yes, frogmen. No, ellls. Handsomest of the ellls, fond of phrases and ideas; slave to his work. Aen—aging, an aging frogman. Isn't there a better word? His golden plumes framing his dark face only barely frog-like. More like a collie or an Egyptian drawing. Green and water mean frog—that is all. Kind, simple Aen. Artellian—strong and competent, golden statue elll, dressed in patterned velvet, firm and wise, like a father. Ellalon—so beautiful, light green framed in blue, now pea soup beside some rocks, and she needs nothing. The life that she lived had been full and good. That's all, and that's enough. And Conn—tall gangly big thing, with an untamed brow; a face lit by fun or wild anger that flashes and goes out, as the lightning of a summer storm; and a capable mind, a brilliant mind that loves sound, words, music and ultrasonic beats, a mind that loves to make it and shape it until it becomes his own, a mind unpredictable and warm, like part of myself, like home and family and pine boughs crackling in the fireplace.*

"Orram, tell me more," she murmured, aware only of his help, not his silence.

For long, vibrant minutes he held her face against his shoulder and transmitted as simply as his patches would allow a set of concepts that defined elllonian existence. Finally, she began to stir and to resist his thought patterns.

"Now I see . . . but I must learn more for myself. Let me go, Orram."

I am ready to face them alone now. It is cleared. Let me go!" She struggled to free herself with a violence that surprised them both.

"Yes," Orram said. "You are quite ready now. I, too, am alien at last."

"You have strength and depth few men could match." She kissed
his fingers as they knelt together on the floor, and without conscious
design their forearms met in an intimate varokian embrace.

Beyond Self

"You have learned, Tandra, that we varoks are hard and brittle—
and too soon you will learn that we are also fragile and difficult. You
have many strengths that we lost long ago. I love your flexibility, your
reasoned passion."

Tandra couldn't quite manage a smile.

"Tandra, tell me what happened here."

"Nothing, really, and very much. Conn was enraged at my attitude
toward eggs. I was less than honest. He had become so horrifying to
me, I couldn't accept anything from him. I didn't want him to exist."

"He no longer spared you?"

"That's right."

"I wish I could promise it won't happen to you again, but I'm sure it
will," Orram said. "Come. Shawne wants you. She is in the nursery. It's
time that you saw all that the nursery contains. If you have accepted
Conn's alienness, then you are prepared. Do you feel capable of it?"

"Yes, I want to see it now."

Junah was waiting outside when they emerged from the food center. "Can I help?" she asked.

"I'm much better, thank you." Tandra saw her as if for the first time.
It was obvious that she adored Orram. The unvarokian quality of her
emotion was clear.

"Dr. Grey is recovered now, Junah. You had better get something to
eat and board the *Nalkah*."

The nursery door was open. Tandra could hear Llorkin's voice within: "Shawne, *va. Sense.*"

The baby saw Tandra and ignored the command, running to her mother instead, shouting, "*Da, lelea.*"

"Well, finally, you speak, Shawne," Llorkin said. Then he turned to Orram. "Why is Dr. Grey here?" he demanded.

"She's here at my direction, G. Llorkin. She will begin her elllonian studies now."

"Are you aware that our life cycle approximates that of Earth's amphibians, Dr. Grey?" Llorkin said, peering expectantly into her face and fumbling in the clutter on his desk for a pen.

Tandra took Shawne's hand. "If you don't mind, I would prefer that Shawne introduce me to her friends first, Llorkin. I recognize your amphibious nature now, and I'm sure that nothing will shock me sufficiently to justify your jotting it down."

Quickly, she surveyed the room. An incubator contained one large blue egg, and within a wall-sized aquarium swam two foot-long humanoid tadpoles. A confusion of toys on the floor surrounded a small, featherless, green elllonian figure, still sporting a sizeable tail.

"Dat's Da-oon," Shawne said. "He goes potty in da *udan*. I do too. This is Malkan. And Ellan is a girl. They can swim real good." Shawne ran over to the tank and thrust her hand in. The two elllonian tads swam toward her and playfully nibbled at her hand. Then, as Shawne swished her fingers through the water, they tried to grab them with their rudimentary prehensile fins.

Orram followed Tandra to the tank. "Their legs are still buds, developing rapidly now. In another two years the tail will become a vestige, and its adult extension, the retractable backfin, will develop until maturity. The hexagonal pressure-sensitive plates mature while the tads are still in the tank. The light green outlines of the plates are already sensitive to heat and ultra-sonic vibrations. Ellan has a large ultrasonic vocabulary already, and they will both learn to communicate with changes in water pressure before they leave the tank. We are lucky to find them here. They spend most of their time in the centrifuge room."

Orram turned from the tank and knelt beside the small elll busily working over one of Shawne's puzzles. "Da-oon is almost four Earth-years from hatching now. Mental development is a bit slower than human's."

Orram turned to Llorkin. "Da-oon and Shawne are approximately the same mental age now, don't you think?"

"Yes, in terms of abstraction and mathematical conceptualization. But the human infant's social age is much lower."

"What do you mean?" Tandra asked.

"She is very ego-centric and possessive. She expresses the individualistic survival demands of a year-old hatchling."

"We don't expect human children to learn to share until they are four or five years old, Llorkin," Tandra said. "We encourage generosity, and babies can demonstrate an amazing amount of it at times, but we also encourage individuality and self-reliance. We are not group-oriented creatures, like yourselves."

"Neither are varoks," Orram assured her. "The ellls school in both a psychological and a physical sense. In fact, they find being cut off from their own kind very difficult. The crew of this base is rather unusual. All had to pass rigorous psychological tests for adaptability to isolation. But you and I, Tandra, are naturally independent souls. We stubbornly refuse to equate ourselves with any other creature. We can't rub elbows with our fellows continuously, as the ellls must. Since they need to school and we require individual territory, the optimal density for our species is comparable to yours, while the elllonian density is maintained at three times that."

"Whose eggs are these? Are their parents known?"

"No. *El* eggs are selected at random and checked for fertility and apparent good health. Application can be made by a group of four to six ellls to raise five eggs. Tllan, Killah, Ohln, and Tallyn are sponsoring these three infants, and a new sponsor must be found to replace Ellalon. They are responsible for the incubation of the eggs, their nursing in the tank until their lungs develop, and their education, which begins upon emergence from the tank and continues for two Jovian years, nearly twenty-four Earth-years. The five sponsors establish a special relationship with their young; they are a family unit of sorts."

"And the unselected eggs are eaten?"

"You have enjoyed many *el* eggs yourself without knowing that they were elllonian," Orram replied. "No doubt the difference in pronunciation between *el* and *elll* misled you." He paused and observed her with an unseen sense. "So that is what happened at the food center. Conn told you, I suppose, in rather crude terms."

"No, that wasn't it. I accused him of cannibalism." She stared at the varok. "Orram, you're reading my mind."

She expected a denial. But the varok touched her chin, and his eyes filled with warmth. "What made you think I was reading your mind?"

Llorkin watched with huge, dense eyes as Orram accepted the woman's hand on his own and they moved closer together.

"Tandra, I need to know. Can you tell me what made you think I was reading your mind?"

"I felt watched."

"But not with eyes."

Llorkin busily noted their conversation. His broad mouth gaped and looked unusually dry.

"Not with eyes," Tandra agreed.

"Where's Conn?" Shawne interrupted. "I can swim with Conn. I do. He says I'm Shawnoon now."

"Conn is going to the moon's south pole, little water Shawne," the varok said with the hint of a smile. "Come, let us brighten the lights so you can show us what Conn taught you while we were gone."

$$- \Delta -$$

Later beside the pool, after they had "schooled" to her satisfaction, Shawne slept, and Orram and Tandra talked. They reviewed Tandra's changing relationship with Conn. They worried about Conn and his anger. They grieved for Ellalon. Orram was convinced they were exchanging thoughts with more than words.

Tandra took Shawne to the food center after the child awoke. Orram stayed by the pool stretched full length on its soft deck, thinking of the diffuse mood-reading that Tandra had been doing. He wondered if it had any relation to her ability to hold him suspended between crippling grief and rational self-control. He was jolted from his thoughts by Artellian's voice.

"Are you quite sure you are out of danger now, Orram?" the master elll asked. "Aen said that you never went completely into your grief for Ellalon." He folded his golden green form onto the deck beside the varok.

"Yes. I am out. An interesting phenomenon really. With Tandra's help, I was able to experience the anger and regret of grief and to maintain some conscious control simultaneously. We have just communicated again on a similar level."

"Orram, are you able to read her?"

"I can read her mood quite easily. Sometimes I need specifics. Also, she reads me, Artell, though she doesn't seem to know it yet."

"How can she not know it? You always know it, don't you?"

"It's a conscious act on our part, the use of the patches. What she does must be an unconscious learned response." He stopped talking and sat up. "I think we should run fertility studies between our species. I'm sure Tandra would be willing to contribute a few eggs."

Artellian jumped to his feet. "Are you mad, varok? We have joked about such tests, but we have never considered them seriously. Tandra has had a difficult time with us. We can't ask her—I think you are in need of more time with Junah. Perhaps Erah?"

"Untie your backfin, Artell. Tandra is a biologist and a philosopher. She will understand that fertility tests are a logical addition to our comparative studies of DNA. Its coding and regulatory chemistry have more similarities than we expected."

"But why speak of fertility as you mumble about patch capability?"

"Both functions are extremely personal ones, closely related in varokian life, are they not?" Orram said.

"True, true, my dear friend. But discussed together only in reference to consummation."

"Yes."

Artellian stood over the almost-grinning varok with a golden head cocked at full tilt. "I think you're asking a bit much of yourself, Oran Ramahlak. Or are you released, already?"

"Already? Do you expect that my emotional release is inevitable—with this human being?

"Isn't release precisely what happened to you after Ellalon's death? Tandra kept you in touch with reason during your grief, did she not?"

"That may have been a phenomenon related to release. But connected to fertility studies? I do not think so." Orram stood up and clasped Artellian's shoulders. "Don't worry, M. Artell. I am well under control."

Taking Orram's hands from his shoulders, the golden elll sighed, then looked at the varok's hands, pondering his unusual gesture. "Take care, Orram," he said. "Take care with all this . . . with Tandra."

– Δ –

While the *Nalkah* crawled around the southern pole of the moon, the elllonian crew at base began their adjustment to Ellalon's absence. For two days—defined by Earth's rotation—they put aside their studies and brought their experiments to a pause whenever possible, while they schooled together in the warm water of the pool around a throbbing nucleus of pressure patterns.

Tandra watched them from the pool's deck as she studied elllonian books. At first the ellls treated her cautiously, afraid of imposing on her, but soon they found in her a new acceptance and a hesitant yearning, so Killah was dispatched to invite her to join in the adjustment.

"Our grief is different from yours, Tandra," Killah said. "Come join the school without Ellalon. Know us again before Conn returns."

Without hesitation, Tandra followed her colleague into the pool, where the ellls gradually embraced her with the gentle tapping of their pressure signals. As the tapping grew more intense, she relaxed and floated at ease in the gentle massage until, finally, acceptance was won. In an unconscious, symbolic act, she entrusted her life to the school and slept.

Killah was the first to notice that she had slipped beneath the surface. Swiftly he dove under her and lifted her face out of the water. In her sleep she took a deep breath and fit her body onto his. And there they stayed for more than an hour, his velvet green form making a bed for her in the warm, throbbing water, while his backfin undulated tirelessly to support her.

Nothing was said when she finally awoke. She clung to Ohln and to Killah for a long time before she climbed out of the pool to return to her laboratory and her books.

The Ellls

In that way, Tandra learned to know the ellls—not as near-human-oids nor as unfathomably alien amphibious beasts—but as mild, handsome, unique creatures of rare intelligence and appreciative nature, who, by good fortune or divine plan, had escaped the worst of nature's demands. They had learned to live happily with existence as they found it, reshaping and exploiting it only slightly for their real needs, rarely for their convenience, and never for their aggrandizement.

One evening soon after the adjustment to Elallon's absence had been made, and a relaxed schedule of analytical work had been reestablished, the elder varokian astronomer, Ahl, came to Tandra as she lay on the bed pad of the room she shared with Orram and Artellian. She was reading The Cultural and Political History of the Ellls of Ellason.

"Dull, eh?" Ahl said, as he sat on Tandra's bed pad and looked over her shoulder.

"Beautifully dull. Yet exciting. Reading elllonian history is like reading about a very large, complex child searching for awareness and meaning in life and finding it, and finding that it is only the beginning."

"So now you love the ellls, Tandra?"

"Even more than I thought I did at first. And I have no more fear of varoks. But, then, I have had fewer delusions about your species, Ahl."

"Orram did not allow them to grow, did he? Do you know that varoks have dreams that lead them astray, too?"

"I'm aware of at least one such problem," Tandra said. She sat up and gazed expectantly at the dark, silver varok.

"Yes. Junah. And she is in some danger, for none of us can reach her, nor reason with her. But not all of our dreams lead us to disaster."

"Do you want to talk about Orram?" Tandra asked, surprised by her own question.

"You read me well, Tandra. I am curious to know how you have unlocked the secret of the master varok's smile."

"A varokian smile is a rare and beautiful thing," Tandra said. She glanced up as Orram entered the room with Artellian. There was something formal in their appearance. Her voice faltered, as Orram's mind seemed to open to her. Abruptly, unthinking and afraid, she denied the possibility.

Artellian sat down close to Tandra on the soft moss floor. "You know, my dearest human, Conn predicted that you would accomplish integration with us . . . Dr. Grey. I was wrong in assuming that acceptance on human terms would be easy, but integration impossible."

"Perhaps only for a dreamer like myself," Tandra laughed. "I think your assumption is valid for most human beings. Acceptance for most will be easy, once your benign nature is known. Everyone wants aliens to land in their backyard. I'm not sure what you mean by *integration*."

"Neither do we, now," the great elll mused. "Be that as it may, you are ready to begin the more difficult work we had in mind for you. You must help us decide whether or not to contact Earth—and how it should be done. In just a few days three human astronauts will be sent to explore the geological formation they call the Straight Wall. We did not expect that Earth would attempt extensive exploration again, especially now that our projections are being realized. Time grows short for many lives on Earth. Somehow, perhaps, we should try to influence the fate of your planet. For the moment, we are convinced that there should be no contact. If these lunar studies continue, however, our presence will be discovered."

"Does anyone besides Jesse Mendleton and myself know of your existence?"

"No one. We have not yet seen any possibility for making official contact with your world, Tandra," Artellian explained, "because there is no central government or agency that all peoples trust. The World Federation is representative only of those who possess military and economic power. If we contact any of the growing ecological regions—Cascadia and Atlantica or others in the north—we immediately prejudice our position with everyone else. All we have to offer is the shock of our alien opinions and experience. We must not jeopardize our credibility."

"The task looks impossible," Orram said. "We must overcome cultural imprints and ancient human survival instincts, but also your remarkable talent for repression. In spite of increasingly sophisticated computer analyses—even the predictable increases in major disasters— many human beings refuse to believe that there is a problem on Earth."

"We also have to concentrate on meaningful contact with Earth as a whole entity," said Ahl. "We can't limit our efforts to the fate of the human species."

"I'm not sure I understand. Do you mean you will stand by and watch millions of people die?" Tandra asked.

"We already have," Ahl said. "If Earth requires a repeat of Varokian history, then we can only grieve, nothing more. I doubt that the human species is capable of the give-and-take required by a dynamic steady state. Therefore, growth will continue, something will give, and I doubt that it will be the human appetite."

Artellian hesitated, looking very uncomfortable standing near the door. "Of course, there is always the possibility of nuclear war when competition for food or water or energy becomes intolerable. Whatever happens, while humans ignore the necessity of restraint, they will have destroyed many of Earth's other species. That is the real tragedy, Tandra, for they are innocent."

"This is sad talk, my friends," Ahl said.

"It's hard for me to grasp the possibility that humans, too, could become extinct," she said. "We have always assumed that we were a super-species, somehow not subject to natural law. Yet we evolved into dominance with superior adaptability, as a result of natural law. How many species will suffer and disappear because of our dominance?"

Artellian stared at Tandra. "Repeat what you have just said."

"Repeat what? That biodiversity on Earth is threatened?"

Artellian looked to Orram for help.

The varok spoke slowly at first. "Tandra, you said that the extinction of Earth's species in the wake of human dominance is to be expected as a function of natural law."

"Did I really say that?"

"It was assumed in your statement."

"Yes, I suppose it was. However, isn't that true? Survival of the fittest is an old biological dogma."

"Yes, Tandra, but not with reference to a total world system," Artellian said. "Survival of the fittest concerns differential reproduction. The strongest normally produce young within a single species, not across an entire biosphere."

Orram sensed Tandra's unease and sought to relieve it. "In many ways your culture implies that nature is a benevolent personality, always looking out for human existence. But the ellls have never assumed a superior stance, and, even though we are the only technologists on Varok, we varoks have had faith in our unique qualities utterly denied by our history. Tell me, Tandra, what are you: humanist, spiritual ecologist, or theist?"

"I'm not sure I understand, Orram."

Orram's eyes were demanding, penetrating. "You will see with the eyes of ellls and of varoks and add your own dimension, if you will only open your mind and let go of your pride. You can understand what I ask. Are you humanist, spiritual ecologist or theist?"

Tandra forced her reluctant mind to work. "If the theist places ultimate responsibility for human acts on God, especially a god defined in the image of man, then, I am no theist. Nor does my idea of Creator give special privileges to human beings, for He is not only integral to Earth, but integral to everything happening within Earth. And I am no longer humanist, for I believe that human welfare, indeed human survival, is dependent on the subjugation of *Homo sapiens* to the total life system of Earth. This must be what you mean by spiritual ecology. Man is not the *raison d'etre* of the universe. Am I talking sense, Orram, or merely reiterating the varokian philosophy I have been reading?"

"Your thoughts are close to those of the varok, Analahk, but they are your own," Orram replied, feeling a surge of joy. "We believe in the unity of existence. Men might use the word God or Allah or Brahman, but we varoks have learned from the ellls that precise definitions and conditions tend to restrict the concept. The point is that there is no reason to believe that our lives are distinct from the forces that shaped them."

Artellian plucked some moss from the wall and munched it quietly, while he opened the water inlet of his sleeping bowl. "I can take only so much philosophy in one evening friends. No doubt we'll make you grow beyond your human assumptions before we are done with you, Tandra. Perhaps we'll even force your view beyond Earth." Without further comment, he climbed into the *uuyvanoon* and slipped beneath the warm water.

"I'm too wound up to sleep," Tandra said to Orram and Ahl. "Will you join me in the observation deck for a while?"

In answer, and as a gesture symbolic of their shared thoughts, the two varoks embraced Tandra with their eyes, and, lost in thought, ushered her slowly toward the food center. There Tandra poured them cups of a tart Ellasonian red algae, which they carried to the observation deck and sipped absently as they stared out over the moon's landscape.

"You have climbed beyond disdain, Tandra," Ahl said. "We will work well together now. You are not alone in shame; we too have felt severe growing pains." He stretched out on a couch and quoted in low, grating tones from the varokian *Songs to Life*:

> Though our minds run narrowly in small, straight rivers
> And never branch nor feed large pools
> As do the flaming crystals of Varok's streams;
> Though Life has now denied us freedom of the passions,
> And we are chained to reason, sanity required,
> Mindless joy denied, forgetful love impossible;
> Though Life is drawn in squares and we dare not tread the lines
> Lest we plunge to destruction on wildfires,
> Cindered at the edge of reason and the fringe of love
> Or the precipice of hate;
> Though Life enchains us,
> Denies us her most precious gifts,
> We have remained her friend
> And found our freedom from her dreaded sister, Time.
> Enchained by Life, yet free now, free from Time,
> Whose passing no longer fills our minds with terror.
> Eternity is ours; and we may once again embrace our lives.

IV. A New Reality

Varok, a rocky captive of Jupiter nearly the size of Earth, coasted around its host at a comfortable distance outside the planet's magnetosphere, camouflaged by a belt of ancient dust and debris. The moon's low albedo, about 0.005, made it very faint to human telescopes. Its isolation from other moons of Jupiter meant it was missed on Earth's photo missions, Pioneer 10 and 11 and Voyager 1 and 2, which were focused on the Galilean moons.

Tectonic tides generated by Jupiter, along with the rocky orb's radioactive veins and molten heart, supported sulfur-driven life, while Varok's tidal and geothermal forces provided enough energy to drive its more creative varieties of carbon- and oxygen-based creatures. Eventually its prolific life had generated an atmosphere similar to Earth's and life forms endowed with diverse intellectual talents.

CONTACT AND DETACHMENT

Slowly the *Nalkah* retraced old paths through the maze of craters southwest of the base, until it reached smoother terrain near the lunar south pole. After a routine stop at the experimental station between the craters Amundsen and Boltzmann, it hurried into the Southern Highlands facing Earth, clambered over the roughs east of Clavius and west of Maginus, and headed for the rim of crater Tycho. There, the rough terrain covered with sharp rocks became almost impassable.

Conn sank lazily into his couch as his webbed fingers played the *Nalkah*'s controls. They moved deftly and surely like extensions of the craft itself. Usually, he loved this rugged part of the trail. He enjoyed the sensuous pounding of the lumbering craft. He relished the challenge of finding the easiest path and leaving the least trace through the extravagant debris, rolling or climbing or hovering over the larger boulder piles with a minimum of shock. He dodged the sudden pits and small craters and swung back before the craft threw everyone too violently. When he grew tired of the necessary concentration, he would shout a warning to Junah, Aen, and Tllan and let the vehicle careen wildly in and out and around and over the tortured landscape.

Now he drove the *Nalkah* as if by instinct. His mind was not on the rocks ahead of him. He felt dull and heavy, too dry, much too dry with all this gray dust surrounding him and the warm, wine-red water of the pool still days away.

Junah, too, was restless. While Aen and Tllan slept, she made the final entry in the South Highland Maintenance Log with some difficulty, then climbed into the couch next to Conn. "You look like you have eaten a *kaehl*'s sour-gland," she said in clipped Varokian.

Conn tried to smile but failed. "Did you ever think you'd get tired of twilight and long shadows?" he said. "Toss the moons!" he roared in Elllonian. "Drown the great-fish!"

Junah startled. Conn's unpredictable fierceness frightened her. "I've never seen your mood so ugly, Conn," she said. "It can't be the loss of Ellalon. Is it the human, Tandra? Is it her sickness?"

"What sickness?"

"I found her in the food center after you left her. She was holding her head in her hands, shaking."

"Is that all?"

"Yes. I called Orram. She left the food center with him a short time later, apparently recovered."

"Human beings are not like you varoks, Junah. They can wallow in emotion and enjoy it almost as much as we do. She wasn't physically ill or incapacitated, just crying. She was probably dancing around with Orram ten minutes later."

"Dancing? With Orram? M. Ramahlak wouldn't dance. He'll probably never dance."

Conn smiled weakly. "Junah, when are you going to learn not to take me seriously? But now that I think of it, don't be too certain that Orram isn't capable of the *Vrankah*. Tandra has him worrying about differences in your species for more than academic reasons."

"That cannot be true. Do I read you correctly?"

"You read me," Conn laughed darkly. "I think Orram went away from that game of feelies with Tandra with a psychological, if not a physical, hard-on, but he won't admit it, even to himself."

"What are you saying, Conn? Orram is always honest with himself."

"I'm sorry, Junah, I'm not being kind to you."

"I lose my grasp on reason when I think of Orram. Conn, may I confide in you? I think it will help."

"Of course."

"I will take a chance and expose what I feel, if you will tell me more about you and Doctor Grey first."

"All right, Junah." Conn sighed. "I'll try. *A-la-oon!* Where can I begin? I'm so sorry I blew off at Tan. Her face, Junah! She looked at me, and all the love was gone. There was nothing left but horror. The tide had gone out, Junah. I wanted her to accept me. *Me*, as an elll. So I raged at her about eggs, of all things."

"Surely she will recover from the shock and remember your good times."

"How I wish I could forget them. I see Shawne paddle to me and Tandra beam at us, so glad I could teach her tad to swim. Every night, when the water fills my lungs, I remember. Then her face comes to me, twisted and frozen with horror—her face, *aeyull! Dankah* on her! *Dankah* on her failure to integrate."

He continued in Elllonian. "Junah, we spent hours with music, and our sound was going to be good. Really good. We didn't need to talk.

Who needs so many words, when you have so much else?"

Junah smiled, acknowledging to Conn that she understood. "Perhaps she was not being honest with herself. The lie will come clear sooner or later."

Conn's face relaxed. "Now spill your beans, Junah. I've done mine."

Junah hesitated. Conn waited while she adjusted to his instantaneous change in mood. Then she put down her natural reserve and dove into dangerous emotional waters. "I treasure Orram's words, his appearance, his voice. I long to meet his arm with mine, to share our minds."

"I'll put in a good word for you." Conn tried to stop himself, but his confused bitterness drove him on. "Forget it, Junah. Orram is twice your age and three times your maturity. The best you can expect is an occasional empathic pat on the head and a mindless poke in the ass."

Conn's words lit the passion that Junah had dared to touch within herself. With an emotional violence that humans rarely suffer, reason and control succumbed, and she jumped at Conn with a scream of rage, tearing at his crown plumes. Instinctively, he dropped the steering bar and struck out to defend himself with a lurching attack that spun the *Nalkah* out of control and sent it spinning over the sharp rim of a deep crater.

– Δ –

Delight bubbled up from a hidden spring within Orram, and he laughed as he watched Killah's reaction to his boisterous approach.

"What sound is this?" Killah chided. "Let me give you a sedative."

"Your tail plumes are curling, Killah," Orram said, peering behind the elll, "but fortunately I am quite sane, just partially released, indulging in a bit of joy, if you will allow me. I am relieved that Tandra has integrated with us. We were cautious when there was no need for caution. From the time she met her first varok, Tandra's assumption has been that fertility tests should be done. Our parallels are too intriguing."

"So, you finally dared a probing on the subject?"

"No no no." Orram's stolid face cracked with a hundred lines of amusement. "She suggested it herself, and I have arranged for you to capture some human eggs."

"So you are released, Orram," the elll said, marveling at the varok's transformed countenance. "Do we have a whole new varok to know?"

"No, I am not released, at least not in the classical sense. Yet, you see now that I am capable of some emotion."

"And Tandra is the cause of this emotional indulgence? Can she help you control it?"

"She could, but she won't, not consciously. What is incredible, Killah, is that I have some control myself. It seems to be related to my patch contact with Tandra. You are given my happy permission to watch it closely."

"I don't like to see you experiment with yourself this way, Orram."

The varok nodded gravely. "I am in no danger, and, of course, Tandra is very strong now. She has found reality and purpose with us. I guarantee that she will not suffer any harm."

– Δ –

Not by the congestive flow of blood, but with voluntary muscles, acting in accordance with reluctant involuntary ones, the varok generated the required sample. He quickly froze part of it. Killah immediately prepared another part for microscopic analysis, DNA sequencing, and viability tests. The rest was allowed to incubate with two meticulously nurtured human eggs, taken with careful timing from Tandra.

During the following hours, Orram and Tandra tended the small incubator like anxious parents, as their biological samples lay poised beneath a recording microscope. Finally, a hint of sperm penetration could be seen in one of the human eggs. Then, as the hours passed unnoticed, the development of pronuclei became obvious. Tandra's glance met Orram's. Then they looked again through the lenses to the newly fertilized egg—and watched it die.

Tandra sighed and started to turn away, but Orram clung to her. His hand was shaking. "Orram?" She turned to the varok and placed her fingers on his patches. "It's only an egg, you know." She looked into his eyes, hoping to find the deep open blue again, but it was closed and dark. "Killah will attempt more fertilizations."

"Of course," he said. His hands had stopped shaking. "A momentary lapse wishing for miracles, Tandra, nothing more."

In the pool room, though disappointed by the egg's death and Orram's denial of emotion, Tandra felt contentment cover her like her soft varokian robe. Several ellls were scattered about the room studying Jesse Mendleton's latest summary of scientific papers, where the most important news was a re-scheduled lunar landing.

A nanochip of Conn's favorite melodies was softly driving lyric sound from the walls. Tandra's mind felt deliciously open, free to explore. She would have her elllonian studies completed by the time Conn returned.

How she loved him now—the free, intelligent loner among the schooling ellls, his easy slouch as he worked over their tapes, his quiet "plunch" as he slipped into the pool to leap and cut through the water. She saw him meet a blue elll briefly in the center of the pool, dive with her in casual acceptance and resurface minutes later, as if there had been no interruption in his swimming. What a stable, joyful, integrated existence his amphibious culture had made for his species and for him—a misfit really, a loner, probably a mutant of evolutionary significance.

Tandra was shaken from her musings by Orram's voice. "I thought that you might like to listen to the humans' lunar landing."

He switched Conn's maze of electronics from stored music to the radio interceptor and homed in on the transmission from the Multinational Space Agency's lunar module.

"Where are they landing this time?" Tandra asked.

"They intend to land on the Straight Wall northeast of the South Horn Mountains and west of crater Thebit."

"It's rough in there, isn't it?"

"It's all right, if they stay just south of the Taenarium Range near the precipice."

As the varokian receiver picked the astronauts' voices out of the moon's airless space, Tandra smiled at the familiar banter. But soon the radio conversation crackled with tense excitement as the lunar craft turned to give the astronauts a view of the Straight Wall.

"There she is. We're right on it. Sixteen thousand at eighteen. Sailing over Birt now. Beautiful! Up a bit. Keep it up. Fifty-five hundred at eight. Eleven hundred at five. There's the Wall. Who-ee, look at that, a mountain climber's dream!"

"Or nightmare," a second voice interjected.

"Roger, Bob."

"One thousand at four point seven. Nearing the Wall, Midpacific. Looks rough over there. Nine-fifty at three point five. Approaching Wall. Twenty-five at two point two. Boulders, by God. Let's try. Over this way. Fifteen at two point one. Poor visibility."

"Can't see a damn thing down there. We're kicking up dust."

"Take your time, Bob."

"Roger, Midpacif—"

The voices were interrupted by a loud crunch, then silence.

Tandra stiffened. "Orram!"

A controlled but frantic call came from the receiver: "Bob! Carliano, this is Midpacific. Can you read us? Jane, can you read us? Inclination critical. Confirm."

Tandra grasped Orram's hand, and they waited interminable seconds. Finally, a thick slow voice grumbled through space, "Roger, Midpacific. Carliano here. *Dove Two* has landed, so to speak. Too much dust kicked up. Couldn't see. Apparently flipped on a large boulder or something and fell flat on our face. Confirm eighty-eight point six."

"Report status, Bob."

"Roger, Midpaf. No obvious damage. What we need is a crane. We're completely over on our side. Jane Wright was thrown against the front panels. She's unconscious. Ted Bardeane seems to be in shock. Hold on while I check them out."

"Orram?"

He looked hard at Tandra. "Can you understand why we may not help them? We could put the *Lurlial* into low orbit and pick them up within a few hours. But our most recent decision was to avoid contact until we could devise an effective introduction of ourselves. There is much at stake, Tandra."

Tandra turned up the volume on the receiver. Minutes passed, and it became clear that the lunar craft was lying helpless on a craggy ledge near the upper rim of the Straight Wall, with no hope of rescue. "You have to help," she said.

"I'll ask Artellian to call the base Directorate together immediately," Orram said.

– Δ –

Hundreds of miles from the toppled *Dove* at the bottom of a small, deep crater, the *Nalkah* also lay helpless, crippled beyond immediate repair. Three gray-green figures sprawled motionless on the craft's cushioned wall, which now lay against the moon's surface, and the fourth figure, Junah, sat in a half-crouch, quivering violently—a creature broken on the rapids where varokian reason and emotion meet but rarely blend.

More than an hour passed before Conn regained consciousness. Without moving, he tested the air and tried his body. Then, momentarily satisfied that the life-support seal of the *Nalkah* was still intact, he sat up and surveyed the interior of the overturned craft. Nothing alarming. Its large balloon tracks were still extended, apparently undamaged.

Then he saw Junah, and he knew that major damage had been done. He crawled to the pitiful brown figure and enfolded her in his arms.

"Junah. Junah. *Ae-yul-ll!*" He searched for a sign of consciousness in her eyes. But there was none. Blank and gray, they stared dimly ahead through her convulsive sobbing.

With Conn's groans, Aen regained consciousness. His shoulder ached where he was thrown against the *Nalkah*, but he got up without difficulty and stepped around Tllan's prostrate body. She was either dead or resting well and needed no treatment, so he turned his attention to Conn and Junah. The blank look in the varokian woman's eyes jolted him into elllonian grief for her loss of consciousness, and he missed Conn's more subtle injury.

Conn tried to stand, but the *Nalkah* reeled from under his feet. He grabbed Aen for support. Slowly, the vehicle resettled in his mind, and he tried again to stand. There was no steady reference. His mechanism for balance on land had ceased to function.

"I'm disoriented," he said. "Call base, Aen, if you can set the probes. We won't get out of here without help."

RADIO CONTACT

Aen's belabored message sped north and west to base—while Tandra listened to the sporadic, quietly anguished conversation between Midpacific Space Center and the stranded astronauts. She jumped from her chair eagerly when Orram reentered the recreation lounge.

"When will you radio the *Dove*?" she asked. Orram's face was grave. "I'm not sure we will, Tandra. Come to Artellian's office with me. We need your viewpoint so we can reach a consensus." He stood very still as he spoke, probing the strength of Tandra's mood.

"The *Nalkah* has also had an accident," he said. "It is trapped in a small crater near Maginus H. Conn has lost his sense of equilibrium and Junah—she has been injured, too."

"You are not telling me everything, Orram,"

"How can you know, Tandra? You read me before I know myself. We will talk later. Artellian is waiting for us now."

They turned to enter the base's small, crowded office. Artellian, Ahl, Llorkin, Killah, and Tallyn were sprawled in awkward angles around a topographical lunar globe which was set into the living moss floor.

Artellian turned to Tandra. "You know how undecided we have been about contacting Earth's human society. Should we let circumstances force us to reverse our current decision?"

Llorkin's large green eyes focused sharply on Tandra and he stood up stiffly. "We are not prepared to encounter more people, Dr. Grey. We have only begun our talks with you, in order to reexamine our options. We had decided some time previously that no contact should be made except with spokesmen truly representative of Earth's total life complex, which, it has been our observation, humans are not."

"If Earth knew of your existence, that point could be made and have some influence," Tandra said, feeling comfortable using Varokian. Her voice was firm.

"There is no hope for world-wide cooperation of significance, not even among human beings," Tallyn said. "I see nothing to do but to watch. After a die-off, surviving mutants might be sane."

Tandra nodded. "I can't blame either of you for your poor regard for human life, but don't forget that we are sensitive, conscious beings. In spite of our adaptability, we suffer as much as any other species."

"I'm not sure such capacity for repression makes for strong animals, Tandra. Perhaps it is best humans die so Earth can try again, eh?"

"No. You don't mean that, Tallyn. You value life—even human life—too much."

"Yes. Yes," Tallyn complained. "But what is most important is the survival of some sort of living-support capability for Earth."

"Yes, Tallyn. Yes. But when humans go, we'll take everything else with us. So if you care at all for our rotting oasis, you'll be very careful not to prejudice any influence you might have." She whirled to face Orram. "You can't let these astronauts die. Eventually it would be learned that you had been here, capable of rescue."

His blank face nodded slightly toward Artellian.

"I believe you are right," said the master elll, "though some might suspect we could do much more for Earth in the category of stop-gap rescues, this, at least, would be expected by all. It would serve as a gesture of good will." Artellian spoke thoughtfully, looking to Orram for agreement. He rolled off the moss onto his feet and opened his hand, signifying the end of the meeting.

Llorkin began to puff and stammer. "I must insist on submitting a contrary report if this outlook prevails," he said. "We cannot predict what effect a sudden revelation of our presence will have on the human population. We endanger this base and the entire life system of Earth in order to save three men."

"I think that you overestimate our ability to influence Earth under any conditions," Ahl said.

"I for one do not intend to stand by and watch the further degradation of life on this beautiful planet," Llorkin announced.

"Then you may return to Ellason on the next ship," Artellian snapped.

"I think it's rather a good play, myself," Killah chortled. "Hopeless astronauts are suddenly rescued by an unknown, benevolent intelligence from outer space. It's a good entrance, I think."

"I agree," Ahl said. "The entrance is as good as we could hope for. The stage would be set for maximal influence. Llorkin, I will take full responsibility for this decision. The cost of this base is not justified for our studies alone. We can't ignore this opportunity to minimize Earth's peak death-load. We will put the *Lurlial* into polar orbit, land near the *Nalkah*, and do what we can there, then make a ballistic shot to the Straight Wall and pick up the astronauts."

"Since one of them is injured, perhaps we should pick them up first," Orram said. "The *Lurlial* is equipped adequately for medical treatment. We don't yet know the nature of the *Nalkah*'s damage. We may have to spend some time there."

"Let us proceed at once," Artellian said. "Tandra, all security precautions will be enforced. No scientific information is to be revealed to the astronauts, except as specified by this directorate. What you may know or may have guessed about the varoks' patch organs and the probable locations of Ellason and Varok will remain private speculation.

"The *Lurlial* will be decontaminated before embarkation. Since at least one of the astronauts is injured, we will reverse normal procedure and wear isolation suits ourselves while *en route*. The suits will disguise us if we deem it necessary. We will effect repair if possible and bring the astronauts back to base only as the last resort. Tandra, you will accompany Tallyn and Orram in the *Lurlial*. Assume responsibility for proper isolation procedures and the maintenance of psychological balance in the astronauts. Come with me now while I make radio contact with them."

Tandra followed Artellian down the hall and into a corner of the hangar stuffed with a maze of transmitting and receiving equipment.

"Vohn, attempt to lock onto Midpacific Space Center and *Dove Two*," Artellian said to the young varok working there. "High frequency directional to Earth, and try the lunar e.m. web to eight degrees west, twenty-one degrees south, full power."

A few seconds later Vohn said, "Full power, locked in and receiving."

At first no sound came from the receiver. Then a slow, steady human voice broke the silence. "No change in Wright. She's still unconscious—looks pale. Bardeane is sedated. I've done all I can for them. I'm going to sleep for a while. Give me a buzz in a couple hours and I'll continue EVA."

"Roger, Carliano. We're with you, exploring every possibility for getting you out of there. Hold on."

"I'm not going anywhere." A grim chuckle was barely audible.

"I'm impressed with that person's stability," Artellian said. "I see no reason to delay."

He absently pulled at his golden crest, set his expression, and flipped on the transmitter. "Calling *Dove Two*. Calling *Dove Two* at Straight Wall. Do you read me?" Artellian spoke into the transmitting web slowly and distinctly without dampening his elllonian accent.

"Midpacific? This is *Dove Two*. Reading you loud and clear."

"Bob Carliano, this is Midpacific. We did not send that transmission. Picked it up here, too."

"Midpacific and *Dove Two*. This is Elll-Varok Science Observation base on Earth's Moon. We can effect rescue of *Dove Two* within one hour. Repeat. This is the Earth Moonbase of Elll-Varok Science. We can accomplish rescue of *Dove* or *Dove*'s crew within one hour. Do you read me?"

"Where the hell's that coming from, Midpaf?" Carliano cried. "It's a damn poor joke."

Artellian continued. "Until we make contact with you again, we prefer, for security reasons, that the location of our base remain unknown. We will cease transmission until our space vehicle is in lunar orbit. Approach will be from the north in approximately one hour."

"Bob, did you receive that last transmission?"

"Loud and clear, Midpaf. What's going on?"

"The transmission didn't come from us. We can't get a directional fix unless they keep transmitting."

"That's your problem. Just get them off the frequency."

"Could you place the accent?"

"Negative. Forget it. I need some sleep. Keep those kooks off my back."

"Roger, Bob. Better watch the language. We're still open."

Tandra turned to Artellian. "It's not surprising, you know, their response."

"Yes, of course," he smiled in spite of his disappointment. He turned off the transmitter and spoke into the base's intercom. "Ready the *Lurlial* for immediate insertion into polar orbit. Decontaminate. Crew: Orram, Tandra, Killah and Tallyn. Isolation suits readied for Conn, Tllan, Aen and Junah."

Tandra ran quickly to her room. As she expected, without knowing why, Orram was there waiting for her.

"How did they receive you?"

"They didn't believe us. I don't think any amount of talking would convince them that it wasn't a hoax."

"Tandra?" Orram stared at his hands and waited for a question to surface in her mind. "Your touch has become an aid, a small part, or an introduction—I don't know which—to a much deeper communication between logic and passion within myself. I need that now, Tandra. I need your help. During the *Nalkah's* accident Junah went negative. She is irrational. She has lost her connection to reality."

Tandra stared at the varok, and dismay darkened her face. "What happened?"

"We don't know. Aen talked to me from the *Nalkah*, but he wouldn't elaborate. Like all ellls, he is too afraid of triggering varokian emotional and rational shutdown. I might have saved her, Tandra. I should have ended our mating when I sensed that she was over-reading me."

"Over-reading?"

"Fantasizing identity with me. Looking for a mind-link, for consummation. Eventually all varoks who forsake reality or reason succumb to their psychoses. But perhaps I could have reclaimed her by making my position clearer. She was reading me incorrectly."

"Reading you?"

"Yes. You are reading me now, Tandra."

She looked into his blank face and made a considered guess. "I sense regret. Surely you can't blame yourself for her breakdown. You never encouraged her, did you?"

"I tried to discourage her, but I was too kind. Read me again."

"Orram?"

"Read me, Tandra."

The woman searched the varok's eyes, but found no clue to his demand. "Do you need something, Orram? Reassurance?"

"There is nothing in my eyes, Tandra." He moved his arm over hers. "Try moving closer. Your sensitivity may be limited to a shorter range than ours."

Timidly placing her fingers behind his ears, she said, "You need support—support in bearing guilt. But you are not responsible for her going irrational."

"Don't deny it. I cannot live with self-delusion. I am varok. I cannot survive if I deny reality. I am partly responsible for her illness. At least I could have postponed it. And again you read me correctly. I bear guilt, and I look to you to bear it with me."

"Orram?" Tandra began to sense the import of what Orram was attempting.

"Read me once more."

She closed her eyes and searched for intuition. Nothing spoke. She relaxed and tried to let her mind go blank. No clear suggestion came. She opened her eyes and looked at Orram and tried to find a spontaneous, obvious answer in his eyes. No. His touch. No. His presence. No. Nothing spoke. "I can't read you now, Orram. I think that the others were only logical guesses."

"Perhaps," he said, going entirely still. "We must board the *Lurlial* now."

Rescue

The ship glided through the hangar locks and leapt into the black lunar sky, then fell into a low elliptical orbit that passed over the poles and skimmed crater Maginus.

"We have you spotted, Conn boy," Killah twanged in English on the Midpacific-*Dove* frequency, hoping to reassure his bewildered human audience of their real presence and good will.

"Go to Harrahn's cave in a fruit basket, Killah, you jerk," Conn snorted moodily. "And don't take all day playing hero. It's not getting any more pleasant down here, you know. Who's your crew, Orram?"

"Tallyn, Killah, Dr. Grey, and I."

"Dr. Grey? The human? You and Killah? That all? How'd you get that thing off the ground?"

Killah laughed in rollicking tones that tumbled and played all the way to the Midpacific Space Center and across the stark wastes to Bob Carliano in the *Dove*.

"Who the hell is this?" he called.

"We'll be with you shortly now, Carliano," Tallyn said, his English heavily accented.

Orram broke into the conversation with data indicating their approach to the Wall.

From the window of the upset lunar ship Bob Carliano had a fair view of the dark horizon. Suddenly his excited voice sent a shock of hope and fear through his anxious colleagues at the space center.

"Goddam if there isn't something up there. A faint glow. It's coming in fast. Looks like a huge kite. It's gone out of sight now."

"Easy down, Orram," Tallyn said. "Engines off. Good aim, varok. We can't be more than twenty meters from *Dove*."

"*Dove Two*, this is *Lurlial*. We are approximately twenty meters directly east. Can you prepare for lunar exposure?"

"Who are you?"

"We will discuss everything when you are safe. We assure you, we intend only your well-being. I repeat: Can you prepare for lunar exposure?"

"*Dove Two*, this is Midpacific . . . *Dove Two*?"

"Midpacific, we are going out. *Lurlial*, Carliano here. Whoever you are out there, we are ready for lunar exposure. Depressurization commenced. I'll check our position. I think we're on a ledge down the Wall about twenty-five meters. In any case, you'll need something to get us out of here. Two of us are injured."

"It will take us twenty minutes to dress for exposure and walk to the rim. We will attempt visual contact first." Orram turned away from the controls and strode to the rear of the *Lurlial*. He spoke into the intercom. "Tandra, I do not see any reason for you to come out. Maybe if they see a human in the ship—"

"Confirmed, Orram. I'll stay here and receive the men."

Orram, Killah, and Tallyn quickly donned exposure gear over their isolation suits, sealed their helmets, and disappeared through the hatch onto the lunar surface. It was treacherously pocked, and strewn with enormous boulders. At intervals the cliff dropped away two hundred meters to ledges below or plummeted the full three hundred meters to Rima Birt overlooking Mare Nubium. The three aliens searched the face of Straight Wall for a sign of the human ship, but failed to see it.

"*Dove*, this is M. Ramahlak. We are at the precipice above you, but we cannot locate you from here. Do you have any light source that will give us a vertical signal?"

"*Dove Two*, this is Midpacific. We have directionals on the interference. Moon is apparent source. We advise caution."

"Affirmative Midpaf. Going EVA again to signal whoever is out there."

"Repeat. We advise restraint in signaling."

"I'll have to respectfully ignore that advice, Midpacific. We're being upstaged beautifully, but at this point we are willing to believe anyone's fairy tale."

"Signal Ramahlak. This is Midpacific. Please identify yourself."

"Midpacific, this is Master Biophysicist Oran Ramahlak, director of scientific operations at the Elll-Varok Earth Moonbase. We are visitors to Earth's moon from Ellason and Varok. Our purpose is scientific observation. Our policy has been one of strict non-interference with human affairs. We will make no official contact beyond the effort necessary to effect this rescue, until we can deal with a fairly representative body from all the peoples of your planet. When such a body is firmly constituted, we look forward to an exchange of information that will benefit us both."

"Please identify Ellason and Varok."

"That information is not available to you. I have defined the conditions necessary for any exchange of scientific or technical data. *Dove*, do you have a signal for us?"

"Depressurization is complete. Hatch open. I'm coming out onto the struts. The ship is in shadow. Light signal deployed . . . now."

"There it is, Killah, behind that pinnacle," Orram said, pointing to his left. Below them a light flickered in the deep shadow and reflected off the gold cloak of the lunar ship, which was wedged almost horizontally between the face of the sheer cliff and a huge angular boulder perched on the narrow ledge.

"We have nothing on the *Lurlial* that will get that module out of there," Tallyn said.

Almost an hour passed before Orram and Killah climbed into the *Lurlial* behind Tallyn and Bob Carliano. It had not been easy transferring the injured astronauts out of the *Dove*'s trap and into the alien ship. Carliano had also decided to take all the documentary equipment he could find.

Midpacific was frantic for news. Carliano had said nothing for the last half-hour except to grunt acknowledgements. He was physically exhausted and, at the same time, in a state of acute tension. He realized the tall, anonymous, square-helmeted figures could not be human. One was stiff and calculated, and his movement had a strange, defined pattern to it; the other was disjointed and powerful, his torso and limbs stacked all out of proportion. Their space suits were definitely not Russian, Chinese, German, English, or Japanese. Their voices were turbid and alien. No human throat could make such sounds.

Carliano stood in the passageway of the strange ship, still dripping from the entry shower, with two aliens beside him and his disabled companions at his feet. Then he watched a figure come toward him looking humanly feminine in spite of her isolation suit.

"Welcome aboard. My name is Tandra Grey. We're almost neighbors. I work at the medical labs near the southwestern megalopolis. I just recently took a leave to do comparative microbiology for the ellls and varoks. We are in isolation garments for the trip, and you will be quarantined at base as a precaution. There is no need for fear and very little risk of infectious exposure."

Carliano decided he had no choice but to trust her. Impulsively he took his helmet off. "You at least look human to me."

"I am," she said, turning to help Killah and Orram remove their lunar exposure suits.

Carliano watched anxiously while his rescuers unsuited. He was visibly disappointed that they remained hidden in their isolation garments.

Killah bent over one of the astronauts. "This one was conscious for a while."

Carliano tried to protest as they unsuited Ted Bardeane, but he was easily overruled, and they carried Bardeane down the hall to a cabin and bedded him down in a dry *uuyvanoon*. At the instant that he touched the soft moss he regained consciousness, took one look at Killah's strange, suited silhouette bending over him, and bolted out of the basin. They were able to subdue him only after a struggle. To still Bardeane's panic, Carliano helped them administer a sedative.

In a temper, Killah left the room to check on the more severely injured woman, Jane Wright, stabilized in another *uuyvanoon*. Orram and Tandra followed.

"This person has had a fracture. There may be a clot," Killah said. "We should get her to base as soon as we can."

"Can we take time for the *Nalkah*?" Orram asked.

Tandra gasped.

"We'll go get your Conn," Killah laughed. "We'll have you two healed together before these humans are out of quarantine."

As the elll grasped Tandra's shoulders affectionately, Bob Carliano appeared in the passageway and watched closely, his mind whirling with curiosity. He followed Orram and Tallyn to the control panel and had to be reminded to secure himself while they arced through lunar space and braked over the lunar highlands.

"Tycho, Street, Maginus," Tallyn murmured into the communicator. "We have Maginus H. Conn, give us locater signal. We have to be choosy just where to set down in that mess. How are you, big elll? Still dizzy?"

Conn's voice mumbled an affirmative, and Aen talked the *Lurlial* down onto a relatively uncluttered space in their entrapping crater.

"Bull's-eye," Aen said for Midpacific's benefit.

"Aen, I think we can jack you up and get you on your tracks," Orram said in an unperturbed monotone.

"Roger, varok. We're ready for you."

"*Dove Two,* this is Midpacific. Can you give us a status check?"

"One minute, Midpacific," Orram said. He turned to Carliano. "Commander, the communicator is here on the control panel. Midpacific wants a status report. Aen, Ramahlak here. Can you continue the expedition with Tllan?"

"Yes. Mare Humorum station needs some maintenance, and we should erase the trail through the Cordilleras. We'll bring Junah and Conn over to the *Lurlial* now. They both need immediate care."

– Δ –

Tandra moved back to the entrance hatch. When she heard the decontaminating shower turn on, she opened the inner hatch and found Conn under the cascade clutching Junah's frozen, blind figure, trying vainly to expose it entirely to the spray. Tandra reached in and helped with Junah. When the shower finished, she led Junah out of the chamber. Conn tried to follow, but he fell into the passageway, knocking Tandra down.

"Conn, let me help you."

The elll remained silent and motionless while she dismantled his lunar exposure suit.

Suddenly, Junah jerked spasmodically and dug her hard fingertips into Tandra's arm. Her eyes grew less than dull and her fingers clutched with their full strength. Tandra set her teeth against the pain and tried to wrench the fingers from her arm, but they tore ferociously into her flesh.

Conn focused on their struggle and threw himself at Junah. She tried to steady herself against his attack and momentarily her fingers left Tandra's arm before they grasped out again toward the source of her pain. Conn grabbed her throat in his wide hands, pinning her down with his legs.

"Conn, stop it!" Tandra screamed, pulling violently at his shoulders. "You're cutting off her air. Stop it. Stop it, Conn."

"She's got enough air. I'm just calming her so you can strap her down. There. Now take her quickly to the nearest *uuyvanoon*. Leave it dry, for God's sake. Then come back and get me."

While Tandra obeyed, he made his way down the passageway with maddening difficulty and climbed into an *uuyvanoon*.

Tandra returned and stood over him uncertainly. "Can I get anything for you, Conn," she said, hating the self conscious timidity that plagued her. "Perhaps Killah has some medication."

"No, no," Conn said, closing his eyes.

"Conn, I've learned to love you—so much more than I could have before. The books—you are a magnificent, beautiful people."

"You've done your homework at last," he said, not unkindly. "But it's too late for us now, Tandra. I need Orram, lots of time with Orram. Even the pool seems too empty. I destroyed Junah with cruel, bitter words because of us, because I was angry and frustrated with you. So 'us' is gone. I can't be your pet lizard anymore. I never should have been. I can't sit up and bark; it just won't work. You know what I mean? You are human, and humans have always seen themselves as masters. We both made the same kind of mistake, Tandra. You are too human for me. And now Junah—"

Conn tore off his helmet, turned his face away from her, and sank into the warm water, letting it flood his lungs and ease the torment that shook his body.

Tandra closed the sleeping basin and stood looking down on Conn, her beloved elll, cradled in moss and sealed in water like a giant, tortured fetus. She would win his love again somehow. But now, the loner needed to school in the manner of fish, needed to mate in the manner of amphibians, needed to rollick in the manner of porpoises—and she would never again know his friendship on her own terms.

ENCOUNTER

Killah had no talent for what human psychologists might call healthy repression. Within the fluid, formless culture of his elllonian fathers, where passions rose and fell with their own impetus and washed over the life-essence of that green species to enrich its collective awareness, there was little need for self-delusion. And no need for tact. Hence Killah was unpracticed in the mind-numbing arts required of human bureaucrats.

As a result, when he talked to Midpacific Space Center about Jane Wright's condition, he saved no adjectives in outlining the necessary surgical procedure. He drew precise though indelicate analogies to the tools he would use, and with considerable accuracy he presented the odds against error in judgment, in technique, and in the physical idiosyncrasies of Wright's injured cranium. His human audience was impressed, even awed, and ready to give him unanimous approval to do the operation—but then the television cameras were set up.

When the first transmission in living color reached Earth showing the competent elllonian doctor, his beplumed assistants, and his array of unfamiliar tools and support equipment, it was immediately cut off from public broadcasting "for reasons of national security," and Killah was besieged with questions about elllonian life and technology. Jane Wright was completely forgotten.

Desperate over the loss of time, Killah called in Orram. His humanoid but strange appearance precipitated a new round of curiosity and fear in the human audience. On the Earth, contingency plans were immediately revised to include attack as well as defense. It was only because Orram's tone was so unwavering and insistent that he was able eventually to pull the conversation back to the wounded astronaut.

Then the human beings began to question Killah's instruments and to debate his proposed technique. There was skepticism about Killah's skill. Finally they decided that Orram would be better suited to do the job, in spite of his explanation that he was a biophysicist not a practiced surgeon, as Killah was. His objections did no good. Killah was gradually ignored, and the questions were directed more often to the varok. Orram patiently redirected each question to the elll, but Killah's answers were largely disregarded.

Carliano obviously understood what was happening. Since he was a little chagrined at the odd display of racism, he tried to be helpful. The astronaut Ted Bardeane was openly hostile. There was little doubt in Orram's mind now; they should have left all video devices on the *Dove*.

Too many minutes passed and still the *Dove*'s command at the Midpacific Space Center could not decide who would decide to allow the repair of the fracture that was endangering astronaut Jane Wright's brain. They could not agree to let the aliens do what they could not, in fact, stop them from doing.

Killah could no longer contain his impatience. With heroic restraint he excused himself from the cameras. He grabbed Tandra away from his would-be patient and tore down the hall screaming, "Do they really believe they have a choice?" Pulling Tandra into the pool past an amazed Conn, then embracing her firmly, the elll took her deep into the clear red water. He remembered in time to tow her to the surface and unburdened his overloaded psyche on his human colleague with a torrent of elllonian anger.

"Never! Never never never have I ever ever wasted so much valuable time," he screamed as he sliced furiously through the water around her. "Never never in all my life have I ever sat on my ass with my feet in my mouth for so long. Sat on my ass and played word games while a normally conscious being lay blind to her own life, losing not just seconds, but minutes, Tandra, long precious minutes of consciousness. She's losing all that life, while they sit around inventing circumlocutions to avoid making the decision to operate. Of all the unfathomable, cruel—you human beings have no sense of priority!" He slammed his hand down on the water where Tandra had been a second before. "To hell with diplomacy. *We'll* make the decision."

Tandra found Conn's eyes fixed steadily on her. Did he think she would be offended by Killah's rage? She smiled wryly at him, as Killah continued to tear up the pool, but he made no response. Behind him, she saw Ted Bardeane enter the room and watch Killah's tantrum with increasing horror.

"We ellls do not repress our emotions," Conn tried to explain. "We get them out and over with in—"

Bardeane turned away and ran from the room.

Suddenly Killah surfaced again and stopped ranting. He rolled onto his back to let the ruby warmth of the pool damp the quiver of his velvet hexagons. Then he leaped through the water to Tandra and placed a dry, lippy kiss on her nose. "Well, that's enough of that," he said with a broad smile, his mood already completely placid. "Let's return to the great debate. A good tantrum like that gets the venom out of the juices in a hurry, right?" He boosted Tandra out of the pool and leapt onto the deck beside her, draping a stocky arm on her shoulders.

"Swim, Conn?" he said to their sullen observer. "You missed the adjustment, and you're still unstable. You'd better take some vibes before you go back to the centrifuge."

"With Tandra? I had better not. I can't fake it." Then he hobbled drunkenly away.

"Conn," Tandra cried, but he walked on and disappeared into the hall.

"This will pass," Killah said softly. "Conn needs your love more than he realizes. Don't abandon him yet, eh Tandra?"

"Me? Abandon him?"

"You're not going to let pride have its way. We ellls are a schooling organism, Tandra. It is difficult for Conn to understand your feeling of alienation from your own species. I think that is why he is still upset with you. Now wipe the eyes. We have surgery to do, Midpacific or no Midpacific."

– Δ –

Conn made his way to Junah's room and sat beside her. A wave of grief washed over him as he stared into her brown eyes. They were dull and empty.

"Junah? It's Conn. Junah?"

He sat near her for more than an hour, calling her name and reaching toward her patch with his mind. It was useless. There was no channel for his thoughts to follow, and he was sickened by the continual spinning of objects around him.

He went to the food center, trying to ignore his injury, and prepared a softly textured meal. He would feed her, exercise her, devote all his time to her cure. He returned to her side and cautiously placed a small amount of food in her mouth. If she refused it, the job would be nearly hopeless; her survival instinct would be too weak. The food lay suspended for a moment, but then she began to chew mechanically. Finally she swallowed.

Conn made his way back to the food center with a surge of hope. Tandra and Killah were there, eating hurriedly.

"We're in for it now, Conn," Killah remarked acidly. "They've made it clear that we are solely responsible for Jane Wright's fate."

"That's the most accurate statement they've made since we contacted them," Tandra said. She watched Conn fumbling toward the fruit cupboard, and a sharp yearning welled up in her. "Conn, Artellian needs help. His throat won't stand much more talk. Midpacific insists on information from a reliable source, an 'elll of authority.' Bardeane's got them all upset again."

Conn's body wavered as he tried to answer. "I'll be with Junah," he said.

"You'll do Junah no good unless you do some time in the centrifuge first," Killah snorted.

"You don't look well, Conn," Tandra said.

"Don't tell me what to do."

"I'll tell you what to do," Killah commanded. "Three hours a day in the centrifuge—minimum!"

"I'll help you with Junah as soon as we have operated on Jane Wright," Tandra said.

"Stay away from Junah," Conn warned and lurched through the door.

"Wright is losing more lifejoy than Conn at the moment," Killah said. "Call Orram and meet me in the lab, Tandra. We'll set up our isolation booth within the quarantine room. Lock that madman Bardeane in the shower if you have to."

In the wake of Killah's decision to operate, Earth needed to be mollified. Midpacific raised such a series of threats and charges that

Killah agreed to set up the television cameras in the isolation booth so that the human audience could monitor the surgery. Killah made the compromise only when Artellian reminded him that their future influence with Earth was at stake. "We can't jeopardize all our chances for effective contact," Artellian argued. "The more exposure we have the better."

In spite of the cameras, the operation was soon done. And when it was over, Killah indulged in another elllonian temper tantrum to clear his head. The tension generated by the skeptical astronauts and their bosses at Midpacific was more than he could absorb.

"Never. Never again will I appear before those *kaehl-din* cameras of theirs. Orram and Conn can do the honors. No thank you! Forget old Kill the Doctor. They would have listened to a three-hour demonstration lecture on alien life while that woman lay losing the precious minutes. Even after we promised them regular broadcasts, they continued to harass me with nonsensical questions. Proof indeed! Well, here I am, not proof enough: laying their astronaut's brain bare in alien quarantine on the moon with instrumentation they haven't dreamed up yet, and they don't want to believe it."

Killah knew that Jane Wright would recover with no brain damage, for the repair had been successfully accomplished. But it was impossible to convince the human beings of the fact. They were determined to sit grim-faced for all the hours that it would take the astronaut to regain consciousness. *Well, let them. Paranoids. Vulturous paranoids! Insisting that their kaehl-din TV cameras focus on the grisly procedure. Miserable, frustrating beings.*

Jane Wright did not emerge into consciousness when Killah expected. Tandra became moderator between skeptical men and disdainful aliens. How easy and comfortable it was to assume a role conversant to all and loyal to none but herself and her child—so different from the activist's part she had discarded long ago on Earth, cynical and defeated. This role would cost her nothing. Her real tension was well hidden in the compromising, calm exterior.

Conn didn't like the affectation, and he told Tandra so. To his surprise she agreed.

"I would much rather take a position and watch Orram and Artellian demolish it than grease along like this," she said. "But it is not possible with men. Pride and money are always at stake. Honest opinion hasn't a chance. Besides, Orram wants to go easy until Wright regains consciousness."

"Why isn't she conscious yet?"

"We don't know, but there should be no real danger. The EEG and mind probe are good."

"Somehow you seem more conscious now, Tandra."

"So you really have noticed. It is because the varoks prod me whenever I doze mentally. Ahl pursues every questionable inflection in my voice. I will never think like a varok, but I'm learning to question my first impressions." She cupped Conn's face tenderly in her hands. "We are in contact again, dear Conn. Can't we extend it?"

For a moment they tasted their old joy. Then Junah's specter rose to destroy it. "No," Conn said. "I don't know where to begin, Tandra. We'd just better leave each other alone. We could do more damage to someone." Reluctantly he turned away. "I must go to Junah."

In spite of the continuing medical debate concerning Jane Wright, Orram's regular telecasts were well received. By the time the astronauts' required quarantine was completed, their immunizations pronounced successful, and their exposure to normal alien flora accomplished (after considerable human objection to the inclusion of the unconscious Jane Wright in such treatment), the world was well acquainted with Tandra's moderation. People liked Artellian's rambling erudition and Orram's bland, masterful composure. Human curiosity was surfacing from within the initial morass of fearful hate. Once the appearance and intelligence of the ells were accepted, elllonian culture had a charming appeal. After all, they had been on the moon for ages; they wouldn't be about to come down *en masse* now. That tall man (what's his name? Orlan?) is quite definite about that.

Orram underplayed his varokian heritage. The harder issues could be introduced once confidence was established.

Killah admitted to no one but Tandra and Orram that he was worried. Jane Wright should have showed signs of consciousness before now. Carefully they considered more corrective surgery and rejected the idea until Wright's danger was clearly defined.

"We can't operate on her again just because political pressure dictates it," Killah said. "We rescued these astronauts for the sake of politics and look where we are—we now run the risk of being more demons than heroes in most eyes."

"I am very discouraged," Artellian agreed. "I have seen faith and an inclination toward trust in too few men. It may be that our efforts on behalf of Earth are quite useless."

Conn's Challenge

Conn played little part in the televised conversations and cultural presentations. In fact, he played little part in anything but the attempt to revive Junah's sanity. As the weeks passed, hope wore thin. Conn regained his health, but his spirit grew raw with fatigue and grief and estrangement from the school. Only his growing friendship with Carliano and his deepening dependence on Orram created enough joy in his life to maintain his elllonian wholeness. Then, like the precious gift of rain on a drought-stricken seedling, the news of Junah's first spoken words reached him.

Conn made his way quickly to her room, and lay down beside Junah on her bed-pad. Should he touch her? Would it help her or drive her deeper? Reality. Life seeks its own, doesn't it? He moved very close to her so that his entire body was in contact with hers. Then he murmured the words that she had said to Erah: "Orram's *alyakah* is Tandra. Junah is here. Junah minds Junah. Say it again. Orram's *alyakah* is Tandra. Junah is here. Once again, Junah. It is true. Junah directs Junah."

He stopped, nauseated with self-reproach. "I was wrong, Junah!" he cried. "Hear me! Orram will always love you as friend, a first friend, his best mate before his *alyakah*. *Alyakah* loves you too, Junah. I love you. I was wrong. I was bitter. I made you suffer for my pain. Conn was wrong. Conn says so. Conn knows it. Know it, too, Junah. *Ae-yul-l!* Junah come to me. Conn suffers."

He tightened his arms around her, and gradually, in warm, mysterious ways he could not know, his suffering penetrated Junah's wall against consciousness. She stirred in his arms and knew nothing but that she must comfort him.

"Conn. *Uuyvanoon*," she said.

Conn leapt for the water inlet to an *uuyvanoon* and set it to half-full. Then he supported Junah as she groped her way across the room and braced her as she stepped into the sleeping bowl. He followed her into the warm comfort and lay beside her, holding her head against his chest.

"Tell me your pain," Junah said with incredible effort, as she stroked the elll stiffly.

"*Aaeo-o!* Junah. Words are difficult for me. Read me, Junah."

"No, no. I cannot. Words, Conn," Junah said more easily, as her full consciousness and some control began to reemerge.

"I have too much to sort out," Conn said. "I loved Tandra. She was special to me. But she would not know me as I am. She refused to know me. I begged her to know that we were elll, but she saw me as a humanoid pet. The shock in her face when she understood about the eggs, Junah! *Aeyull!* I knew then that she would hate me for being such a creature. Harrahn's tooth! I'm a creature that eats its own eggs, a creature that mates only for pleasure. They care so much for mating, these human beings. They care more for how things are done than why they are done. At times I hate her for her humanness. And I hate her all the more because I love her and want her—for what I don't know—and I am jealous of every moment Orram spends with her, every moment that he can accept her for what she is—whatever that is—and I can't."

"Jealous, Conn? That is not an elllonian emotion." The comment was perfectly normal, but Conn did not notice.

"Yes, jealous. A terrible human emotion that no sane elll has any business feeling. What an irony, eh? I blame Tandra for making me feel jealousy and personal desire. Yet I know it's not her fault. I hate her prejudices and love her closeness and ease, and I am bitter that she refused to know me. How can I sort this out? I might as well be a varok. I'm just a mass of emotion, not rational at all."

The word rational jolted him, and he sat up to look at Junah. The amused glint in her eyes told him that she had returned to a natural, controlled sanity. Great crystal green tears boiled up in his eyes as she smiled at him and accepted his prolonged, intense embrace.

"No one could stay repressed under the onslaught of language like that," she said. "I don't know what all your words mean, but the flavor is unmistakable. I must find Orram, now. Where is my robe?"

Conn didn't wait to help her. He ran from the room, and, with an ear-shattering whoop that soared past the humans' sonic range, burst into the pool room where the crew and the astronauts now spent much of their time. He threw himself against Orram, Tandra, and Artellian, tumbling them all into the water. Then, wild with joy, he leapt out of the pool and shouted down at them, "Junah's back. She made it. I got her back." With that he dove on top of Orram in an embrace that took them both to the bottom of the pool.

In stark contrast to his entrance, Junah walked quietly into the large room, a beautiful silver and brown goddess, commanding and statuesque. She accepted the welcome of the jubilant ellls with controlled pleasure as her mild dark eyes searched, then found Orram climbing out of the pool.

He approached her, questioning, measuring with silent probes, until their forearms met and their fingers slowly interlaced, growing strained in each other's firm grasp. Then—surrounded by silence and a roomful of tense, watchful ellls, two bewildered humans, and one silent woman awaiting consciousness in her chair—they sought a solution to their relationship.

The pool room breathed with them and waited, while they spoke without words.

Dreams repressed. Now forgotten, Orram's patches read from Junah.

Admiration. Friend, Junah read from him.

Yes. And no longer mate.

Erah?

Not necessary.

But your need?

Irrelevant. Partial consummate release with Tandra. Unexplained.

Is the mind-link possible?

Perhaps. Complications for Tandra.

Tandra loves you.

Yes, but far too well. Exaggerated admiration.

Which you deserve. Her view of you: very little distortion.

There is hope in that.

And danger, for you. Emotional overload.

Danger also for Tandra. Consummation, the mind-link, may not be enough for her. It also implies imposed alienation from Earth, from her biological imperatives.

Her choice. Make it possible, if that is what you need to protect yourself, Junah insisted.

No. Other cultural factors operable. Pressure too great to impose on Tandra.

You are too protective. She is strong now. She gives you partial release? You remain rational when emotion attacks? How can that be?

Unexplained. Still uncontrolled. And she is unaware of her ability. It occurs with close contact.

Then touch is tolerable?

Yes.

And you savor her mind.

You have known that.

Settled! I desire your happiness. You will never consummate with anyone else now.

Junah! Do not force her. Do not tell her. It is too much to ask.

Junah smiled, dropped Orram's hands, found Tandra and approached her. Taking Tandra's arm in her hands, she pressed it against Orram's. A hushed murmur traveled through the ellls. They pressed around Tandra and Orram now, and a chant began. Slowly at first, it gradually gained momentum, then broke into a varokian melody. Artellian tried to stop it, and Orram shook his head, denying the demand, but with hesitation. That hesitation was enough to drive the ellls on. The tempo of their song suddenly increased, and they began to stamp insistently.

Tandra was bewildered. "Surely not the *Vrankah.* The ellls wouldn't demand that of you, Orram."

Suddenly, Orram's hesitation was gone. His feet joined in the syncopated beat of the ellls' stamping and his hands began to tell a story with the flowing varokian melody. Or was it an invitation? The meaning became more clear as Tandra watched his hands talking to her, inviting her to come to Varok or to him or to both. Without volition her feet began to move with Orram's and her hands retold his message. They danced in unison then, the flowing movements of their arms contrasting with the changing hard beat pronounced by their steps.

When the story was told, the invitation complete, the carved mahogany varok and the soft human woman stood locked in mutual awareness.

"And Junah?" Tandra asked.

"She has reemerged into a state of mature reason," Orram said.

The music continued then with a slower beat, and the two astronauts watched the ellls dance. Some varoks moved with the pulsing rhythm, distorted and extended by the moon's light gravity. Ellls cavorted in the angular style of their own species, which took them into the water more often than not. Tllan passed trays filled with fermented Ellasonian fruit and rich, dark nuts. A celebration was in full swing.

Tandra saw that Bardeane was watching with growing disgust. "It's unpardonable that the ellls should exhibit such joy, while Jane Wright sits like a vegetable, destroyed by their crude surgery. I'm getting Wright out of here," he snapped. "She needs rest."

He started to wheel Wright from the silenced room when a distinct groan of protest emerged from the medical chair.

Killah leapt toward his patient and shoved Bardeane aside. "Make another sound if you are conscious, and we'll really celebrate," he shouted.

Obediently Wright mumbled, "Sound," and managed a weak smile at the sight of this weird green character who seemed so interested in her recovery.

The celebration broke into full bloom then. Cameras were brought in to record and announce the event. Indeed, as Jane Wright emerged into full consciousness, she responded to her alien benefactors with such an infectious, intellectual joy that she inadvertently boosted Artellian and Orram's online ratings. Confidence on Earth grew, and it was decided that the astronauts should stay at Moonbase several more weeks.

– Δ –

Now that Junah was fully recovered, Tandra hoped to reestablish some contact with Conn. She tried bringing music to him, she invited him to school, she even approached his *uuyvanoon*—but he refused her with strange, mixed messages: "I don't have to stay here for anyone," or "All I give you is pain," or "It can't mean what we ought to mean, like Orram."

"Conn, join the school," Killah insisted, "so they won't have to readjust to your absence."

Tandra realized that when he tried, he had little success; essentially he remained estranged from the ellls.

He voluntarily approached no one but Orram and Carliano.

With some relief, Tandra saw that the astronaut became a substitute for the school—another accepting, open mind who loved life and relished experimental sound, as she had.

Orram, meanwhile, had as little success bringing Conn closer to Tandra as he had earlier trying the reverse. His psychic link with her, however, grew stronger and stronger.

He joined her by the pool during the evening meal, as he often did now. "Tandra, during the celebration last week we danced a kind of *Vrankah* during which you were tracking me. It is a much more specific function than mood-reading. The fact that you accomplished it so readily indicates that your mind-link potential may be considerably more extensive than we thought possible."

Tandra looked at him as if puzzled.

"Do you understand what I am telling you? This is extremely important, this tracking that you have done. If the men should question you, please tell them it's a dance, a game we invented."

"Some game," Conn said drunkenly from behind Orram, his mouth crammed with rich, potent fruit. "You're treading on thin ice in more ways than one, M. Ramahlak. You seem to assume that Dr. Grey here is one of us. She is not approved for security information, you know. You were talking about tracking, right?"

"I have told her no specifics, Conn. You should know that I have good reason to trust her entirely. You would do well to rediscover that yourself."

Conn's brow deepened and he dropped his head. "You'd better fly or give up your wings, *Vrankah* din."

"Don't be ugly, Conn," Orram said.

"What do you mean, Conn?" Tandra asked. "Take those berries out of your mouth. You're drunk."

"Leave-me-entirely-alone!" Conn hissed, grabbing Tandra's wrists fiercely. "Everything you vomit is a command. You have learned nothing."

"Release her!" Orram shouted.

Conn backed away at the sound of Orram's command. "They didn't put all the details into those books you read, Tandra dear. Varoks can't forever walk a tightrope between rationality and subjective human droppings. And they can't afford to play around with emotion, especially sensual emotion, as much as he has lately. I'm not talking about the kind of crack-up Junah had. I'm talking about strong emotions, mind-links without release—"

"There is nothing more that Tandra needs to know about it, Conn."

"First myself, then Junah, and now Orram. How many of us are you going to destroy before you leave here, Tandra?" Conn strode unsteadily away from them toward the pool.

Tandra did not need to look at Orram to know that he shared her bewilderment. "Surely I haven't been the cause of destroying you," she said.

"Remember that he is elll, Tandra. His emotions vacillate wildly and quickly. Conn is suffering from some very mixed feelings toward you, and he is dramatizing my danger."

They joined hands and followed Conn, passing the astronauts, who stood watching them with a variety of expressions on their faces. Ted Bardeane rose to stop them. "What is this?" he demanded.

"What is what?"

"This!" he shouted, knocking Tandra's hand from Orram's grasp. "I've seen enough. First that dance and now this. You represent human beings here, by whoring with aliens! You degrade us all."

"I have done nothing to shame anyone. Man degrades himself; he doesn't need any help from me."

"God, I should have known. You're a Stabilist!"

"A what?"

"You know damn well! Are you a Stabilist or not? What side do you take?" Bardeane shouted.

"What is a Stabilist?"

"Hold it, Ted," Jane Wright said. "How long have you been at this base, Dr. Grey?"

"Almost five months."

"And have you had any news from Earth lately?"

"Very little. My life has been-focused in other directions."

"Yes. I understand. Our focus has also changed since we have been here."

"Don't tell me you don't know about the Stabilists!" Bardeane said. "They have gone wild. They don't care how they get their way now."

"Let me explain," Wright interrupted. "The Stabilists are, in effect, a revolutionary party, demanding that all economic and population growth must stop immediately. They organized when the human death rate suddenly rose. They are completely out of patience with any attempt at gradual transition or rationalization. There have been increasing numbers of industrial bombings and two assassinations. The situation is extremely dangerous now, for the people of many countries are divided on the stop-growth issue."

Another rare silence settled over the pool room, as the ellls surfaced to listen. Killah exchanged a knowing look with Orram. The conversation was leading toward a confirmation of the impressions they had gained from their first experiences with human society. The astronauts' first fearful reactions, the interference with the surgery, the Moonbase broadcasts so easily misinterpreted—all led to the same conclusion: humans were not ready to listen to an alien voice.

"The position you take in this controversy, Dr. Grey, could have significant influence," Carliano said thoughtfully.

"Isn't her position clear already?" Bardeane exploded.

"I am interested in no one's position but my own and Shawne's," Tandra said.

"You write yourself off very easily," Conn said.

"My species has written me off." The conversation had not mattered much, before Conn entered it. Now Tandra's voice and body shook with emotion. "The solutions are clear, Conn, the limits are defined, but men still fight and claw for control. They leave nothing for the future. Your pool may be the last clear water Shawne will ever see, the stars from here, the last stars. And there is nothing I can do to stop them."

"So they're stupid or greedy. I can't follow their thinking. But it's no reason for hate."

"They are tearing apart Shawne's future, Conn. How can you blame me? I don't want to teach her survival tactics. I want her to live with beauty."

Orram's cool, steady hands covered Tandra's tight grip on Conn's arm. "You care too much," he said to them both. "It is misplaced."

"So that's your game," Bardeane said to Tandra. "You'll choose no side because you don't have to. You'll sit around up here in pink bathtubs with your damned survival instincts, while the rest of us fight it out."

"Yes, we probably will," Orram said. "It has become clear since we contacted you. In the end we will have no other choice. There is nothing we can do if humans choose an irrational course."

"But where is the rational course?" Wright asked, with an admonishment in her voice more analytical than Bardeane's. "The stakes are very large. No one can escape. Every person's choices affect every aspect of their life, sometimes in opposing ways."

"Yet people see it in terms of battle," Tandra said with an old familiar grief tightening her voice. "You have no capacity for political accommodation, much less economic compromise. You can't imagine gearing production to the return of materials or restricting yourselves to local resources. You don't think people could survive without powered contraptions. They couldn't possibly walk to work or have fewer children or live in simpler homes. You refuse to see that we must do with less of everything or we will soon have nothing—certainly not a life worth living."

V. COMMITMENT

Many Jovian years ago there were no varoks on Varok. The forebears were magnificent winged bipeds, who ignored their excesses until the resulting ecological catastrophe initiated horrendous mutations in their genetic codes. The survivors of the Mutilation retreated to the hot acid plains far to the east. Over many ages of Varok their children and their children's children became a tough and adaptable new species, survivors of the forebears' overindulgence, determined that the populations and the level of consumption would never again grow beyond control.

We varoks are happy to be taller, but we are also sorry to have lost our marvelous wings. That's why we call it the Mutilation. I'm afraid we lost much more than just our wings. The planet's early tragedy is now written indelibly in our genes. The Mutilation bared the ends of the forebears' nerves and muted the hormonal response between sexes, making emotionally-prompted physical contact difficult for us varoks without a mind-link. A dynamic readjustment to the steady state is still our constant challenge, so that nothing will become scarce or poisoned again, ever.

Here beneath Mt. Ni Orram grew up, and his father taught law to the ellis of the Forested Sea. Later, as a young man at the Concentrate, Orram became a biophysicist, as well as a distinguished amateur in philosophical history. Not long ago he was designated master.

Conn met Orram at the Concentrate in Ahl Vior, and they became close friends. They spent many pleasant hours comparing the ways of Varok and Ellason with the ways of Earth, which Conn was studying at the Concentrate.

Now, so Conn tells me, he has a serious personal issue to solve. Please help him, as best you can.

A communication to Tandra Grey
From Orserah, Orram's mother

BEYOND LOVE

While scientists on the blue planet Earth grew more frantic for details of the aliens, Bob Carliano, Jane Wright, and Conn spent their time together with Conn's sound equipment in the recreation lounge.

"How does that translate?" Conn asked, as he fed his ultrasonic recording into the low frequency synthesizer.

Carliano listened to the rich music for a moment and nodded his head in approval, as did Wright. "It's wild—but beautiful. You've combined some of the best styles from all three planets."

Conn felt a surge of appreciation for the astronauts, not unlike his first reaction to Tandra. "I'll leave this one alone then. Do you want to take a duplicate back with you? No regulations against cultural exchange. I'll copy this onto one of Tandra's old SVD's. They'd probably confiscate mine for chemical analysis and ruin my music."

"They'd confiscate a lot more than that, if they could," Wright said.

"You sound like Tandra," Conn complained, suddenly confused. What was it about these humans that drew him in?

Carliano didn't hesitate to probe. "What's the problem between you and her? You pick at everything you can find. She's no different than the rest of us."

"That's half the problem."

"She loves you like a brother."

"That's the other half of the problem. I'm not human."

"She's beyond that now," Carliano said. "I know what she went through. She's spent a lot of time with me trying to explain what happened. She knows you're elll. Good grief, how could she miss? I still lie awake nights trying to believe you're real. And what a shock you give me every morning. Real honest-to-God alien intelligence. Every nerve in my brain wants to pull back and deny it. 'No,' they say, 'I am Man, the image of God. This elll is only imitation.'"

"You've had a long tradition touting that."

"Once in a while we get a glimpse of the stars, and now we know that the probability of life on some of those exoplanets out there has got to be high. Still we come home believing we're God's great gift to the universe. Think what we're exposed to all our lives: The moon! Hooray! We've done it again! 'Man—'humans' to be politically correct—the king of Earth, now prince of the heavens,' a pope once called us. Can you blame us for being a bit nearsighted? We'll no doubt go over the cliff with head held high, breeding like rabbits, jittery as lemmings, proud of our humanity to the end. We're all products of this incredible no-think. It takes time to adjust. Don't blame Tandra. She's grown out of it now, and I'm getting there slowly."

Wright looked squarely into Conn's wide eyes. "Bardeane will never make it though. He still sleeps with a knife under his pillow."

"And you?"

"I gave it back to him. I've had my nose in all the books Artellian could dig up. It's just an intellectual exercise for me. No sweat."

"Have you told Llorkin all this?"

"We couldn't get rid of him for the first few weeks. Yes, he's got it all down in red and white. He seems more convinced than ever that rescuing us was a mistake."

"We may never know," Conn said, "but we're in it now—with a size-able audience guaranteed when we deliver you to Midpacific."

Carliano was silent for a moment. "You're not planning to land the *Lurlial* in public?"

"I assumed we would. So far we've been received rather well."

"But why sacrifice yourselves?" Carliano asked. "You wouldn't en-joy living in the Bronx Zoo."

"You mean that, don't you?" Conn laughed. "You'll never catch an elll indulging in martyrdom."

"Then don't take any chances when you take us back. Don't an-nounce our return. Set us down on an island somewhere. We can sal-vage signal devices and survival gear from the *Dove*. There are influen-tial characters who would go to any extreme to get some alien material to study or to sell. And there are nuts at all levels determined to blow the alien menace out of the sky before it attacks. Then there are bureau-crats determined to enhance their national prestige by getting a piece of you before the other guys do. Do I need I go on? I'm serious."

Conn's eyes narrowed. "Perhaps we've been a bit naive and sloppy in our thinking lately. Let's go talk to Artellian."

– Δ –

Carliano's suggestion was adopted. The *Lurlial* made a side trip to the downed lunar craft at Straight Wall and retrieved its survival gear. The alien craft traveled in minimal time to Earth, hoping to deposit the astronauts on a remote corner of an island not too far from Midpacific Space Center before they were spotted. They found an island Carliano suggested and sacrificed a small pod, so their human guests wouldn't have to parachute to Earth.

When the pod had landed safely, Conn initiated full acceleration, and the *Lurlial* pulled away. High over Earth, Conn listened as the astronauts made radio contact with their colleagues at Midpacific.

"What do those coordinates mean, Carliano?"

"They mean we're sitting in the middle of someone's pineapple plantation waiting for a pick-up."

"What do you mean *pick-up*? Aren't the aliens bringing you in?"

"No. They had a previous engagement, Midpacific."

"You can't let them go. You've got to bring them in."

"They're awfully shy," Carliano said.

"Where are they now? Where are they?"

"About one hundred kilometers straight up, I'd guess, Midpaf, but—"

"What are they doing? Why aren't they bringing you in?"

"They've got strong survival instincts, Midpaf. Radio contact established, Conn. You'd better bug off."

A new voice broke in like the crack of a whip. "Hold them there, Carliano. That's an order. Midpacific security, scramble more jets. We can't let them get away."

"Hey, wait a minute. When do we get a pick-up?" Carliano yelled.

The *Lurlial* disappeared into the sky above the ocean, leaping in a great arc toward the North American continent.

"Where are you taking us, Orram?" Conn hollered. "We're not making orbit."

"I don't intend to go into orbit; that's what they'll expect. No one will look for us, where we're going. Artellian picked us as crew for this trip so we would have some time to relax together. He hoped we could resolve our relationships before we returned to base."

"More likely we'll dissolve them."

"Just that, Conn. Your humor turns the air sour around you. Where is the life-joy that usually emanates from your plumed brain, *aloon*?

You're still not adjusted to the school without Ellalon. We'll land in the Rockies, in the San Juans where you and Tallyn picked Tandra up. The snow will still be on the ground there. Junah, what do you think? Tllan? You're least involved. Tandra? Llorkin? Shawne?"

"Let us risk it," Junah said.

Llorkin and Tllan and the child nodded in agreement.

"It should be beautiful there now," Tandra murmured.

"A bit cool for *eeflin*, but I'm game," Conn said. "The isolation suits will keep us warm enough."

He and Conn headed the *Lurlial* toward their favorite isolated basin in the San Juan Mountains southwest of Denver, and expended a good deal of energy maneuvering their ship over its rocky slides and aspen trees. The basin cradled a fragile pool of icy water collared with pine and fir and the delicate greens and yellows of marsh grasses. The morning sun skipped lightly over the deep blue of the lake and glanced sharply off the *Lurlial* as it touched down on soft brown earth carpeted with snow-soaked pine needles. Soon the EV Science colleagues and Shawne emerged from the belly of the 'pregnant bat' *Lurlial* and began dressing her in a camouflage of snow and pine boughs.

After the inevitable snowball fight, Conn and Tandra, Tllan, Llorkin and Junah lay on the snow-dappled edge of the sky blue lake and watched the changeless rim of rock that surrounded them capture and release white puffs of clouds. They drank in the hot sun and the crisp thin air of the high country, while Shawne chattered on with endless questions about the trees and jays and pine cones. Orram improvised a sled from the *Lurlial*'s galley equipment and spent more than an hour tumbling up and down a small snow bank with the toddler.

"It's so beautiful here," Junah murmured when Orram finally sat beside her to recover his breath. "Reminds me of home. How long can we stay?"

"We have provisions for ten days. We can stay for eight if we're not discovered."

Conn stretched his legs and absentmindedly pulled at the thin material of the isolation suit encasing his sensitive hex plates, as he watched Tllan toss bits of snow into the freezing water.

"*Aeo-o!* Look!" she said. A small rabbit-like animal appeared from behind a pile of rocks at the far end of the lake and darted across the meadow. "Is that a rabbit?"

"I think it's a pika," Tandra whispered. "They're very rare now."

"Looks delicious," Conn growled, throwing out his tongue full length and licking his face plate.

"Conn, you scared it away," Tllan protested.

He ignored her. "Come on. Let's go for a swim." He pulled off his helmet and threw it to the ground.

"No, you beast," she said. "Do you know how cold that water is? Look at you! You're violating the air. Get your helmet back on."

"No water could be that cold. In we go, *leel. La oon!*"

They ran to the water and hollered with the cold, then again when they fell deep off the shore's sudden drop off. Clasping her with his legs, Conn dragged Tllan deep into the lake.

A moment later the surface of the water boiled and trembled, then exploded with the thrashing of struggling ellls. Orram jumped up and watched with alarm as Tllan attacked Conn, thrusting the hard tips of her stiffened fingers into his groin. He sank, and the woman glided to the edge of the lake, accepting Orram's hand and stammering furiously, "I—I'm not going to be used as a—a depository for his problems in that freezing water." She strode to the *Lurlial*, yanking at her helmet Conn had knocked askew. Conn had not yet surfaced.

"He can't take that cold much longer," Tandra said. Before Orram could stop her, she dove into the icy lake.

Deep in the crystal water Conn doubled up with his head clasped between his knees, convinced that he must be experiencing every kind of pain known to the elllonian mind. In vain he tried to shut it out. Tllan's rejection—a rejection he had never experienced before—compounded his self recrimination, and that, together with the maddening, unresolved emotions he felt toward Tandra, triggered a death-wish. Life-joy was gone. His mind was beginning to close upon itself when he felt Tandra's firm grasp around one shoulder and across his chest. He did not resist as she towed him to shore, supported him, with Orram's help, to the *Lurlial*, stripped off his isolation suit, and bedded him into an *uuyvanoon*.

Warmth crawled over Conn's body, and he felt the pressure of something else enter his water. At first he knew only love—then Tandra. Here in his water. He pulled a large volume of the soothing liquid over his gills and into his lungs. Soon, as she massaged his dangerously cooled body, he was able to savor the awareness of life again.

"You're treating me like an elll," he whispered in a water-logged lilt.

For a long while she massaged him, until he nestled underwater against one of her breasts, cupped the other in his palm, muttering something about elllonian women not coming equipped with pillows. Then he slept.

When Llorkin found them a few minutes later, he gasped and stared and rushed off to write in his piles of plastic. Orram looked in, smiled broadly, and went on. Almost an hour later Tllan passed the room. Tandra called quietly to her, "Ease Conn's head off of me, will you, Tllan? I'm wrinkling up like a prune in this warm water."

Tllan slipped her hand beneath Conn's head and lifted it gently as Tandra slipped out of the basin.

"How could you go to his water, Tandra?" Tllan said. "He has been disgusting—and especially unkind to you. Of course, Llorkin has failed to reach him, and the ellls at base have done all that they could. He has refused to join in the adjustment since Ellalon. The pool isn't enough for him anymore. He's been indulging his loner tendencies far too much."

"Is it fair to call it indulging? Conn extends himself very far as an individual. He went beyond normal elllonian limits with me and Orram and with Bob Carliano. Then he was able to reach Junah when no one else could. Are all loners like that, Tllan?"

"I suspect so. No one knows yet."

"Unusual individuals like Conn are not easily accepted in human society," Tandra said. "And of course ellls would not be accepted. Bob Carliano was right. You would be put in a zoo. Your wit, your intelligence, your elllonian emotions would be cause for nothing but amusement or scorn."

"Orram thought you were no longer so bitter," Tllan said uneasily. "Lately you have been more in tune with life. You are so accepting, so full of awe. Now you seem to speak with hate."

"It comes in waves. I hate what I am. I hate myself for the way I let concern for money and convenience make me live. I no longer want to be human."

Tandra's voice grew suddenly tighter. "Why should I take Shawne back into their fouled nest? That's what they made of Paradise. They took Eden and didn't rest until they had made Hell of it. Well, you can have your Hell, mankind! And may you rot in terror with it!"

Suddenly a befinned hand grabbed Tandra's shoulders, whirling her around as another flew hard across her cheek, knocking her against the *Lurlial*'s moss-hung wall. Conn stood over her, his face distorted with rage and stained with tears. He shook violently as he fought to control himself. "Will you ever stop thinking of yourself? You are mankind. You and Bardeane—you're just the same."

The words tore at Tandra, but she said nothing.

Conn turned away, his prehensile handfin held limp.

Orram had watched the entire encounter. He immediately followed after Conn. "You hurt her more with your words than with your slap. What you said is not true."

"What do words matter? She didn't even flinch."

"You want her to be emotional like an elll? She is somewhere between us, Conn. Sometimes hidden and repressed like a varok, sometimes open and volatile like ellls. Remember, we are all imperfect, and more or less reprehensible, in unique ways—in your insistence on sensual expression, in our susceptibility to emotion, in the human beings' need for individual uniqueness and cultural superiority. Are you going to make the same mistake she made? Can you love her as human?"

Conn's eyes widened with understanding as the concept walked through his mind. "I don't know. Orram, I really don't know."

– Δ –

During the long, free days by the pine-scented mountain lake, the elll, the varok, and the human being searched for the keys to the loner's mind with little success. Conn remained incoherent under a load of unfamiliar emotions that most ellls would ask the school to share, rather than carry alone.

In the evenings Conn, Tllan, and Llorkin would climb into one *uuyvanoon* and school as best they could until Shawne and Junah asked them to join in varokian games.

Tandra and Orram reserved that time for themselves. They walked together at sunset, enjoying the changing light, discovering small creatures and plants along the lakeshore, and exploring the frontier where their minds met.

One evening, as Orram gently probed the resistance of Tandra's mind, she consciously tried to open it to him and finally succeeded. He gasped with the sensation of falling into the abyss of her consciousness. He pulled back hard to regain his equilibrium and finally settled himself on its periphery as an observer. From then on they often found words unnecessary.

In the open moments beneath the pine trees, Orram bathed deeper and deeper in the tides of Tandra's consciousness. Tentatively at first, then with growing sureness, he grasped her fund of reason, while he lowered himself into the dark caverns of his own emotional potential. First, his annoyance with Conn, then deeper frustration with the elll, then intense desire to see him reconciled with Tandra.

Yes. He could bring himself back out of it. No loss of reason. As with Ellalon's death, he could experience emotion and maintain control. *Tandra*, he exclaimed ecstatically, silently, *what an incredible experience!* There was no answer, only a slight surge of positive mood, which Orram incorrectly interpreted as awareness on Tandra's part that she had given him her mind. Consummation was possible, but he would not seek her human touch.

Tandra never realized that she succeeded in opening her mind so well. And it did not occur to her to probe the varok's willing mind in turn. How could one do such a thing? It was unthinkable.

Conn watched this relationship with deep concern for Orram. He sensed the strength of the varok's desire to join Tandra's mind. Normally that joining made sensual sharing possible, sometimes imperative, for varoks. The problem was that his fear of imposing himself on her was as strong as his desire. Few ellls knew, as Conn did, that such emotional denial in a varok could manifest itself physically—that involuntary muscles could act in direct opposition to those controlled by emotions, resulting in excruciating pain, such as that suffered by a panicked woman in the labor of childbirth.

So it was with Orram. In ever more frequent waves, the force of his determination to leave Tandra untouched drove against his desire to lose himself in her yielding mind, until suddenly, on their sixth walk in the mountain's crisp beauty, he could contain the ancient exigency no longer, and his conviction paid the price of pain.

He had taken her hand as they left the *Lurlial*, and their forearms met accidentally as they both reached to examine a perfectly shaped pine cone lying in a snow bank. Laughing, they struggled for possession of the cone, until Tandra won it and raced for their favorite tree to bury it in the soft bed of pine needles. Orram ran after her, grabbed her around the waist as she knelt down, pulled her over and back on the soft ground, then lay quietly beside her, reluctant to let her go, knowing he must. Suddenly, he was contorted with a spasm of pain. He doubled up and writhed away from her, his face contorted with agony. He uttered no sound.

Tandra sat up and grasped his shoulders. "Orram, what's wrong? Orram?"

For many seconds he could not make his voice work as the pain tore through his groin. Finally, he forced breath from his throat: "A moment. I will be all right."

"No, no you won't. You're in terrible pain. I can see it."

"*Aeyah*, Tandra." His mind leaned into hers and his emotion found expression as he groaned with pain and humiliation. "We're fragile, we varoks. I don't have enough strength for you."

"Orram, it's senseless to suffer so." As she spoke, she placed her forearm against his, and her words began to melt the denial that tore at his body. "No accusations can hurt me."

"You know," Orram groaned.

"I look for nothing beyond us here. Let me love you."

"*Alyakah*, my Tandra," he said, and the joy of consciously shared passion swept him out of the stranglehold of pain into full, welcome release as their bodies sought and found each other in easy acceptance.

For a long while they lay in their conjugal embrace—the varok's mind open and expectant, but unprobed; the human content with giving a moment's help, expecting nothing more—until they felt the cold air attack them. Then, shivering happily, they dressed each other and huddled beneath the pine tree watching the stars grow brighter in the deepening night.

REJECTION

Like most ellls, Llorkin functioned best when he was involved with a group. It was natural for him to make his belabored pronouncement while the *Lurlial*'s passengers were all together in the galley, relaxing with a meal of bitter-sweet Varokian fruit and chewy, dried *kaehl*. "After some deliberation," he announced, "I have formulated my recommendation to Director Artellian that Dr. Grey terminate her service with us now."

Tandra felt panic rise and paralyze her.

"There are several reasons," Llorkin continued. "It is certainly most logical and efficient. It would save us another trip to Earth when Dr. Grey's period of service was to have ended. There is no reason for her to return to base. Shawne is here. Since further contact with Earth is pointless, further discussions with Dr. Grey on how best to aid in such a contact are also pointless."

"Shawne," Tandra thought. "At least you could keep Shawne."

Junah interrupted. "The fertility tests have not been completed. They are very important."

"I have received communication from Generalist Killah," Llorkin said dryly. "Another human egg has been fertilized, and eight divisions have been observed."

"Orram! Tandra!" Tllan jumped up with excitement. "There may be a chance."

"Whoopee," Conn grunted.

"I, too, regard it as tragic," Llorkin said. "It can only confuse and encourage an already complex relationship between Master Ramahlak and Dr. Grey. Another reason for my proposing an immediate termination of Dr. Grey's services is that her personality has involved two of our staff in disturbing, indeed, disrupting, affairs. Her continued presence is detrimental to the mental serenity of Conn and the physical and mental health of M. Ramahlak."

"Horseshit," Conn muttered.

"I have good reason to believe that M. Ramahlak is in an irreconcilable position. You, yourself, have expressed concern for his health, Generalist Conn. In the interest of the base I recommend that Dr. Grey be returned to her home immediately."

"And I propose that she be offered a staff position at the base with full rights under the EV Dictate," Junah said without emotion. "She has been invaluable to us as a microbiologist and social critic, and her broad insight into the human situation is essential to our most effective handling of Earth's continued education."

"*Aeyull,*" Conn said. "You went *deäcuh* for Orram less than four weeks ago, and now you want to keep Tandra around forever."

"Conn, don't be foolish," Tandra said.

"Don't call me a fool," he screamed, the words tearing through Tandra like a cold chisel.

Junah stood before Conn and extended her hands to him.

Tandra saw that he was startled by her intimate invitation. Timidly he grasped her fine brown hands and waited while her patches read the tone of his mind and tasted the flavor of his emotion. He tried to hide it from her, but it was useless.

"Don't misplace your concern, Conn," Junah said. "I no longer grieve for what I know could never be, but I think you are grieving—a strange, longing grief, mixed with anger. Why, Conn? I can't see, why are you grieving? Orram is no longer in danger. He and Tandra are successfully joined in mind. He is released, emotionally and physically."

Conn jumped to his feet and faced Orram, his eyes narrowed and wild. "When?" he demanded. "How do you know, Junah?"

The galley fell silent while his furious question reverberated harshly. Then his brow deepened with regret. He touched Orram's shoulder, "I'm sorry. Forgive me," he said, and left.

"Conn!" Tandra called and followed him.

"So this is how you get your free ride off Earth."

"Conn, will you listen to me?"

"No. You listen to me. How do you care for me? I don't get it. Do I go on watching you with Orram, loving you both, yet cut off because I can't sniff brain waves? Our minds mated once, too, Tandra, mated in music and foolish star-games. But that's not enough. I live by touch. Where do I fit in? Are we isolated, we ellls, alone in this solar system with two identical mammalian species, wagging our backfins and hoping for a few scraps from your table? Do we have to watch a universal mating from the sidelines, yearning for a communion we can never share? Go home, Tandra. For Harrahn's sake, go home to Earth and quit tormenting me."

He turned away to indulge his frustration. Then, a moment later, the boiling emotions gone, he looked back, as if he expected to find Tandra waiting for him, but she was gone.

– Δ –

When Tandra rejoined the others, Llorkin was repeating his views into the communicator. "I have therefore concluded that Dr. Grey should stay on Earth and return to her home immediately."

Tandra heard Artellian's voice. "Is Tandra there? I would like to talk with her about this."

"First let me make this counterproposal," Junah said, taking the communicator. "I believe that Llorkin's premises are exaggerated, and that Tandra is needed as advisor in human affairs and as bacteriologist. I propose that she be offered a staff position with EV Science. I will have the case ready for presentation as soon as we arrive back at base."

"Let me speak with Tandra."

The others made room for Tandra by the communications center. "Yes, Artell?"

"What do you think? Do you want to go home now, Tandra?"

"I have no home. I don't understand what is happening to Conn. I have done nothing to simplify life for Orram. Perhaps Llorkin is right."

"The choice is yours, Tandra. I can't guarantee that you will be given an EV position, but I'm sure that Junah will make a formidable case."

"The original purpose of my visit to base has been accomplished," Tandra said, as if detached. "Contact has been made."

"Agree," boomed Tallyn's voice from the speaker. "If you care for Earth, you will return. Knowledge of us is needed there. Go now. Otherwise you will look to us too much, work on more emotions and never go."

"Exactly exactly exactly," shouted Llorkin. "She will precipitate Orram's emotional demise—aggravate Conn's neurotic trauma."

"I assume that you can substantiate those charges," Artellian said. "Tandra?"

"Orram?" Tandra looked to the varok for help.

Her eyes were dark and brilliant, but too full and difficult. *I want you to go back to Moonbase with us*, Orram thought, sure that he was telling her, since his mind was completely open to her expected probing. Then in soft sandpaper words he said, "Why try to change what you cannot change? Why project yourself on the world when you hate to, when you feel you will be trying to make impossible what you know is already inevitable?"

Tandra understood his words as a challenge to her integrity—kinder than Conn's, but just as direct. She failed to recognize the open blueness of his eyes, to follow his thought. There was no choice. "I'll have to return," she said, her throat tight and unwilling.

Orram nodded. He was sure that Tandra had read his desire and had rejected it. Apparently, he had assumed too much. Though she had opened her mind to him, she was not varokian, merely accepting—loving, surely, but driven essentially by intellectual needs and desire for growth. He had imposed on her far too much. He would say no more.

The crystal blue depths of Orram's eyes finally let Tandra go, and she felt the impact of that release as surely as she felt the estrangement from Conn. Abruptly, she turned to speak into the communicator. "I would like never to leave you, Artellian, so Shawne and I had better stay on Earth now, so we cost you no more."

EARTH

Tandra sank back to Earth only half-conscious of herself and everything around her, knowing what she must do, knowing it would stop nothing. But being swallowed up again by the human-dominated planet was much worse than she expected. The tiresome gray-black sky above, the concrete beneath, the demands, all too human—all closed in on her, shutting her in so that escape to silence and beauty seemed hopeless. Even the pines were gray. Where was the crystal blue of her childhood?

"Remember the Milky Way, Shawne? From the Moonbase

observation deck it spilled across the sky like fairy dust." How could she keep these memories alive in the child? "There at base you knew what you were made of—what you were a part of."

But what was she a part of here? The faces around Tandra were pale and strange. The eyes were blank and difficult to read. The ears were large and pink, apparently used only for pulling and scratching and hanging things on.

She searched her mirror for some clue to her identity. She was undeniably a human creature, but the vision in the glass was more alien than the shadowy ghosts of Conn and Orram, staring at her with unseeing eyes from the television screen.

She soon stopped watching their presentations. The loneliness they accented was far too painful.

She sought out Jesse Mendleton and found some relief in the support he offered. He shared her concern for Shawne. Already, only a few months into their return, the child was becoming indifferent to the life around her. She was beginning to assume that she should have all the manufactured accoutrements that others assumed they should have.

Tandra feared that Shawne's awareness would be dulled, that she would lose the sensitivity to natural phenomena that the ellls had taught her, that simple things like the gentle touch of the ellls' moss skin or the dancing reflections on the pool would no longer be enough. Tandra resolved to save the remnants of elllonian influence in the child if she could, if she had enough time, so she quickly set aside her fear and her yearning grief, as an elll might, and hurried through the motions of her assumed task.

She told everything that she could bring herself to tell about the aliens. She wrote tirelessly and granted all interviews, hoping to saturate the curiosity of the reporters and their readers. She accepted all speaking invitations, and she conferred with an assortment of government officials from around the world.

Most affable was the President of the World Eco-region Federation. A glimmer of real hope surfaced in Tandra. Here was a man of influence who understood. Of course, no treaty with the aliens would be proper unless it was written and signed by a body representing all of Earth's peoples equitably, which, he was sorry to admit, was not true for the World Federation yet.

He smiled warmly and spoke of the need for perspective, for the growth of the human mind toward accepting the give and take of balance. He defined balance as total recycling and equitable distribution of the Earth's resources, with a stable population count.

Economic de-escalation to such a steady-state? A foregone conclusion. Disruptive? Yes, during the adjustment, but far less disruptive than the present course to human degradation and death. "We should get on with it as soon as possible. Won't you help, Dr. Grey?"

She believed him. She took him literally, as she would a varok. She devoted all her time to helping the environmental lobbyists. Her message was sure and inspiring. The president was behind them. He not only understood the problem but was committed to attaining the steady state as quickly as possible. They could drop their defenses, forget the hypocritical reality of political maneuvering, and state baldly what was required.

The environmentalists swelled with hope; many awoke from the deadening apathy that had followed their growing disillusionment; some dared to admit their sympathies with the Stabilists. They reformulated their proposals in less compromising language and believed they would now be realized. Tandra Grey—confidante of the aliens— had reassured the Federation President that his deepest beliefs were logically and practically correct for the planet Earth. Nothing could stop them now.

– Δ –

The telecasts continued from the moon, with Conn and Orram sharing the duty of programming. Historical and cultural presentations were easy; world model confirmations and projection analysis were not difficult, but suggestions for reaching stability were impossible. They were not taken seriously.

As the months grew bleaker, Conn watched every detail of Tandra's work. At first he couldn't understand it. But with Orram to guide him, he eventually forced his thought patterns through their necessary logical channels and learned to understand the complexity of her mind.

To verbalize his own rampaging emotions was more difficult. He wore a wet-sweater all of the time now, for he rarely entered the pool. Orram was almost enough. But not quite. Though they tried every technique known to varokian psychology, they could merge few patterns of their minds. Orram easily read Conn's mood, but he could not follow the elll's thoughts through his great complex of deductive channels. Cautiously he conditioned himself to accept and empathize with Conn's raw emotion, but the risk was ominous, more so because it involved the resolution of Conn's ill-defined jealousy. Gradually, however, they grew as close as those species could, with Tandra a compelling, silent link between them.

Still, words were as difficult for Conn as touch was difficult for Orram. Conn learned to drop his sensual caution with the varok and to rely on Orram's warnings, but occasionally he would rage uncontrollably with frustration at himself or at his unsatisfied sexual and schooling instincts. Then the bemused Orram would drive him to the pool. "I am not a hermaphrodite, my dear friend, and I flatly refuse to fill all your needs. *Uleoon!*"

Besides, the pool makes my chest feel heavy and uncomfortable, he thought to himself.

– Δ –

Jesse Mendleton sat between Tandra and Maurice Glene, Chairman of the World Life Coalition, wondering what to say next. It wasn't going well. They seemed to agree in outlook, but they couldn't reach an understanding on matters of policy.

They agreed that the governments of Earth had waited too long before starting the adjustment to steady-state economies. As a result, a vital resource—which might be food or potable water or some industrial rare-earth mineral—had often disappeared from an area or industry very suddenly, with disastrous results to the population dependent on that resource.

Tandra and Glene also agreed that legislation the environmentalists had won—cap and trade pollution controls and conservation measures—had been largely ineffective, for they were too easily suspended in crisis situations. The "natural disasters"—massive death from starvation and bad water, noxious substances, extreme weather, flood and drought—could not be prevented. The people of Earth had chosen to let the death rate climb, not to lower the birth rate.

Philosophically, Tandra agreed, she was a Stabilist. She believed in the transition to a stable condition of minimal resource use and equitable wealth distribution. But violent attacks on the principal means of production were insane. She would never agree to aid the Stabilists, if that was their policy.

Glene seemed to understand what was needed for long-term security. When she made her position clear, he opened up to Tandra.

"We live in a state of emergency, Dr. Grey. There is not enough water for both agriculture and the cities. The Eco-region Federation president had to choose. He has no intention of initiating the conversion to a steady-state. He will apply bandages forever in order to keep his friends in business. Advocating the reallocation of demand to a reasonable level is too much of a political risk, for any man, convictions or no convictions."

"Then you have given up all hope of an orderly slowdown? Surely, the president understands Varokian stability economics. He knows that the world's total stores of vital resources can be estimated and recycled equitably."

"Of course he understands that. But he understands immediate economic pressures far better." He paused. "It would be a nice solution, but it won't work."

"No one has seriously tried it. How can you know it won't work?"

"You can't force a man to live a smaller existence than he can buy," Glene said thoughtfully. "People won't live for some indeterminate, stable future. Death from malnutrition or lung poisoning comes slowly and quietly to individuals. People react only to huge disasters for a short time, rarely for a distant future."

Tandra felt herself withdrawing. "Perhaps you are right."

– Δ –

"Time has gone very slowly for me these last few months," Orram said, as he arose from Killah's examination table.

"I miss her, too," the elll said, assuming that the varok was thinking of Tandra. He did not look away from Orram's medical records on the base computer.

"Of course," Orram continued. "At first I thought that Tandra's absence was the reason for my lethargy. Then this cough began. It has deepened. I feel very tired, Killah, all the time."

"You have lost some lung capacity, Orram. The growth has spread. It is like no malignancy I have seen in varoks. Yet it has come on you too gradually to be common disease. I'm not sure what to prescribe yet, except bed rest. Let's give your body a chance to throw this off. Meanwhile I will check Tandra's books. Perhaps you have picked up a human organism, something like TB."

Orram agreed to put aside his work, and he rested well, but the feeling of weariness was not relieved. Soon he was forced to sleep as much as the coughing would allow.

Though Killah was unable to culture any pathogens from Orram's sputum, he decided that Orram might have tuberculosis. He spent many hours synthesizing the human drugs PAS and streptomycin and administered them to the varok.

When there was nothing left to do, Killah and the ellls grieved for Orram's loss of life-joy. They waited anxiously for some improvement, but their master varok continued to grow gray and thin. They began to wonder how they might get Tandra to return to them.

LOSING HOPE

"You must make your followers realize, Dr. Grey, that we are all concerned for the environment, but the economic health of the world is of first priority. Furthermore, our energy needs continue to grow."

Tandra winced at the clichés, especially the word "needs." Maurice Glene had been right. The president was a master politician and little else. He knew how to mouth the proper philosophy at the proper time. He had used her to gain time, to learn who among the environmentalists were active Stabilists.

"You are going to let them strip-mine all this acreage in spite of the loss of arable land, in spite of the knowledge that the Stabilists are prepared to stop it at any cost." Tandra felt herself drawing away from the discussion, even as her anger rose.

"You are a friend of the aliens. The Stabilists rely on your advice."

"That is no longer true. You have betrayed them through me. Your promises of beginning the industrial readjustment have been ignored, and now ruthlessly broken by stripping this land for its coal. The Stabilists will no longer listen to anything but decisive reversals in policy. The bombings have started again. Most of the people are with the Stabilists now."

"I can't believe that. This insurrection will easily be put down."

"You are going to let violence and nature do the leveling job, aren't you?" she murmured, only half aware of him now. "You can't conceive of denying invention or leaving power unused, as the varoks do. You will do nothing toward securing the future."

"Dr. Grey, it is economically dangerous—"

She rose and walked away from him, unhearing, oblivious to the insult she dealt him.

"I hold you responsible for any more violence, Dr. Grey," the president called angrily after her.

– Δ –

What makes me keep ranting? Tandra wondered bitterly as she looked out at the sea of hard faces before her. *There is no way I can make them understand.* But she continued, in one final effort to dissuade the Stabilists from violence. "You can't force a steady-state solution. There must be consensus so change can be gradual and not disruptive. Allowed pollution levels must be reduced slowly. Resource quotas must be established at existing values, then gradually reduced to sustainable levels. Men must learn to temper their needs."

"More do-nothing political lies!" a Stabilist shouted.

"We're through waiting!"

"We must stop them! Destroy their fowl strip mine!"

Tandra felt numb. "More violence will teach nothing. You've got to care for men's lives in the process of re-education or they will learn nothing but hate."

"It's too late to care about a few men's lives," someone shouted.

"You must look beyond yourselves," Tandra continued. "You are generating hate that will continue in your children." She was very, very tired. There was nothing more to do after this. It was time to quit and take Shawne away to some place quiet and clean and safe.

"She's been bought!" Uncompromising stares met her bewildered eyes.

"Try to understand me," she begged. "You must become devoted to living simply. Deny the spoilers their market. Then your children will learn, and others will see and understand."

A groan of irritation rose in the crowd, and several people stood up to wave her off the podium.

"Please listen."

The crowd pressed in. A comforting hand took Tandra's arm and invited her to step down. Eagerly she took it and looked into the despairing eyes of Jesse Mendleton. She welcomed the final knowledge he gave her. Her effectiveness had run out. She was finished at last. Only a few jeering comments followed them out of the hall. In very little time she was forgotten by all but too few, but she would never know that.

"Shawne has been too long among those who care too little," she said to Jesse. "Human society has become alien to everything I believe, an enemy to everything I care about. I must take Shawne away, quickly, before she forgets the ellls. I must find a place to raise Shawne strong but sensitive, with a real knowledge of what life might mean if one learned to love all of existence."

– Δ –

Almost a year had passed since Tandra's return to Earth, when suddenly Conn missed the steady input of news about her political activities. He asked the Midpacific Space Center for help in contacting her, but they claimed they could not find her. Conn panicked. *Why would she suddenly drop out of sight?*

He went to Orram. The varok had lain quietly determined, clinging tenaciously to his life, but gradually weakening through the long days. He could not talk without great effort. His only advice was the name of Jesse Mendleton. But uttering that name brought on a torrent of wrenching coughs that sounded as if they would split his lungs. At this Conn became incoherent with grief for Orram's pain, blaming himself for driving Tandra away.

Hours later Killah found Conn still grieving. He tried schooling with the loner, but there was no help for Conn in the pool, so they climbed out onto the deck and talked.

"He can't take much more damage to his lungs, can he, Killah? Varoks have a greater oxygen requirement than we do."

Killah's eyes grew wide with empathy. "I'm trying everything I can to keep him conscious, Conn. Once they lose touch with reality, varoks can suffer brain damage and die of oxygen starvation quite suddenly. He's under high oxygen pressure continually now. I've given him the injection mask."

"Great God, you mean if he loses consciousness we'll never get him back?"

Killah nodded soberly. "I wish Tandra were here. I need her help. Junah has already initiated proceedings to clear her for a staff position with EV Science. What would her presence do to you, Conn?"

Conn's grief was momentarily flooded by hope. Killah felt his answer in the high ultrasonic.

"If Llorkin blocks Tandra's candidacy, I'll issue a legal restraint on the grounds that he's obstructing base objectives—and if Orram dies, I'll charge him with murder," Conn stated.

"His objections are no longer valid," Killah said. "It's now quite obvious that she can cope with mentalities and cultures alien to herself, even those on her own planet."

"Killah, this request to clear Tandra shouldn't be routine. Let's label it urgent. Artellian!" he shouted for the master elll. When Artellian did not answer, Conn stuck his head into the water and bellowed ultrasonically.

Immediately, Artellian surfaced and sliced toward them. "What was that for?" he asked. "The pool is still quivering."

"This request for Tandra's staff position must be treated as urgent. And we need a full clearance for her so she can try to reach Orram if he should lose consciousness."

"Reach him?" Artellian asked.

Killah nodded. "I have good reason to believe that if Orram loses consciousness, Tandra can make diffuse contact with him. There is known human potential for low frequency reception and transmission, and Tandra has tracked with Orram."

Junah approached to listen, as did Llorkin and the other ellls in the pool.

"Tracking is very limited, Conn," Artellian argued. "You're asking that we clear Tandra for complete defined contact. That's nearly equivalent to the mind-link's consummation."

"Artellian, you know that last year Orram reached Tandra with diffuse mood-reading," Junah said, "but you may not know that it became a common form of communication between them, culminating in their mating, as the mind-link requires."

"Yes, I thought so," Conn said, and a wide grin split his face.

"You see? You see?" Llorkin shouted. "She broke him. That's why he's dying. She broke him. He had resolved not to consummate their mind-link. She broke his resolve. Varoks can't stand that, you know."

"Your rantings contain some truth," Conn said, forcing his eyes into a disconcerting, calm roundness. "Now sit down and listen. Orram had gone so deep into her mind that he went into sexual link-need on one of their sunset walks. He wanted to beat it down with anesthetics, but Tandra realized what had happened and offered a lot more than physical relief. Her message was loud and clear: complete acceptance, insistent love in the present, no strings attached. He nearly lost himself in her mind it was so wide open."

"Did Orram feel that continual, detailed mental contact was possible with Tandra?" Artellian asked.

Junah seemed a bit wistful, but she smiled. "His exact words were, "I believe we have achieved the mind-link."

"I suggest that we delay no longer," Artellian said. "Llorkin, do you have any substantial objections to offering Tandra a full clearance and a staff position with EV Science?"

"She is human," Llorkin snapped. "I insist on conducting a complete psychological analysis."

Conn catapulted to his feet and slammed his hand against the moss-lined deck. "Llorkin, will you get your sonar melons out of your cloaca? Tandra is more than human. We may lose Orram!" The wild anger of the lonely elll had nowhere to go but back into elllonian grief. Throughout the night he thrashed and paced in and around the pool, then back and forth to Orram's room, hour after hour, until Killah feared for his sanity. And still he refused to join the school, even when they realized Orram had lost consciousness.

– Δ –

"I have talked directly with Jesse Mendleton," Artellian told Junah as they sat quietly by Orram's bed. "None of his news is good. Some time ago Tandra left Shawne with Mendleton and drove away. He said that Tandra didn't know where she was going—only that she had to find a place for Shawne, that she would return for the child as soon as she could. The federation police are also looking for her, but so far they haven't connected her with Mendleton. He was smart to keep our contact with him secret."

"Why do the police want her?"

"For sabotage, and apparently for treason, also. A stockpile of weapons and explosives was found in her house. Mendleton believes they were planted. They need a scapegoat for the recent bombings. She is accused of fomenting civil war."

"I remember Mendleton telling us about her last appearance with the Stabilists," Junah said.

"Mendleton feels that Tandra will be safe while she travels. She won't be in heavily populated areas. Right now he's more concerned for Shawne. There have been charges of neglect. Tandra didn't want Shawne exposed to the socialization schools, so she kept her home without authorization. He has heard that the child will be taken from her soon."

With those words, an intense wave of fury crashed into Junah's perception. Conn! Junah whirled to face him. His eyes glared with determined rage; then he turned and ran toward the hangar.

For a moment, Junah and Artellian stood stunned. Then they guessed the loner's intentions.

"I had better go with you!" Junah called, running after Conn. She was too late. The *Lurlial* had already left the hangar.

– Δ –

Conn shut off the braking engines at forty thousand feet, activated the glide wings, and waited while the silver bat soared silently into the murky lower atmosphere of Earth. He scraped to a stop on a wide grassy slope and set off on foot in the direction of an insistent beep in his helmet.

He shuddered at the hideous excuse for air and double-checked the seal on his isolation helmet, to prevent any of the human waste from clogging his lungs.

The terrain was not rough, but he stumbled with fatigue and the unaccustomed pull of Earth's gravity. Finally, he saw a figure standing near a waiting buggy on the road below. The figure signaled for him to stop. It was Jesse Mendleton. Impatiently, Conn waited while the man climbed to meet him.

"Conn?"

The elll grasped the man's arm gratefully. "Where's Shawne? It's my fault she's lost a whole year of her life down here."

"There. In my car."

"And Tandra? Where's Tan?"

"I'm not sure. She called yesterday, and I told her to be at her old homestead. I don't know if she'll be there. You haven't got much time. You'd better just take Shawne now."

"We'll make time," Conn said. "I've got to get Tandra out of here. The steady-state philosophy hasn't had its martyr yet. She's become the symbol of human failure, and now it's time to hang it up on its cross. That's the way of human history, isn't it?"

Mendleton nodded grimly. "The human race is busy committing suicide, and they don't want to be reminded of the fact."

They came to Mendleton's solar buggy, and he stood baffled as Conn began circling around it, bobbing up and down and making mocking threats. Shawne was jumping up and down on the seat inside, happily joined in the game. Then Conn disappeared, the toddler jumped out to pounce on him, and he captured her with a long-armed hug.

"A whole year's growth I've missed, Shawnoon. You're huge! And already three years old. Let's go find your mother, okay?"

Mendleton noticed that the elll's grief for Tandra's lost year did not re-emerge during the ride. It had been expressed. Conn was completely, joyfully engrossed with Shawne now.

Miles later they drove onto a dirt road that wove haphazardly through an old orchard, past houses built of scrap plastic and automobile shells. At last Mendleton recognized a pattern of juniper trees on the hill above an old frame house, and there he stopped.

Conn got out of the car, glad for the dimness of the night, which allowed him better vision. He whispered to Shawne and Mendleton to stay quiet, then tried the door to the house. It was locked. He circled the house, noisily trying the windows and back door. He stopped to listen. Something had moved inside. He tapped on the door. No answer. Quiet.

"Tan?" Conn whispered through the door. "It's Jesse Mendleton. I've come to take you home."

The door swung open, and Tandra stood there, frightened, but expectant. "Conn. Thank God!"

Conn tore open the screen door and pulled his helmet off, forgetting the taste of the air for an intense moment.

"How soft, how open you are," Tandra said. "Open and vulnerable—"

"A sprouting weed, Tan. I've learned a lot, but I need your storms to make my stems strong. I need your fertilizer to grow more—"

She laughed, interrupting him, and their tears ran as they came together in a prolonged hug.

When at last she pulled back to look into his eyes, he smiled down at her and took her face in his webbed fingers. "How I've missed you! When I think how you crawled into my water—you went more than halfway to know me again. Then I woke up in some mental blind alley and found you really gone. I would have sold my soul to have you in the *uuyvanoon* again with me. The pool was no longer enough, nothing was enough, so I walked the Earth with you this miserable year, followed your every move, began to understand your every thought, learned to tolerate your unfathomable human emotions. And I longed for you. My pool is dry and empty without you. Please come home to me."

Tandra moved into his arms again and spoke with gentle pressures and undulations along the length of his lean, tiled body—spoke clearly and easily the language he had begged for many long months ago.

"I think I've finally sorted out pride and jealousy and bitterness and love, Tan," Conn said, "all these individual emotions that you stirred up in me. But now what do we do? I am still an elll. An elll's deepest relationships always involve sexual contact within the school."

With his suggestion, Tandra moved again within his embrace.

Conn exploded with joy. "At last I have my answer. You do love me. You accept me. Totally! With no hint of repulsion. That's enough, Tandra. That's all I need."

She swam deep and easy in his emerald gaze, seeing the dimming lenses for what they were.

A broad smile rumpled his face. "Have you had enough down here, Tan? Will you come home now and stay where you belong?"

"Stay?" Tandra asked hesitantly. "Shawne must go with you, but--"

Conn put a soft, webbed glove over her lips. "Don't try to rejoin the human race, Tan. You can't assume the role of caretaker now. It's too late. You're wanted for sabotage and treason. They won't allow you to do anything more now, and I won't allow you the role of martyr."

Tandra's eyes widened. "It's more painful to give up on Earth than I thought, Conn. She was once so beautiful. Now, with these bombings, they add more horror to the rape. We were given a precious gift, and they continually abuse it. They use it and destroy it; they take it utterly for granted."

"Listen to yourself, Tan," Conn said, smoothing the quick tears from her eyes. "'We' has become 'they.' Come home with me now. Our Shawnoon is in the buggy waiting for us."

They drove as quickly as they dared, a strange vehicle filled with mixed emotions—tension and relief and curiosity and joy and apprehension. Conn would not talk about Orram, and over everything was a fear that the *Lurlial* could have been discovered.

Finally they reached the long, flat hill which hid the *Lurlial* from the road. Everything seemed undisturbed.

Mendleton followed as they circled cautiously toward the ship. He stood apart as Conn, Tandra and Shawne climbed in. Minutes passed. There was too little noise. Then the elll reappeared in the hatchway.

"Better come along with us," Conn urged.

"To the Moonbase?"

"Why not?"

Mendleton could find no answer and no desire to reject the invitation. He climbed in, and within minutes the stocky silver ship rose with quiet power toward the moon.

Quivering with impatience, Conn eased the ship into orbit and sent it toward base. Mendleton sat beside him at the controls, admiring the broad, gloved fingers darting competently over the command deck.

"There," Conn mumbled, stripping off his isolation suit and ignoring Mendleton's startled reaction. "Call me if anything moves on this data readout." He pointed briefly to a calibrated set of concentric circles, and, without another word, heaved himself out of the control room and down the passageway in search of Tandra.

He found her braced against weightlessness in an *uuyvanoon,* enfolding Shawne in her arms and staring out of the porthole. Conn grasped the edge of the sleeping basin and knelt beside them, but only Shawne turned to greet him.

"Tan?" Tentatively, afraid to intrude, he placed a hand on her shoulder. She took his fingers eagerly and clung hard, while she watched the Earth sink beneath her. "Tan, it's all right," Conn said. "Life finds a way to go on. Eventually Earth will reclaim her own."

"I wish I could be so sure," Tandra said. "I wanted you to see it, Conn, the way it was—"

"I did, you know, for a moment, with the bear and her cub. They are strong, wedded to the Earth. They'll survive."

Conn stared at the back of Tandra's head, while emerald drops of empathic grief and longing gathered on his brow plumes. He took the dimming lenses from his eyes, wiped the tears away, and whispered in Elllonian, "Tandra, divorce yourself from Earth; I am too alone."

She tore her gaze away from the swirling blue and white orb below. Her mind locked deep and sure into the once-fearful black void of his naked eyes, and his gentle touch of moss brought her home to him again.

The elll couldn't find words enough to tell her about Orram, but she knew they would face something difficult together. For many hours, then, while the *Lurlial* glided toward Earth's moon, the elll and the two human beings clung together, watching Earth grow ever smaller, shimmering silent and alone in space.

Home

"I have another passenger, Artell. Jesse, where are you? Watch the gravity." Conn laughed, steadying the man as he emerged from the *Lurlial* in an unaccustomed isolation suit.

"You're very welcome here, Jesse Mendleton," Artellian said. "You've been an invaluable friend. Seems a bit rude to shut you up in quarantine right away, but we had better play safe."

"I don't mind," Mendleton said.

"Tandra, welcome home," Artellian said, embracing her warmly with his large golden-green arms. "I was afraid we'd lost you. *Aeo-o* Shawnoon? You are getting very large." He picked her up with a surge of joy and set her tenderly on his hip.

"Conn," he continued gently, "your privileges and duties under EV Science are suspended until your criminal actions are reviewed. You are confined to base. Automatic penalty for violation will be permanent removal from E-V Science."

Tandra turned to Conn.

"You might say I borrowed the *Lurlial*," Conn said with a wry smile. "When Jesse reported that they were going to take Shawne from you, I freaked." He straightened out of his slouch and put his arms heavily on Tandra's shoulders. "Llorkin was threatening to block your return. I had to get you out of that horror down there, Tan. But I had to bring you home for a second reason." His eyes were wide and glistening. "I haven't been able to tell you. It's Orram. He's dying."

The shock lasted one long terrible moment. Then Tandra grabbed Conn's hand and ran through the silver-red halls of the base. As she released the sealed doors and stepped into the isolation room adjoining Killah's lab, she saw the unconscious shell of Orram lying on his back, his face gray-sallow and thin and his breathing noisy. She grew deathly pale.

Killah led her away from the restless form as he continued the terrible struggle for breath. "Come, Tandra," he said, grieving for her pain. "Review what I have done with the sputum samples. I need your help. I don't know what to try next."

They retreated to the lab, and with great difficulty Tandra set her mind to work. "Tell me everything you know about his illness," she said, as Killah prepared a sample of Orram's sputum for microscopic examination. "When did he get sick?"

"It's almost impossible to pin down, Tandra. He began feeling tired about a month after he returned from leaving you on Earth. Then he began losing weight. The cough didn't become severe until a few weeks ago. I found abscesses and drained them, but I wasn't able to culture anything from sputum until recently. Now I may have a few colonies on these tubes."

Tandra peered at the minute drops of yellow on the surface of the semi-solid nutrient. "Could be TB. Are they acid-fast rods?"

"And gram positive," Killah nodded.

"What drugs do you have him on?"

"He's on PAS and streptomycin, but he should have responded by now, shouldn't he? I put him on the drugs when I first suspected TB several months ago."

"Let me look at these slides." Tandra's fingers deftly pulled the microscopic vision into focus. Then they slid to the manipulator, and her mind wandered visually through the cloudy blue microscopic world, until her eyes and her fingers were arrested by a magenta flash. She swung the slide back and stared at a cluster of broken red rods scattered in a bluish tangle. "Kill, have you ever had a uniform acid-fast take?"

"No, I don't think so. But my technique isn't accurate with your stains. I can't distinguish their differences visually, you remember."

"And those colonies were grown at twenty-five degrees, centigrade, weren't they? Let's put them under the scope."

With a delicate scalpel they lifted one of the tiny drops of ferocious life into a scope sampler and set it under the lenses of the low-powered scanning electron microscope. The colony was like an aged dew-drop, wrinkled and yellow.

"Not much doubt now," Tandra said. "But I want to look at that smear again." She returned to the high-power microscope and continued her survey of Orram's sputum. Another magenta tangle. She closed in on it. "There, Kill. We're in luck."

He switched on the infrared source light and peered down through the maze of lenses. "Branching forms. Then it could be fungal."

"Yes. It's not TB. There's no granular material. It's Nocardiosis, but I don't see how he could have picked it up. It's usually found in soil and not directly transmitted between persons."

"Could he have picked it up on your trip to the mountains?"

"Improbable," she said, remembering their happy scramble for the pine cone beneath their tree, "but most likely. We should have stayed in isolation suits up there."

"Can't help that now."

"Let's get him on a sulfonamide right away, Killah."

"We should be able to synthesize that without too much trouble. Though I'm afraid it may be too late."

Through the artificial night and into the next day they nursed Orram and worked at synthesizing the new drug. The hours were not long enough, the minutes far too short, as they labored over their rows of culture tubes and watched with mounting terror Orram's ever more difficult breathing. Finally, the drug was ready.

Cautiously, throughout the next week, they eased the varok onto the foreign chemical. Heart rate up slightly. Then down again.

Tandra slept on a moss pad by his side, refusing to leave even when Killah or Conn was on watch. Often Orram's coughing allowed no one any sleep.

They pushed the dosage up, but his cough became steadily worse. The rare fungus was notorious for its resistance to treatment. Many days passed with no reason for hope.

Most work lay undone at the base, while the ellls and the varoks teamed to provide relief and support for Killah and Tandra. Conn's hearing before the directorate was held informally over dinner one night, and the order to pick up Tandra and Shawne was made retroactive. Llorkin abstained, as little able as any other elll to swim against an emotional tide that concerned the safety of children.

The directorate then wanted to clear Tandra for patch understanding, but she could not be persuaded to leave Orram until she was convinced that she had done all she could. Then, reluctantly, she told Artellian she was ready. She was willing to try to learn how to reach the varok through patch contact, if they thought it was possible.

– Δ –

Exhausted and discouraged, Tandra sat in the middle of the floor in Artellian's office surrounded by Conn, Artellian, Llorkin, Tallyn, and

Killah. Ahl and Junah sat straight and tense, concentrating on every aspect of Tandra's consciousness, probing as deeply as they could.

"Exhaust all doubts relating to our mutual trust with Tandra," Artellian announced succinctly, and the directorate began its work.

Killah was brief; he said that his mind had been made up long ago. She should be on the staff.

Tallyn stated that his prejudices toward Tandra were largely dissolved. He had come to respect her for her attempts to reach Conn before she returned to Earth and for her persistent efforts there during the last year. Nevertheless, to erase all doubt, he would wait until Conn had spoken.

Junah, through a series of questions, examined Tandra's personal reaction to her psychological collapse and return to reason. No prejudice or confusion there—rather, a clear understanding of varokian personality and profound appreciation for their cultural problems. "Just one more question," Junah said softly, then waited. "Do you read me?"

Tandra looked at the varok and almost blurted out that she felt acceptance pouring from the alien's patch organs. But she remembered Orram's caution concerning patch information and remained silent. "I'm ready for your question, Junah," she said.

"You have already answered it, Tandra. You have been aware of our security regulations and quite cautious even here. Now you should know that all members of this directorate are aware of your ability to read diffuse patterns and to transmit them."

Llorkin and Ahl in turn drilled tirelessly with questions that had no answers—or too many answers—questions that invaded every corner of Tandra's life and consciousness. She soon became very tired. She began to seek refuge from the continual barrage, until she found it difficult to control her annoyance as Llorkin's questions grew thinner and then, before they stopped, meaningless.

The varok, Ahl, continued relentlessly, as was customary, pursuing her breaking point. But before long a clear message reached his patch organ: "Please," it begged, "let me go to Orram. My integrity will break only with physical exhaustion." Abruptly, Ahl ended his questions and nodded to Conn.

Folding his long legs across each other and curling his brow into a thoughtful knot, Conn began to shape his thoughts into words, but he failed. "Orram is losing too much time with this nonsense. Come here,

Dr. Grey," he said, pulling her down onto the floor beside him. "Talk to me in a way I can understand. There have always been too many words between us." He wrapped his long arms and legs around hers and pressed his lean, tiled body against her softness, half expecting her to protest their public intimacy. But instead, she shifted slightly so as to increase contact with him.

Artellian glanced around the room. "Tallyn?"

"No questions," he said, nodding his massive, wildly plumed head with satisfaction.

Ahl stretched back in his chair and pulled thoughtfully at his silvered hair. "We are neither gods nor worthless specks," he said, "but our mutual consciousness binds us together for all time. You have accomplished honest communication with two very alien species, Tandra. We congratulate you."

"Tandra," Artellian interrupted, "do you consider yourself a good security risk?"

For a long moment she said nothing.

"Should we share our technology with the Federation, if it should become a stable and representative world government? Varoks have developed photovoltaic technology to a high degree of miniaturization and efficiency. But I don't think you realize that our backup systems are controlled by quantum computers and powered by controlled nuclear fusion. Shall we give Earth the extra time that our technology can provide?"

Tandra's face paled as she realized the magnitude of Artellian's challenge. "You have never seemed so powerful. You could have imposed yourselves on Earth long ago." She gazed around the warm green and silver-brown circle of once-alien faces. "No. I am quite sure, Artell. Human society is not mature enough to utilize such power responsibly. If you provide Earth with unlimited power now, the problems of overpopulation and overuse would continue unchecked, so that suffering would be greatly magnified in the end."

Artellian stopped pacing and extended a golden webbed hand to Tandra. "This hearing is closed. Your trust in us is no longer in doubt."

"My trust in you?"

Artellian's great eyes yawned wide with affection. "Go to Orram now quickly," he said.

Tandra and Junah exchanged a glance, then arose together and crossed the hall to Orram's isolation room. In spite of the oxygen-injection mask, his breathing remained irregular and labored.

"You have communicated diffusely quite often, Tandra," Junah said. "Transmit to him now in much the same way. I can't tell you how, since you have no patch organ. Yours is apparently a learned response. Whatever you have done before, do it now more intensely, with concentration, only beware of letting your consciousness dominate."

"I'm not sure what you mean, Junah. Tell me something I should do, something to look for."

"This may be an elusive thing for you, like a speck of dust in the eye. It might help to touch him as you begin to make contact. You have guessed most of the patch organ's functions."

Junah paused and then continued carefully. "You remember that Conn checked your EEG pattern before he first contacted you. That low voltage detector and analyzer was modeled on our patch organs. We can read not only diffuse moods, as you have done, but we can also execute specific mind reading on a conscious level, but only the current stream of thoughts. On a subconscious level, thought patterns can be followed, if conditions are favorable."

"Perhaps you can reach him more easily than I," Tandra asked.

"No, surely not. He was attuned to you, searching for you in the link you had established. Open your mind and go to him, Tandra."

Tandra leaned over the bed where Orram's feverish body struggled for oxygen. She held his limp hands in hers and tried to flood his patches with a call to herself. The call envisioned everything that he had meant to her, everything that had passed between them. She struggled against her wandering mind, trying to focus her thoughts and emotions, but the focus eluded her, and she found herself yearning diffusely or grieving already.

Gradually, as the hours passed, her consciousness left the room, its sound and its feel, its warmth, even its light. The focus narrowed and magnified her self-awareness, striving, yearning, loving Orram. Tentatively, she moved away from the awareness and tried to extend it toward him. Then, as her focus steadied and grew sharper, she stole brief instants to listen for a reply, for any projection from the unconscious varok. There was nothing. She returned to reinforce and concentrate awareness of her total being, before she attempted to build her extension to him.

Orram, the concept of being that was Orram, grew in her mind and held and grew steadier and stretched toward her own self-extension. She strove to focus the concepts of both of them, to make them meet. But then she became anxious and lost the entire vision. She sank to the floor. She had seemed so close.

"You must sleep, Tandra," Junah said. "If you do reach him, you must be able to hold him until he has come through this crisis."

Tandra slept for several hours. She dreamed that Orram was slowly sinking into quicksand as she reached out for him, their hands just failing to touch.

She awoke with a start, quickly cleared her mind, pressed his fingers to her temples, and sought to recreate the concentrated self-awareness. It came back quickly. She was alone again, in limbo, reaching to Orram, but now she searched continually for a response from him. She strained toward the impression of him, and she imagined his response. She tried to bring her image of him toward herself. They leaned together a little more, almost touching, just a little more—

Suddenly the vision evaporated and she felt herself in the presence of Orram's awareness. He had been waiting for her; she had been too narrowly focused.

Joyfully, she basked in his knowledge, his dread, his love, and she provided a link with reality, a directive to his body, a strength he no longer possessed. They remained together through the night and into the next day.

Afraid to break the subconscious communicative trance between the woman and the varok, Killah administered emergency sustenance to them both. Late on the fifth day, Tandra and Orram emerged slowly into consciousness. The room materialized around them, regained its walls, then Killah's medical instruments, the bed pad they shared. At last they rediscovered their bodies, as they touched and saw and heard each other again.

– Δ –

Through the next few weeks, as Orram began to regain his health, Tandra and Conn rarely left him. Gradually they reestablished their intimate awareness of each other, until it became habitual and constant.

Long forgotten incidents came back into Tandra's memory. Seen in perspective, as they talked, her childhood became a vivid scenario, pleasantly relived with Orram and Conn. Indeed, she shared more of it with Orram than she realized, as he explored her thoughts with her, sometimes finding them before she got to them herself.

One day, the oxygen injector was finally put aside. Orram began to talk about Varok—about the moist warm evenings when several moons could be seen between the swirling gas clouds, about the ever-changing light, now deep orange or red, then pale yellow or green, now dense, then thin and fragile.

He described his family—his aging mother, still the master of the gardens, tending each fruit tree and moth with great care; his deceased father, a writer of some distinction and his mother's consummate mate; his brother by his mother's first mating, approaching the middle age of sixty with unusually little direction in his life; and his son, Orticon.

The knowledge of Orram's adolescent son on Varok was nothing more than a pleasant surprise to Tandra, for she was already comfortable with the varokian family structure. Its composition was determined solely by individual choice, and could have included Orram's former mate, his son's mother, as easily as not. Orram smiled to himself. Tandra was gradually entering his mind by habit, but she did not realize it yet.

"I remember my early childhood as being the most pleasant time of my life," Orram said. He loved to watch the sky change from masses of dimly lit color to black luminescence. He would lie on his back on the warm ground, fingering the tender new shoots of looping snarl, as he watched the black sky for an occasional glimpse of the other Jovian moons. Later, at new light, he would spend hours looking for crystals buried in rocky cliffs near his home. Overwhelmed by the secrets they might hold, he would hide among the huge rocks and pick at them with a stick, searching for a glimpse of color or a planar surface.

As Tandra listened, Orram's voice gradually faded to an echo, and she became that boy—stooping over a crumbling hillock of rock, looking for a better tool than the stick, remembering the laser pencil he carried around his neck, using it to pick at the fragile minerals until at last he found another crystal.

"It's an emerald!" Tandra shouted.

The little girl then led the young varok back to her mother's dresser, where she stole a peek at the beautiful emerald ring her mother kept there. Together they carefully slipped it over their small finger. Gently, so as not to destroy the union, Orram guided Tandra's mind back to the present. There, in the medical isolation room at EV base, she saw herself through his eyes. She was totally with him, joined with him in mental consummation.

– Δ –

Conn found them still wrapped around each other, breathing in unison, a shared dream drawing a smile across both their lips. He guessed correctly what had happened and tried to retreat from the room, but before he reached the door Orram spoke. "Conn, don't go."

Tandra stirred at the sound of Orram's voice and sat up to welcome the elll. "No, Tan," he stammered. "Privacy is sacred to varoks. I—"

"Don't you think we know that?" she smiled.

Orram sat up with difficulty and extended his hand with Tandra's. "Please, Conn, we want you to be a part of us. Join us if you will, or leave us if you must, but don't reject us for superficial reasons."

Orram's soft words erased Conn's doubts. His brightly framed emerald eyes widened, as he took their hands and let them pull him onto the bed and into their arms.

Such a tender scene, wrought with profound significance for three excellent beings and their respective species, should have found a fitting ending behind a velvet curtain. But the varokian hospital bed support, made lightweight for space travel and never intended for three adults, collapsed with a crash. The ensuing exclamations and hoots of laughter brought Killah bursting into the room.

"What are you doing?" he shouted, delighted at the chaotic tangle of bed and beings.

"By l'Ran, we don't know!" Orram exploded, "But whatever it is, it's good."

"We're schooling, Kill, old fish. Can't you tell?" Conn laughed. "I've found myself a dry school."

– Δ –

His period of quarantine finally over, Jesse Mendleton rapidly become a happy addition to the base. His bemused appreciation for everything alien had given a light touch to the previously leaden days. And now that Orram was out of danger, they could all relax with pleasant memories of their first contacts, joyfully recounting the difficult, subtle exchange of information they had accomplished before Tandra had been chosen for direct contact.

In spite of all this experience, Jesse Mendleton went into a state of high excitement when they received a video signal from Varok.

"It's Orticon!" Conn hooted, as he pushed Orram's medical chair toward the communication center.

Orram reached for Tandra's hand. "Kneel in front of me," he said, "and I'll give you the translation." He sat tense and unmoving while his son reported on his progress at the Concentrate and on the general state of Varokian life. Then with exposed palms the boy saluted his father, and Orram's hand pressed hard against Tandra's as she felt within him the tug of desire for home, for his son.

"Forwarded message from Ellason coming now, Father," Orticon said.

A hazy picture centered on a group of ellls submerged in deep water lit from below. They hung suspended by the gentle waving of their feet and backfins. One heavy-set figure with a magnificent crest approached the transmitting plate and began to speak. His words leaped and tumbled fluidly, but he wasted none on formalities.

"Thought we'd send you a piece of direct news to make you homesick, Art. You probably need a leave, and Conn must be dried up like a Varokian *kaehl* by now. EV Science wants you to convert base to a minimal automatic monitoring operation and prepare to come home. Broadcasts to Earth may continue from Varok. The expense of full operations is no longer justified. We have learned much from the initial decline in Earth's life-quality, but you needn't pay the price of watching the major die-offs.

"Your telecasts sound good, but too divisive, as we predicted. We're convinced Earth knows what it's doing. The choice to allow massive natural catastrophes is obviously deliberate. We've seen no cut-backs in production to force population stabilization.

"Don't waste any time getting home, Aen. Artellian, pack up everything of security interest.

"Congratulations to staff Senior Microbiologist Tandra Grey. Security registered. I assume she will accompany you to Varok. *Uleoon*."

The plate went blank.

Tandra sighed deeply as the last glimmer of her persistent hope faded. "So much for Earth," she murmured. "I don't know what I was hoping for."

Artellian drew her face into his broad hands. "No tears, Tandra. Life is lived well by many other stars. You have gone beyond Earth, eh? Human beings will leave a fascinating fossil record for those to come."

– Δ –

Late on June 24, while the crew lounged intently around the pool, Artellian witnessed the formation of the Oran-Grey-ElConn Family, with mutual rights under EV Law similar to those of power of attorney on Earth. When the formality was completed, Conn took Tandra's hand, found her third finger, and slipped onto it a graceful swirl of moon glass that beautifully enthroned a small sapphire, a large diamond, and an enormous emerald. "For sentimentalistic female scientists, a token of loving commitment, so that none will misunderstand." He grinned enormously. "Some useless human customs have a certain unmentionable quality. I apologize to Orram that the stones are not quite in true proportion to our planets' sizes. Orram, I have made one for you, too."

The varok accepted his ring with visible emotion.

"Shawnoon, here is yours," Conn said, slipping a tiny duplicate onto her pudgy finger. "And," he sighed, "I have made one for myself." He produced the fourth ring from his palm and handed it to Tandra.

"I don't think you'll stand it," she laughed.

The crowd of ellls pressed closer to watch her push it onto his large reluctant finger. "M-m, no," he murmured, as it touched his delicate interdigital web, "I want it to stay there. It feels like a, like a kind of pool."

With that the ellls mobbed them with noisy shouts of congratulations. After a long, clamorous, haphazard meal, Tandra and Orram stretched out on the mossy deck next to Conn, who lay with his head in Tllan's lap translating into English the words to *La I Lea*, the tender mating duet of the ellls:

You are to my life its living.
Come now, confirm it to me.
Renew my life with touch, with roll, with wave.

You are to my breath its breathing.
Come, share your touch with me.
Restore now my being with yours, with mine, with all.

You are to my self its growing.
Come now, lock your body in mine.
I know not of life but through you, with you, in you.

You are to my soul its homing.
Come take now my love in yours.
I am what I am for I'm with you, I know you, I love you.

Throughout the day and into evening they lived life's most precious gift of moments, and the celebration never really ended, though the varoks sensed the approach of embarkation and the ells grieved their kind of grief for the splitting of the crew.

Epilogue

Tallyn and Ahl commanded the *Ranat* and Conn the *Lurlial* for the voyage to Varok. Tallyn, Tllan, and Llorkin would take the tads and the incubating egg on to Ellason with Aen, who wished to spend his last share of life on his home planet. Orram, Conn, Junah, Artellian, Killah, and Da-oon traveled to Varok, intending to guide Jesse Mendleton and Shawne and Tandra around that planet for several Varokian years.

Their plans were disrupted by unforeseen events on Varok that challenged their deepest commitments to that planet and sent them back to Earth, eventually. But that is another story, told in Nautilus silver medalist *The Webs of Varok* and its sequels—*The Alien Effect* and *An Alien's Quest*.

APPENDICES

A. A History of the Archives

3631 *ir* (Earth 5000 BCE) - Events recorded in *The Unheard Song*.[1]

3634 *ir* (Earth 4962 BCE) – Amanok writes his memoirs.

4225.8 *ir* (Earth 2020 CE) – Tandra Grey born on Earth.

4228 *ir* (Earth 2047 CE) – Shawne Grey born on Earth.

4228.3–4228.4 *ir* (Earth 2050–2051 CE) – Events recorded in *A Place Beyond Man*,[2] revised as *The View Beyond Earth*.[3]

4228.4–4229.5 *ir* (Earth 2051–2064 CE) – Events in *The Webs of Varok*.[4]

4229 *ir* (Earth 2059 CE) – Aman Telariahn (Amantel) publishes Amanok's memoirs as *The Unheard Song*.[1]

4229.8–4230 *ir* (Earth 2068–2070 CE) – Oran-ElConn-Grey family events recorded in *The Alien Effect*.[5]

4229.8–4409.7 *ir* (Earth 2068–4202 CE and beyond) – Biological Events recorded in *The Alien Effect*.[5]

4230 *ir* (Earth 2070 CE) – Events recorded in *An Alien's Quest*.[6]

1. Penscript Publishing House, 2022. 2. Charles Scribner's Sons, 1975.
3. Penscript Publishing House, 2014. 4. Penscript Publishing House, 2012.
5. Penscript Publishing House, 2014. 6. Penscript Publishing House, 2016

B. Glossary

adjustment. Intense schooling of ellls, in which strong pressure signals, electro-sensing, magneto orientation and ultrasonic messages are rapidly exchanged underwater so that accommodation may be made for the absence of a member of the school or for the addition of a new member.

aeo-o. Elllonian expression of intense pleasure.

aeyull. Elllonian expression of intense pain.

ahlrialka tree. Huge spreading, plant-like growth on the hot acid plains of Varok; it produces dense, tasty reproductive lumps.

alahranon. The colorful, swirling mists that surround Ellason, whose surface is almost totally covered by warm oceans.

aloon. Elllonian noun, usually used with affection to mean something like wet slob or water bum.

alyakah. Varokian word for a mature, well-integrated female who would be desirable to any creature as a mother or wife.

arl. A large, brilliantly winged, moth-like creature of Varok, eaten by ellls and varoks and considered a delicacy.

Arlaht. Varokian landcraft adapted for lunar exposure. See Nalkah.

brilln. The tiny, brilliantly-plumed water bird of Ellason.

challall weeds. Delicious, rigid, leafless plants which grow on the low hills of Ellason.

consummation. Total mind link, achieved by varoks of the opposite sex who have no mental reservations between them so that complete subconscious mind-scanning can occur.

dankah. A potent, intoxicating tea, made from the Varokian plant of the same name.

deäcuh. Elllonian noun for isolation, quarantine, or loneliness and torture, all of which are synonymous in the minds of ellls.

directorate. Full title: Elll-Varok Earth Moonbase Directorate. The council of ellls and varoks at EV base, which makes policy decisions on behalf of EV Science.

Dove Two. World Federation-built three-man interplanetary space shuttle.

el eggs. The large, blue eggs laid by elllonian females every six Earth-weeks.

Ellason. A heretofore undetected self-heated planet of Sol with gravity equivalent to about twice Earth's gravity. Its orbit is three times as far from Sol as Pluto, hence laser communication necessitates a delay of seventeen and one-half hours, Ellason being some eighteen thousand, eight hundred and seventy-seven million kilometers from Earth. Continental masses on the warm, black giant are small, and the deep, black seas are enormous, glowing with ruby-red warmth near the heart of the planet.

elll. An adaptable, aquatic, life-loving species of Ellason, equipped with a formidable array of sensory organs.

Elllonian. The system of throat sounds laboriously devised by the varoks and ellls to be spoken by ellls in the varokian audible range to facilitate communication between those two species.

Elll-Varok (EV) Science. An organization of ellls and varoks that directs the scientific experimentation and observation conducted by those species and acts as depositor, summarizer, and interpreter of accumulated knowledge and verifiable fact.

EV base. Earth-moon observation station of Elll-Varok Science, set into the edge of a crater eleven kilometers in diameter, located north-west of crater Schlüter at 1.50° north and 89.5° west in the d'Alembert Mountains of Earth's only moon.

EV Dictate. The working agreement between the species of Ellason and Varok, which defines obligations, responsibilities, options, and assumptions inherent in their dealings.

Generalist. Abbreviated as G. An earned varokian designation signi-fying the acquisition of thorough, detailed knowledge in a broad area of related studies, as, for example, physics, chemistry, astronomy, geol-ogy, from the area of physical sciences. Between specialist and master.

Gurahn. Mythological beast designed by the 11-leyoollanl to repre-sent the total experience of the planet Varok.

hedonic glands. Sensory organs whose stimulation gives pleasure, and often sexual stimulation, to ellls.

hoats. A tangy, black edible root of Varok which sports feathery chartreuse leaves.

integrated. An elllonian concept to describe the state of being when an individual of another species becomes a part of the elllonian school in a way that implies total acceptance of the ellls; in general, to accept oneself as no different from those around one.

kaehl. A delicate, easily tamed Varokian animal with silky, pink, branched hair that drapes in long strands about its tiny body and over its large red nose, causing it to trip habitually as it attempts to run. It incubates its eggs in an abdominal pouch and protects itself with an acrid spray from its sour gland. The dried meat is tasteless but nutritious.

kaehl-din. Elllonian invective. Din means fecal matter, kaehl spray, and in general, any repulsive substance.

kaehloid. Literally, furry beast. The elll's nickname for species with hair.

la l lea. Elllonian; title of the tender mating duet of the ellls; literally— have a mating with me.

leel, la oon. Elllonian; literally—female, you do water (swim, woman).

llaoon grass. A soft marsh grass of Ellason.

11-leyoolianl. A species of creative great-fish of Ellason who perceive the significance of experience and express it in a manner most easily understood by their communicants, often by modeling clay represen-tations of their ideas as progressively complex symbols.

lohn bird. A plump, football-shaped animal with large webbed feet, stubby wings, a ridiculously small, bill-less head, and a coat of deep red and pink parasitic moss that drips with a heavily perfumed liquid. One of two species on Ellason capable of flight.

L'Ran. The Elllonian word for the blue star-planet, Earth.

Lurlial. Varokian-built exploratory space cruiser, fourteen meters long, bat-shaped at full glide extension, with capacity to carry eight two-meter beings comfortably, eleven if necessary. The craft has an indefinite range, minimal noise, needs little landing space, and has an extremely low radar cross-section.

Master. Abbreviated as M. Highest honorary recognition by varoks of expertise in a broad area of study, with some understanding of all knowledge, demonstrated by wisdom and restraint in integrating and applying to real problems the acquired concepts. Artellian is one of twenty living ellls to have received the honor; Orram, one of two thousand varoks.

Midpacific Space Center. An international Earth launching site and control center for space exploration, funded by the World Federation.

Mutilation. The period of time in Varokian natural history in which the varokian species mutated from magnificent and normally sensual winged intellectuals to unduly sensitive bipeds incapable of experiencing emotion rationally.

Nalkah. Varokian-built landcraft which rolls, climbs, or hovers as needed for rough terrain. This model was modified with lunar exposure seals, pressurized with an oxygenated atmosphere, and provided with heat shields. A crew of one to six can be transported in considerable comfort in its elllonian-designed couches.

oeln. Edible fish of Ellason, large and gray, with cool arrow-shaped patterns visible to ellls as dark lines in the infrared environment of Ellason.

-oon. Elllonian suffix implying water or wetness.

pallonions. Ellasonian credits. A promise of postponed payment in goods or services whenever requested. Agreements are honored and enforced between all members of species capable of keeping promises.

pallons. Elllonian unit of measure, about twenty-three meters, the length of an elll's arcing leap over the water from a fast swimming start. The similarity of this word to the word *pallonions* is probably a result of the ancient ellls' sense of irony and humor.

patch organ. Round, featureless plate of tissue behind the ears of varoks that detects low frequency electromagnetic signals, often voltages produced by mental and nervous activity of nearby organisms.

Ranat. Thirty-meter varokian space cruiser designed to carry forty passengers over long distances.

reading. Sensing another individual's mood, emotion, or trend in thought. One function of the varoks' patch organs.

release. The ability to experience emotion and to function rationally simultaneously. An ideal state achieved rarely by varoks and only with the aid of a consummate partner.

school. Any number of ellls who inhabit a particular environs or locale and who relate by schooling. The ellls' normal social structure.

schooling. Functioning collectively and sharing awareness as if a group were one individual.

Sonarplate Apraxia. A debilitating disease affecting the hexagonal plates of ellls, caused by a viral-like agent. Untreated, it disrupts sonar meshwork function, hence ultrasonic reception and communication.

Songs to Life. Ancient varokian poems written anonymously during the Mutilation. The first verse of the poem translates as follows:

> *Though long denied Life's gracious gift of flowing free,*
> *In currents wild and lifting down, thrown tumbling,*
> *Lifted up, thrown down, and swept without control,*
> *Our minds unlocked, in gray mists swirling bright with crystal hue;*
>
> *Though elegance denied and flight subdued,*
> *We find Life's beauty in her gifts*
> *And take her favors where they fall.*
> *Though all our visions racked our minds with pain;*
> *Though sound grew dense and ruined quiet senses;*
> *Though mind-filling silence became unknown and unknowable;*
> *And new life came to us, imperfect yet yearning for consciousness,*
> *Heavily distorted, torn by savaged genes*
> *And thrown upon misery to writhe in horror for years denied;*

Though Life came not with joy or promise,
But used us for her mindless purpose-
Or too mindful-none can know-
We still survive, thankful for new strength,
Molecules still conscious in forms perhaps wiser.

Specialist. Abbreviated as S. Varokian designation for those acquiring specific knowledge in one field of study, such as physics.

stabilist. A person belonging, usually covertly, to a revolutionary group on Earth advocating the destruction of the means of production if necessary and the violent overthrow of the World Federation in order to achieve a stable (steady-state or no-growth) economy.

ta. An English word used by ellls to mean any young being or new life.

tracking. Sensing and imitating the precise muscular movements of another individual, one function of the varoks' patches (in conjunction with spinal nerves).

udan. Varokian style bidet-toilet.

uleoon. Elllonian affectionate farewell, from *u* (go), *lea* (mating) or *leoo* (live) or *leoon* (love), and *oon* (in water, deliciously wet).

uuyvanoon (-l, plural). Sleeping basins designed by and primarily for ellls. They are made of a tough, flexible synthetic imbedded with a thick growth of moss, shaped like a bathtub, and provided with a warm water inlet and a sealed cover for space flight. From Elllonian: *u* (go), *uyan* (beyond), *van* (knowledge), and *oon* (in water).

uyen l'e advant. . . Elllonian; Furthermore, I am convinced that . . .

Varok. A dense, barely habitable, hidden satellite of Jupiter, thought to be associated, at least visually, with the Great Red Spot. At its closest, it is less than 600 million kilometers from Earth; communications delay is at least 32 minutes.

varok. The dominant intellectual species native to the planet Varok, formed by mutation from the winged forebears, having lost their ability to fly and to tolerate emotion rationally.

Varokian Concentrate. An institution of Varok open to qualifying individuals of any species who are admitted as students to acquire—by high-speed microvolt implantation into the memory—established fact, non-interpretable information, and thought techniques. The integration and application of this knowledge is acquired at other institutions through continuing studies, leading to the designations apprentice, specialist, and generalist.

Vrankah. A dance invented by ellls and performed by varoks only in close sympathy, usually in consummation; often used as a public announcement and celebration of legal commitment between varoks. The dance requires spinal anticipatory patch organ reading—tracking—by one partner as the other matches the rhythmic clapping of the ellls with his feet and tells a symbolic story with his hands.

wet-sweater. A shirt made of the most moisture-retaining, softest, and most delicious of Ellasonian mosses, kept alive by periodic moistening and feeding.

World Environmental Charter. A document signed by many nations of Earth to ensure the safety and cleanliness of the world's oceans, waterways, air, and soil, whose provisions were subsequently ignored or suspended for reasons of emergency shortages, international security, or economic disaster.

World Federation. A world government of Earth with limited sovereignty but growing enforcement capability, formed primarily out of economic necessity.

World Life Coalition. A religious organization working for the enforcement of the World Environmental Charter, actually a front organization for the Stabilists.

Carolyn A. (Cary) Neeper, PhD raised her family in the US Southwest with her husband and a friendly menagerie of dogs, fish and fowl. An avid proponent of sustainability and steady-state economics since the 1970s, she studied zoology, chemistry and religion at Pomona College and medical microbiology at  the University of Wisconsin–Madison. Cary paints landscapes and animals in acrylics, including the cover art for *The Archives of Varok* series.

The Archives of Varok

In an alternate 21st century Solar System, Earth learns that we have neighbors too intelligent, too nosy, and too near to ignore. . . .

The View Beyond Earth

Two offworld species, disturbingly human and altogether alien. Microbiologist Tandra Grey finds new hope for an ailing Earth and her own future when she makes first contact. Revised and updated from Neeper's 1975 classic, *A Place Beyond Man* (Charles Scribner's Sons).

The Webs of Varok

Silver medalist, Nautilus Book Awards 2013; Finalist, ForeWord's Book of the Year Awards 2012. Tandra leaves Earth for the ancient sustainable culture of Varok, with its promise of stability for her young daughter. But a genius with a hidden talent sets her eye on Varok's wealth — and Tandra's alien soul-mates.

The Alien Effect

Raised on the Jovian moon Varok, Shawne returns to Earth to help her devastated home planet build a new civilization — one that can thrive for millennia. She and her mixed family face unexpected lessons in love and personhood, unaware of the long-term consequences of their collision with life on Earth.

An Alien's Quest

Only two decades after first contact, even Earth's people know of Haralahn, the great-fish spiritual leader on distant Ellason. Shawne seeks his guidance in a quest for meaning that draws everyone she loves away to the Kuiper Belt and into a genetic mystery on the watery home planet of the ellls.

The Unheard Song

In this Archives of Varok prequel, a humanoid invader and aquatic native struggle to communicate in their race to ensure peace and a sustainable future for the wild seas of Ellason.

www.ingramcontent.com/pod-product-compliance
Lightning Source LLC
Chambersburg PA
CBHW022038240626
47154CB00007B/2471